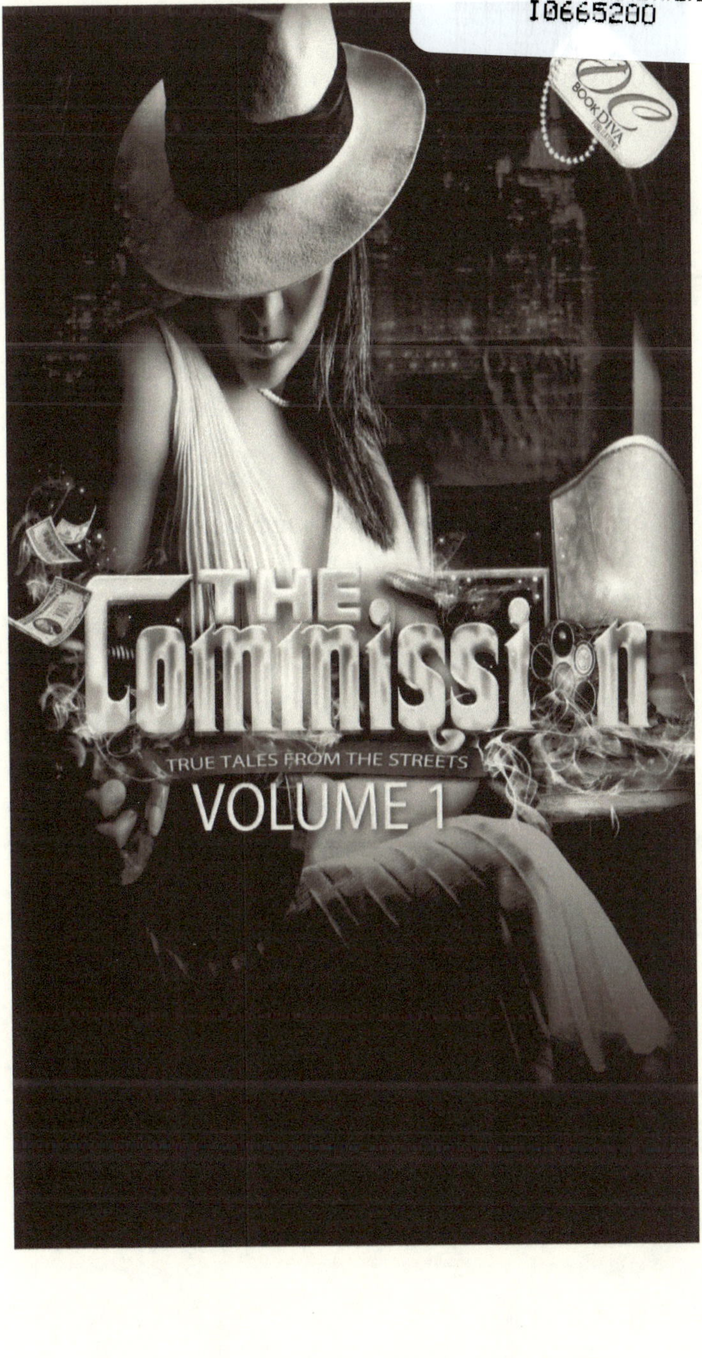
THE
Commission
TRUE TALES FROM THE STREETS
VOLUME 1
BOOK DIVA

ISBN: 978-0-9887621-2-1

Library of Congress Control Number: On file

Publisher's Note

This is a work of fiction. Any names historical events, real people, living and dead, or the locales are intended only to give the fiction a setting in historic reality. Other names, characters, places, businesses and incidents are either the product of the author's imagination or are used fictiously, and their resemblance, if any, *to real life counterparts is entirely coincidental.*

DC Bookdiva Publications

#245 4401-A Connecticut Ave

NW, Washington, DC 20008

dcbookdiva.com

The Commission

Dedicated to

Marion Dixon – Bey
Your support means the world to
me.

DC Bookdiva

Stella

DC Bookdiva

Chapter 1

Friday Afternoon 4:38pm
Southwest, Washington, DC

The hard knock on the door woke Ms. Haddy up from her peaceful afternoon nap. This was the only time of the day when she could sneak in a few hours of sleep, without being disturbed. Which was usually right after her soaps went off the air. "Hold on dammit. I'm coming" she barked. She reached over and grabbed her cane from off the floor. At sixty-eight years old she needed the cane to assist her because of her bad hip; an injury which was the result of a car accident five years earlier. Bang! Bang! Bang! "Goddammit! I'm coming! This better be worth it!" Ms. Haddy yelled out. She stood up and walked over to the front door.

After looking out the small peephole a smile came to her face. Quickly she opened the door. "John, where the hell you been? It's been two damn weeks." she said as he walked inside the house.

"Hey Ms. Haddy, I been on vacation with the wife and kids", he said, going into his pants pockets. Ms. Haddy stood there eyes beaming as John pulled out a large roll of bills. She watched as he peeled off three crisp one hundred dollar bills. "How long will this get me?" he asked.

"Wow, you must really miss her." Ms. Haddy said as she took the money and placed it inside of her bra. "However long you need, she's upstairs in her bedroom." John watched as Ms. Haddy walked back over to the couch and sat down. "What's in the bag?" she questioned.

"A few toys I picked up while I was in Vegas", he said with a devilish grin. Ms. Haddy shook her head and thought to herself, *He's a goddamn freak.* Then she replied, "Just keep it down, the neighbors been complaining the last few days."

"I'll try my best." John said as he began walking up the stairs.

Ms. Haddy eyes followed the tall, skinny white man until he was out of sight.

John was a regular. A white man that couldn't resist some good, young black pussy. He yearned for women of color and often fantasized about weird things he wanted to do with them. At Forty-eight years old, he was a married man with two children, making over one-hundred thousand a year as the VP at the downtown bank, but nothing in his life satisfied him enough to keep him away from his Nubian lust. No matter the consequences or risks, he had to have it because black women were his secret addiction.

As Stella sat on her bed she could hear the footsteps of a man coming toward her bedroom. Her eyes watered but she quickly wiped them. She hated this, for her it was worse than death. But, she vowed never to let a single soul see her vulnerable side. Stella had lived a hard and rough sixteen years. Since the tragic death of her mother everything quickly went downhill. By the age of eight she had tried to commit suicide, and by ten years old she had her first sexual experience with a man twice her age. At twelve years old she was introduced to cocaine. Luckily, she didn't' enjoy the feeling of getting high, so it became her first and her last hit. The saddest part of all this, is that right under the roof, where a

DC Bookdiva

young child should be protected and shielded from such occurrences, stood her grandmother who not only encouraged these acts, but allowed all this to go down.

Chapter 2

"Come in." Stella said, after hearing the knock on the door. The door opened and John walked into the bedroom. Stella quickly noticed three things; the lustful grin on his face, his dick which was ready to explode out of his pants, and the black briefcase he was carrying.

"Hey beautiful, I missed you." John said, as he started to undress. He watched as Stella stood up off the bed. Her dark, smooth complexion on her 5'7 frame was a sight for sore eyes. At sixteen years of age, Stella's body was that of a young goddess with curves in all the right places, attached to the most gorgeous face. She was beautiful, which for her was a gift and a curse.

Stella unsnapped her bra and it fell to the floor, exposing her firm but soft to the touch, 36- C cup breasts. She grinned at John seeing the beads of sweat pour down his forehead. Then she slowly pulled down her panties, as she stood there like a mannequin in a department store. Her pussy was shaved bald, just the way he and most men that visited her liked.

"Before we start do you have what I asked for?" she said.

"Yes mother I have it … everything you asked for mother!" John said, reaching for the briefcase.

He sat his naked body on the edge of the bed and placed the briefcase across his lap. When he opened it there were a few sex toys inside: a 12 inch black strap-on vibrator, a long-thick black whip, handcuffs, a book and a small white envelope. He passed the envelope to Stella and said, "It's all there mother, five hundred dollars cash. Just like all the other times I come over, I make sure it's all there."

"Thanks John, just remember never tell my grandmother about our secret deal, and everything you ask me to do for you I will."

"I promise mother, I will never tell her." he said, as he crawled up on the bed.

"I also brought you another book to practice your reading and writing,"

"Thank you." She said.

"Anything for you mother." John said, as he began to masturbate.

"Stop that! Wait for me." she said.

"Ok, Ok I'll wait for you mother."

Stella took the book off the briefcase and stared at it. The book was called 'The Basics of Writing, Reading, and Mathematics'. She sat the book on her dresser and joined John in bed. After climbing on top of John she pinned him down. "Now you're gonna do everything I tell you to do! Or I'm gonna spank your ass!" Stella shouted.

"Anything mother! Anything you want!" John replied. Stella got off of John and grabbed the whip from out of the briefcase.

"Stretch out your whole body across the bed." she instructed. John quickly did as he was told, and with each demand he was being turned on more. Stella clutched the whip inside her hand and raised her arm high in the air. She looked down at her naked, white prey and felt the hatred she had for him and all the other men she serviced. They were nothing more than the scum of the earth, human predators devouring everything good and pure in their path. Using their money, power and influence to manipulate the poor and uneducated.

Chapter 3

Ms. Haddy sat on the coach going through her small stack of lottery tickets. "Damn I can't win to save my life." she barked. The doorknob turned and a beautiful brown skin female walked inside the house. "Hey grandma" she said, walking over and giving Ms. Haddy a kiss on the check.

"Hey Lisa, how was school today?"

"Fine, I got an A plus on my computer lab test. The teacher told me that I'm her favorite student."

"Just like you're my favorite granddaughter."

"Where's Stella?" Lisa asked.

"That bitch is upstairs with another trick … probably suckin' dick right now."

They both started laughing.

"Here," Ms. Haddy said, passing Lisa two hundred dollars.

"Thanks grandmom."

Lisa was Ms. Haddy's seventeen year old granddaughter and there wasn't anything in the world she wouldn't do for her. She made sure Lisa had the best clothes and shoes, and she even brought her a new 2010 Toyota Camry so she could get back and forth to school. Unlike Stella, Lisa was allowed outside of the home, and could do the normal teenage girl things, like having a boyfriend, talking on the phone, going to the mall and just enjoying her life. But for Stella, she wasn't given the same privileges. She wasn't allowed to attend school, have a boyfriend, or go shopping. She could only eat, sleep and fuck the long list of strangers that paid Ms. Haddy for a good time with her. It had been this way since Stella first got her period at ten. Stella had become Ms. Haddy's own personal whore. Her body paid for all the bills, even the car note on Lisa's new car. Ms. Haddy hated Stella with a passion but loved Lisa with all of her heart, and no one knew why. It had been this way for so long that everyone was used to it.

As Ms. Haddy and Lisa sat on the couch conversing they could hear the loud moans coming from upstairs. But these weren't moans of passion. These were moans of a sixteen year old crying out for help. As the loud moans continued, Lisa snuggled up with her grandmother and began telling her all about the wonderful day she had.

Chapter 4

Stella was down on her knees with John's rock hard dick inside of her mouth. She was giving him the best blowjob of his life. She had thoughts of biting his dick off, but she needed him more than he or anyone would ever know. He was an asset to her and had been for the past year. John secretly brought her books to read and gave her money for performing kinky sex acts on him, which Ms. Haddy knew nothing about. There were also times where he would take a break from their sexual play and teach her how to read and write. It was their secret and she made him promise that it would stay that way.

When John started to cum, Stella wrapped her arms around his ass and grabbed him tightly, then made sure she swallowed every single drop.

"Ahhhh...Ohh Mother!!!" he yelled out in ecstasy.

She hated what she had done but it was all a part of her plan. She made it her personal goal to satisfy John and every other trick that came into her bedroom. She knew that most men thought with their dicks and their lust for sex left them vulnerable. So she was determined to be the best and they could come back for more, so she could get something out of it. And they all did.

"John sit right here." she said.

Like a young child he ran over to the bed and sat beside her. "Yes mother, what is it?"

"Did you do what I asked you to do for me?" she asked.

DC Bookdiva

"Yes mother." John said, as he reached for his pants and took out a small envelope. "Here mother, just like you asked me."

Stella took the envelope and looked inside. For the first time all day a smile came to her beautiful black face.

"Thank you so much!" she said, excitingly.

"Mother can I ask you something very personal?"

"What is it?"

"Why does Ms. Haddy treat you like a slave?"

Stella took a deep breath. She thought about the question and just shook her head in disbelief. Silence feel upon the entire room. For a moment they just stared at each other before she could come up with a response.

"I don't know why but as long as I can remember it's always been that way. Ever since my grandfather killed my mother." Stella paused as the memory began to surface and the pain of her loss intensified. "Sometimes I wish I could just die ... or get far away from this place." She uttered.

"Don't worry mother, twenty four hours and it will all be over." John said, as he begin to get dressed.

Chapter 5

One hour later, John was rushing out the front door and hurrying to his suburban home, back to his wonderful wife and kids.

Lisa was inside her bedroom, sitting on her bed, talking on her cell phone. She was a spoiled brat that got everything she asked for. Ms. Haddy rarely told her favorite granddaughter no, and if she had to tell her no, it was only because Stella hadn't made enough. So she would call over some of her tricks so Lisa could have what she wanted. Together, Lisa and Ms. Haddy, made Stella's life miserable. From physical to verbal abuse, they were the tag-team from hell.

Lisa got off her cell phone and placed it down beside her, then she raised her arms and let out a long yawn before calling to Stella.

"Bitch! Hey Bitch come here!" she yelled out.

Moments later Stella walked into her bedroom. She was so tired it could be seen all over her face.

"Bitch did you wash all my clothes?"

"Yes Lisa, I washed, dried, and folded everything ... just like you told me." Stella said, as she sat down in the empty chair.

"Bitch stand up! I ain't tell you to sit down." she snapped.

Stella stood back up, her tired eyes quickly filled up with hate. Deep down she couldn't stand Lisa. They were first cousins but they both despised each other. Stella had reason to hate Lisa. For the way she spoke to her and how she treated her like a personal servant all

DC Bookdiva

seemed like a justifiable reason for the hatred she had. But Lisa's reasons were unfounded. Stella was never mean to her and the only reason she could have hated Stella, was listening to the lies and horrible things their grandmother had put in her mind. Ms. Haddy had told so many lies about Stella that Lisa just began to believe them.

"Bitch what did you cook today?" Lisa hissed.

"I made spaghetti ... do you want me to warm you up a plate?" Stella asked.

"Yeah, I'm hungry ... close the door behind you and hurry up."

Stella turned and walked out the room as she thought, *Only twenty four hours*. The thought brought a smile to her face but her soul was crying a river of tears. All she ever wanted was love but love never found her- only its twin brother-hate- who came to her side daily. After Stella warmed up the plate of spaghetti, she added some extra sauce--two mouthfuls of spit, and then she stirred it all up and headed upstairs.

"Here you go Lisa." she said walking into the room. When she passed her the plate she watched as Lisa started eating the spaghetti.

Lisa being aggravated by her presence, she shouted, "Okay, you can get out Bitch!"

"No problem." Stella said, as she walked away with a devilish grin.

Chapter 6

A few hours had passed and Stella had sex with two other men. A Puerto Rican guy named Carlos, and a fifty year old black man named Mark. They were both her Friday regulars. In fact, Friday's were her busiest days. For most of her clients it was their payday. For Stella it was hell. The only good thing about it was that most of her sex clients were minute men. She had mastered and taught herself how to contract her pussy muscles. So most of the men she had sex with would cum and be done in less than five minutes. Stella also found a way to make some extra money by giving sexual favors and fulfilling fantasies for additional cash. She never allowed it to get to Ms. Haddy. Stella was smart, she had been secretly been saving up her money for the past three and a half years.

As soon as Stella got out of the shower and dried herself off with her towel, there was another knock on the door. After a long sigh she said, "Come in." The door opened and a stocky, dark skinned man walked through the doors. He stood about 5 foot 9 and weighed almost two hundred pounds. He was dressed in blue jeans, a red polo shirt, and had a pair of Timbs on. He showed no emotions and his presence was terrifying.

His name was Rambo and he had a reputation as a cold blooded killer on the streets of DC. Stella had found out from one of her other tricks, that Rambo beat three homicides, each victim was a woman. He carried

DC Bookdiva

two guns with him wherever he went and he slept with both guns under his pillow. Stella stood there in complete silence. Whenever Rambo came over they rarely talked. It was nothing more than a fuck and he enjoyed beating up her tight young pussy. He also would give her extra cash to satisfy his anal sex addiction.

Stella watched as Rambo got undressed. Scars, tattoos, and gunshot wounds covered his dark muscular body. He was only twenty seven years old but his body look like it had been through a life time of battles-on the streets and in prison. Rambo walked over and joined Stella in the bed. She gave him the best sex he'd ever had, but he'd never admit it. He was turned out by the young teen and not a Friday passed without him seeing Stella. If nothing stood in his way, he'd make sure to be there on Saturday.

When Rambo laid back, Stella crawled over and placed his long, hard dick inside her mouth. She knew tonight was going to be a long night because unlike most of her tricks, that only last a few minutes, Rambo was filled with stamina.

Chapter 7
Friday Night
9:35PM

Ms. Haddy sat on the couch, listening to the raw sounds of sex coming from Stella's bedroom. The headboard slamming up against the wall seemed to go on forever. She could hear Stella's cries and moans echoing throughout the house. A smile always came to her face and she yelled, "Fuck dat' lil' bitch's brains out Rambo! Fuck her good!" She grabbed her pocketbook and took out a small picture of her husband Sam, who was serving a life sentence for murder.

"Why Sam! Why did you do it?" she asked herself. "How could you do it!" she continued.

The tears from years of pain and heartache escaped the confides of her old eyes. "Why , why!" she cried, as she placed the picture back into her pocketbook. She sat back on the couch and rested her arms across her chest. Past memories played inside of her mind, the good ones, bad ones, and the ugly ones.

Lisa's eyes were tightly closed as her slim naked body was laid across the bed. With her vibrator in her right hand she begin masturbating. Hearing Stella getting her brains fucked out in the next room, turned her on. Not only was Lisa jealous of her cousin's great looks and beautifully sculpted body, but she wanted a piece of the action she got. Lisa was still a virgin but not a day went by that she didn't fantasize about having sex. She wanted the kind of sex that Stella had with Rambo, the hard, rough kind. As Stella's moans grew and the headboard continued to bang against the wall, Lisa rubbed the vibrator against her clit.

She could feel her body preparing for an intense orgasm. Suddenly a gush of warm, silky liquid flowed from her pussy. She placed her pillow over her head in case she couldn't keep control of moans. This was her third orgasm and as she leaned her face into her pillows she let out her vocal release. Every Friday she made sure she was home when Rambo came over. Just hearing him fuck Stella made her want him even more. Each night he came, she'd lock her door, undress and lay across her bed with her vibrator as she imagined Rambo fucking her. She secretly yearned for him, he was her dream thug. A beast in the bedroom and a gangster in the streets. The headboard continued to bang, Lisa took another deep breath and grabbed her vibrator for round four.

Chapter 8
10:47 PM

Stella laid across her bed physically drained. Her entire body felt as if it had been hit by a Mack truck, and she could barely move a muscle. Her mouth, pussy and ass were all in excruciating pain because Rambo showed her no mercy. He took a 100 milligram Viagra before every sex session he had with her. He wanted to fuck her like no other, while releasing all the built up frustration he had inside. Street life was taking its toll on him and sex with Stella was his temporary escape from all the madness that surrounded him on the DC streets.

She watched as Rambo got dressed and put on his boots. He tucked both of his guns under his Polo shirt, then walked over and sat down beside her.

"You alright, shorty?" he asked.

"Yeah, I'm fine daddy." Stella muttered.

"My stomach hurts a little but I'll be okay til' tomorrow." she grinned.

"Here." Rambo said, passing Stella a hundred dollar bill.

"You a beast, shorty." he told her. Rambo walked over towards the door, then turned toward her and said, "I'ma see you tomorrow, shorty ... around the same time so rest up."He then walked out the room.

In the hallway he briefly stopped because Lisa was standing in her doorway with nothing but her panties and bra on. Lust was all over her face and Rambo could sense she wanted to be fucked. Word on the street was she was a virgin but was ripe for the picking. The DC streets spread the news, good or bad, quickly. Rambo winked his eye as he passed her room and whispered, "One day, shorty."

Lisa replied, "You promise?"

Rambo just kept walking down the stairs. Lisa returned into her bedroom. After six orgasms she was tired and ready for sleep. She knew Rambo would be back tomorrow, so she had a lot to look forward to and needed her rest.

"You enjoy yourself Rambo?" Ms. Haddy asked.

"Yes I did!"

"Same time tomorrow?"

"Yeah, I'll be back." he said with a smirk on his face.

Ms. Haddy's eyes followed Rambo out the front door. She knew Stella was upstairs laying on her bed, balled up in pain. Then, once again there was a knock at the door. A fat light skin man walked inside and handed Ms. Haddy two hundred dollars. "Big Love she's nice and ready for you. Ain't been fucked all day." she lied. Ms. Haddy placed the money insider of her bra and laid back down on the couch. She felt no guilt or remorse for pimping her own granddaughter. It was the only joy she had in her old miserable life.

Chapter 9
11:52 PM

Stella sat there on the edge of the bed, watching as her last customer for the night walk out her bedroom, and she was glad he was gone. Big love was a 296-pound man who breathed heavy and sweated intensely. Every time he laid on top of her body she felt like she was being suffocated and buried alive. Not to mention the smell, that seemed like he had been doused with a pound of Gorilla shit. Horrific. She did her best to endure the foul smell, and his one hundred dollar tip was enough for her to close her eyes and get through it.

After hearing the front door close, Stella opened her door and tip-toed down the hallway to the stairs. She saw Ms. Haddy knocked out on the sofa. After getting something to eat and drink, she walked over to the couch. Standing over her grandmother, she just couldn't help but stare. *How could my grandmother be my enemy,* she thought. A whirlwind of emotions ran throughout her confused mind. She wanted answers to her many questions. For a few minutes she watched as her grandmother peacefully slept. Snoring on every inhale. Ms.Haddy craved a good night's sleep because she had constant nightmares, which awakened her from her sleep at least once a night. Her dreams were filled with violence and death was always her outcome.

As Stella walked away from her grandmother tears rolled down her eyes. She was so tired of this life. It had to be better somewhere else, she thought as she walked into her bedroom. She locked her door and tears continued to fly off her face, as she got on her knees.

Stella reached under her mattress and felt around for the hole she had made. When she found it she dug inside and started to take out the stacks of bills. Once all the money was removed from her hiding spot, she sat on her bed and began counting the money.

An hour later she had finished counting the twenty seven thousand, six hundred and thirty five dollars that she had saved from the last three and a half years of prostitution. She looked at the money and knew it would come in handy soon, then she placed the money back into its hole and sat on her bed with one of her books. She loved reading, even though she wasn't the best, she enjoyed it because it gave her an escape. She enjoyed urban novels and as she read a few pages of Eyone Williams', *The Cross*, a smile came to her face. She laid the book on her chest and her eyes were staring out the window as she whispered, "Twenty hours more and it'll all be over." The hours couldn't move fast enough. Nervousness swept through her body as she thought about Saturday ... the day she had waited her entire life for.

Chapter 10
Saturday morning...
9:13 Am

When Stella woke up she had to do her daily chores. Clean all the bedrooms, clean the bathroom, the kitchen and do the laundry. Then she had to make Ms. Haddy and Lisa breakfast. This was the only life Stella had known, catering to people who showed no signs of appreciation.

"Bitch come here!" Ms. Haddy yelled. "Bitch where are you! Come here!"

Stella ran down the stairs and straight to the kitchen where Ms. Haddy and Lisa were eating breakfast. "Yes grandmom ... I mean MS. Haddy." Stella said, with a nervous look on her face.

"Bitch did you take out the trash?"

"No, not yet...I was waiting--"

"Bitch shut up and don't say another word!" Ms. Haddy snapped. She reached out and grabbed a handful of Stella's hair. Then she slapped her as hard as she could. "Bitch you know every Saturday morning I want the trash out!"

"I'm sorry. I won't ever forget again." Stella said, as she tried her best to hold back her tears.

"You better not or else I'ma whip that ass with that extension cord again."

"I won't forget, I...I ...promise." Ms. Haddy released Stella's hair from her grip and watched as Stella hurried off.

"That stupid bitch don't ever learn!" Ms. Haddy barked.

"Maybe you need to whip her with the extension cord just to remind her how it feels. It's been about a week and I think she's overdo." Lisa said.

"I'm tired, maybe tomorrow. Sunday's always a lil' slow with tricks so I'll have some time tomorrow. Plus I need to relieve some stress." she said, as they both began laughing.

Inside her bedroom, Stella was on her knees with her hands folded and eyes closed. "God where are you? Why must I go through so much pain...If you hear me God can you please help me escape this made world...Please God I beg you." Stella wiped her tears and got up from the floor, because she could hear Ms. Haddy and Lisa downstairs laughing. She quickly collected all the trash and took it out to the curb. Before going back inside, she looked up at the beautiful blue sky. The sun was beaming and the wind was clam. *Today was a wonderful day,* she thought. "God I'm counting on you." she said, before reentering the house.

Now it was time for her to get ready for the busy days of Saturday's. In just a few hours, there would be a line of hungry predators waiting to see her. To fuck, beat, kiss and violate Stella, and escape their realities, live out their fantasies, all while ruining her reality. *If I can only make it for just fifteen more hours,* she thought.

Chapter 11
Late Saturday Evening…
7:52 PM

Four men and one woman had already come and gone. Stella never had sex with another woman before, but this one came with her husband; and since they were paying customers Ms. Haddy didn't see why they both couldn't be serviced. At first the woman said she only wanted to watch but she quickly joined in and gave her husband the best 39th birthday present he ever had. After they left, Stella kept looking at the clock. Today time was moving slowly and she was anxious. She paced the hallway in anticipation of the late evening.

"Come in." Ms. Haddy said, hearing the knock on the door. John walked inside with his briefcase in his hand and a big smile on his face. He passed Ms. Haddy three hundred dollars and walked towards the stairs. He knew his young Nubian princess was upstairs waiting for him. All day he had been lusting and fantasizing about her. When he walked into the bedroom, Stella was laying across the bed naked.

"What took you so long?" she asked.

"I was trying to get away from my wife and kids. Plus there was lots of traffic." John answered. He sat down on the bed and opened his briefcase. Then he took out a book and a Polaroid camera and passed them to Stella.

"Here you go mother, just like you asked me." he said.

"Thank you John. I want you to take some pictures of us while we make love." she said.

"Anything for you mother." he said, as he began to undress.

John quickly joined Stella in bed and began taking pictures of them fucking, him giving her anal sex, and of her performing oral sex on him. They had taken over twenty pictures and John asked, "Why do you want these pictures?" Stella quickly responded,

"For memories John. I love you and I always want to be able to go back and look at the fun times we share together."

"Promise me you won't show anyone these pictures." he said.

Stella pulled John close to her, rolled on top of his pale, white body, then stared into his blue eyes and said, "I promise John, this is our little secret."

"I love you mother."

"I love you, John. Now be quiet and let mother finish taking care of you." Stella put both of her hands around his neck and slid his dick inside of her pussy. It was small but she had a thousand ways of making him feel like he had the biggest dick in the world. Four more hours, she thought to herself.

Chapter 12
10:15PM

Before John left Stella made sure he told her the location of his job. She told him she would come by and visit him one day. Stella had John strung out and he would do anything she asked. He didn't question her motivates when she said things that would usually require his red-flags to go up. For her services, John paid her five hundred dollars and he thought she was worth every penny.

After taking a shower Stella laid across her bed patiently waiting on her next trick, Rambo. She had been waiting on him all day long because he was the key to her freedom; her deliverer from years of pain, tears and misery. When she heard Rambo downstairs speaking with Ms. Haddy she was a ball of nerves. Still, her mind was made up and she was determined to go through with her plan.

Rambo walked into her bedroom and locked the door behind him. Dressed in all back, he looked like a walking shadow with his black hoodie, boots, pants and gloves. The way he was dressed made her think he'd just come from murdering someone. Rambo sat down in the empty chair next to her bed and began to undress. Stella watched him place both guns on her dresser, a 38 and a 9mm-both fully loaded. When he was undressed he walked over and got in bed with her.

"One minute, I have to use the bathroom." she said. Rambo watched Stella get up and walk towards the door. Then suddenly she grabbed both of his guns from the dresser.

"What the fuck is you doing." he said.

"Shut the fuck up!" Stella said, pointing both guns at his head. He closed his mouth seeing the serious look in her eyes. He knew she wouldn't hesitate to shoot him, and he didn't want to take the chance that she was bluffing.

"Stand up motherfucker...No I mean child-fucker!" she yelled. Rambo stood up from the bed with both his hands in the air.

"Do you like Lisa?" she asked.

"Huh?"

"I said do you like Lisa?!"

"Yeah, she alright, why?"

"Because I want you to fuck her!"

"Well you don't have to point guns at me if you want me to fuck her." he said.

"No, I don't want you to just fuck her...I want you to rape her ass! And fuck her the way you've been fucking me--with no mercy! If you do this, I'll give you your guns and your money back."

A grin came across Rambo's face. He didn't know what all this was about but he didn't care either. He had wanted to fuck Lisa anyway.

"Okay, I'll fuck the shit out of her young ass!" he told Stella.

"Then I can get my guns back, right?"

"Right," Stella said, aiming at his head.

"Now come with me".

Rambo did as he was told and walked out of her room. *As soon as I get my guns back I'ma kill everybody in this house,* he thought to himself.

Chapter 13

"Who is it?" Lisa asked, hearing the knock on her door.

"It's me, Rambo." Lisa jumped off the bed and rushed over the door. She didn't care that she was naked. When she opened the door Rambo pushed her back inside and grabbed her. Stella stepped into the room behind him, pointed both guns at both of them.

"Bitch what is you doin'?" Lisa asked.

"Shut up bitch and learn how to fuckin listen!" Stella said, closing the door behind her.

"Rambo's got something for you…"

"Why are you aiming those guns at us Stella?"

"Bitch I said shut the fuck up!" she laughed then said, "How does that feel?"

"Okay Rambo, go ahead and fuck that bitch brains out!" Stella directed.

Rambo put his hand over her mouth and threw her onto the bed. After he pinned Lisa down, he spread her legs apart. She tried to push him off but she was no match for Rambo's strength. In one quick motion, Rambo thrust his hard, long dick deep inside of Lisa's virgin pussy. "

Ahhhhh!!!" she tried to yell out through his fingers. Rambo fucked Lisa like a possessed man, who had served 20 years in prison. He was brutal with every stroke.

Lisa wanted to cry, scream and yell for help but her cries sounded no different than those of Stella's constant cries to Ms. Haddy when she was getting her brains fucked out. As Rambo pushed his dick deeper and harder inside of Lisa's severely swollen and beaten pussy, Stella watched in enjoyment. This bitch had finally known the pain and misery she was enduring, and how it felt to know no one would do a damn thing to eliminate the hurt.

Rambo swiftly turned Lisa's weakened body over and spread her ass cheeks a part, then rammed his Viagra operated, rock hard dick in her ass. She let out cries that reached the heaven's but only fell on deaf ears. Tears ran down her face and she called out to God until her vocal cords ached and the pain silenced her voice. There was no one that would run to her rescue; she had to endure the brutal wrath of Rambo.

Rambo came in her ass and didn't even pause. He turned her onto her back and began fucking her pussy with a stronger force. It was as if he got a second wind and wanted to blow her pussy to pieces. In a final attempt for help, Lisa yelled out, "Please God somebody help me!" and it echoed through the house.

Ms. Haddy was lying across the coach and she smiled, then said "Fuck that bitch brains out!" She had never heard that intense of a scream before but she was glad to know Stella was being fucked until it hurt. However, these screams of anguish were all coming from the grandchild that she loved with all her heart, Lisa.

Chapter 14
11:30PM

When Rambo had finished, he got up and stood over Lisa's tired, desecrated body. Blood from Lisa's ass was all over the sheets and she was stretched out across the bed unable to move. She also had no voice to call out for help, her body had shut down.

"Move over there." Stella told Rambo. He did as he was told and moved away from the bed.

"Bitch!" Stella yelled. Lisa did her best to turn her head towards Stella.

"Turn around bitch!" she repeated.

Lisa turned around and looked into her eyes. Stella had the 9mm pointed at her head and the 38mm pointed at Rambo.

"This is for all the pain and misery you put me through." She then pulled the trigger twice. Lisa's body lay slumped on the bed. Stella had shot her twice in the head.

"Damn what the fuck she do to you." he said.

"It's what she didn't do that got her killed." Stella replied.

"And what's that?" Rambo asked.

"She didn't love me." she said.

Rambo knew this shit had turned all the way serious and didn't say another word. He had just watched her murder her cousin and she enjoyed it. Life didn't seem to have meaning and he didn't know if she was thinking about adding him to her shit-list. All he wanted to do was get out of this house alive because he was going to put this crazy bitch down.

"Come on, we're going downstairs." Stella said. Rambo looked at Lisa's dead body and shook his head before leaving the bedroom.

"You promised to give my guns back." he said, trying to see where her head was at.

"I am but get downstairs first."

"I'm naked."

"Yes because you have one more woman to fuck, then you can go." Stella said.

"Huh?" Rambo replied.

"You want me to fuck your grandmom?" he asked.

"Yup, just like you fucked Lisa." Stella said, as she kept the guns aimed at his head.

"This is some fucked up shit! She old enough to be my grandmother!"

"Shut up and do it. She aint your grandmother, she aint nobody grandmom...she's a

fucking pimp!" Stella said.

They both came downstairs nude and found Ms. Haddy trying to hide behind the couch. She had heard the gunshots and instead of trying to see what was wrong, she just hid.

"Bitch you can come out." Stella demanded.

Ms. Haddy peered her head from behind the couch and was shocked. She never thought she would see Stella aiming two guns aiming at her, and she felt like she was having a heart attack.

"What the hell is going on Stella?"

"Shut up bitch!" Stella told her.

"Who you calling a bitch, Stella? I'm your grandmother." Ms. Haddy said.

" You aint my fuckin grandmother! Bitch get undressed or get shot!"

Chapter 15
11:42 PM

Stella and Rambo stood back and stared at Ms. Haddy's old, wrinkled body.

"I don't know if I can do this." Rambo said.

"Do it and you'll get your guns, I promise."

"Do what? I'm too old for sex...I haven't done that in over ten years!" Ms.

Haddy shouted.

"Well you're gonna get fucked tonight!" Stella said.

"Bitch you better kill me after this. I swear to God I'm gonna get you for this." Ms.

Haddy yelled out.

"Don't worry about me grandma. Just try to enjoy getting fucked." Stella said, as a big

grin came across her face.

After a long sigh, Rambo walked over and joined Ms. Haddy on the couch. He laid her back and climbed on top of her. He spread her old, varicose vein legs a part and rammed his dick inside her. She yelled out, "Dear God." but he continued to fuck her in hopes this shit would all be over quickly. As he fucked her harder and harder, Stella stood over them, enjoying each moment but never letting her guard down. She clutched the guns and if Rambo tried anything she was ready. "Fuck that old bitch brains out, rip her pussy to death!" Stella shouted.

Twenty minutes later, her grandmother lay on the couch passed out. She had been fucked so hard that she fainted.

"Now I did what you asked, can I get my guns back?" Rambo asked.

"Sure." Stella said, as she shot him five times- three in the head and two in the chest. He slumped where he stood, surrounded in his own blood. The gunshots woke Ms. Haddy from her fainting spell.

"You killed him! You killed him!"

"Shut up bitch! Just shut your stupid old ass up!" Stella said, as tears started to fall from her eyes.

"Tell me why you hurt me so much?" Stella asked.

"Why?"

"Stella please put those guns down."

"No. Answer my question...why have you hurt me, always? Why did you curse and beat

me? What did I do to you?"

Ms. Haddy watched as the tears fell from Stella's eyes. It had been years since she saw her cry.

"Because of your mother." she answered.

"My mother?" Stella asked.

"Yes...your mother and my...and my--"

"Your what?" Stella demanded to know.

"My husband! You're his fucking daughter!" Ms. Haddy said.

"What are you saying?" Stella asked.

"I'm saying my husband raped your mother and nine months later my daughter had a child by my husband!"

"You're a fucking liar!"

"No, it's the truth Stella...that's why he killed her. She had finally decided to go to the Cops!"

"So you knew about this?" Stella asked.

"Yes, he was all I had...I loved that man to death. I know how you must feel but he was going to leave me if I didn't let him have sex with your mother." Ms. Haddy began to cry out.

Stella was in disbelief. All these years she had been abused and destroyed behind these horrible acts that her grandmother could have avoided.

"Why would you hurt me, what did I do to you?"

"Because...I blamed you and your mother for all my pain. Your mother was young and beautiful and all he wanted was her. He would only be with me if I let him rape your mother."

"You're disgusting! You're worse than the devil...How could you let your husband rape your daughter!" Stella shouted.

Ms. Haddy just lowered her head as Stella scolded her and reminded her how foolish her decision was. Then Ms. Haddy muttered, "I'm sorry."

Stella walked closer to her grandmom and asked, "What did you say?"

"I said I'm sorry."

"No, tell the devil you're sorry." Stella said, as she looked Ms. Haddy in the eyes. "Maybe he'll forgive you." She shot her twice in the head. Ms. Haddy's body fell to the floor. Stella ran over to get Ms. Haddy's shirt and began wiping down the two guns, to remove her fingerprints. Then she placed the 9mm in Ms. Haddy's hand and the 38 in Rambo's. Upstairs she ran to get dressed and get her luggage. She quickly gathered her money and placed it securely in her suitcase, then headed downstairs to wait for her cab. She didn't know if her plan would work and at the point she didn't care. But she knew it was time for her to face a new chapter in her life and to regain her freedom.

While she waited for the cab, she wrote a letter to the local police department.

To whom it may concern:

This man is John Smith and he's a pedophile and a rapist. These pictures are of him with a 16 year - old. He's the Vice President of the DC National Bank. Please get him off the streets because he is a danger to our society.-Stella

Once inside of her cab, she placed the letter inside of an envelope and asked the cabdriver to take her to the police station. When they arrived in front of the station, she ran inside and asked the clerk, to make sure the chief of police got the letter, and then she ran back out to the cab.

Stella made her way to the train station with the ticket John had brought her to New York City. Even though she was scared to leave the only place she knew, she knew she couldn't stay. She had to start over. This would the beginning of the end...

A Gangster's Past

Robert "Big Dee" Williams

APRIL 2001

"Please, please, please just give me this one pack," pregnant Angie pleaded. "I swear on my baby's life I'll go to rehab tomorrow." For added effect, she rubbed a hand over her huge stomach.

"How many months is you, ma?" Tre asked in his own distinct accent, then looked down at her stomach.

"Six months," she replied, as they stood in the doorway of one of Tre's drug houses, where she'd stopped him on his way out. Tre ran and controlled the majority of the heroin houses on the west side of town, and even though he sold drugs, he was strict on his rules. One of his major rules was to never to sell to a pregnant woman. Angie had been buying dope from the same spot for years up until she got pregnant. At first, she hid her stomach, but when she began to show and Tre's workers noticed, that's when they cut her off. Tre looked at her stomach again. She was huge. His thoughts were broken up when she reached out and grabbed his hand.

"Come on baby," she begged. "Just this one pack, pleeeaaase?"

Angie wasn't a bad looking chick and was used to getting what she wanted. She was young and she kept up her appearance.

"Come on Angie, you know how I feel about them babies." He grabbed her by the arm and swung her around. His eyes went straight to her ass. "But damn, you do look like you been taking care of yourself." He turned and opened the door he'd just walked out of and told one of his workers to come to the porch.

Seconds later the door opened again and one of Tre's workers named Q stuck his head out of the door.

"Yeah, what up Tre?"

Tre held one of his hands out in front of Q, but kept his eyes on Angie.

"Let me get a pack Q."

Q hesitated and Tre turned his attention to him, and Angie flashed Q a sly smile behind Tre's back.

"But - ," Q said in an effort to protest, but was cut off by Tre.

"But nothing!" Tre barked.

"Just give me a pack, Q!"

Confused, Q reached in his pocket. Tre's number one rule was to never sell drugs to pregnant women, but Tre was the boss. He pulled out a pack and placed it in Tre's extended hand, then turned and went back in the house shaking his head. Tre gave Angie the pack and she snatched him into a hug and kissed his cheek.

"Thank you Tre baby," she said seductively.

"Yeah, whatever," he said dryly. "Just make sure you take your ass to rehab tomorrow."

Angie walked off into the dark night with her head down and the feeling that Tre was watching her; she picked up her pace and hoped that he didn't notice that she didn't give him any money. When she was out of sight, Tre flipped his hood over his head, and jogged to his car just as the rain began to fall. Behind the wheel he turned the wipers on and laughed at Angie and how she thought he'd forgotten to get the money for the pack he'd given her.

*****

Robert "Big Dee" Williams

Tre had a habit of playing the numbers, and every night before he went home he stopped by the number house. He opened the back door of the house and looked out. The rain was coming down harder now, he ran to the car. Once inside, he grabbed the ignition and began to turn the key. A tap at the window startled him and made him reach for his pistol. With a hand firmly gripped on the pistol, he looked over to the passenger side of the car it was just his cousin Duke.

"Goddamn Duke!" placing his hand over his heart.

"You scared the shit out of me."

Duke, with a trembling hand inched the flame of his lighter to the cigarette in his mouth and took a deep pull.

"What up cuz?" Duke asked without even looking at Tre. He blew out the smoke he'd just inhaled then took another long pull, this time Tre, noticed his trembling.

"I ain't mean to scare you." He looked to the driver's seat at Tre.

"So what numbers you play?"

Tre didn't answer immediately, he just turned the ignition over and pulled off. The rain crashed against the windshield and every few seconds the sky roared and lit up with thunder and lightning.

"You know I play my momma and grandma birthday every day." He looked over at Duke and lightning struck at the same time. Duke had a bland stare on his face.

"Come on Duke, you know I play the same numbers every day."

The passenger window slid down an inch and Duke thumped the cigarette butt out and rolled the window back up before the water had a chance to seep in.

Robert "Big Dee" Williams

"So where you headed to Duke?"
Duke shrugged.
"I don't know. I was really just out and about."
"You hungry?"
"Naw, I'm good Tre."

There had been some talk going around that
Duke had gotten into some trouble, Tre wasn't sure, but
then again he knew how Duke was. Duke was a go
getter. If he didn't have something he was going to get
it by any means. When they were younger they had
been close, but as they grew older space had grown
between them and that caused them to veer off on two
different paths. Tre had always been the hustler and
leader, and Duke a renegade. Now a days they usually
only got together at their cousin's barber shop to blaze
weed or at a few family functions they did
attend. Besides that, if Duke was around, then Duke
wanted something.
"Yo Tre?" Duked called out through sniffles and
waited until he had his cousin's attention. He continued
anyways knowing that what he was about to ask for was
taboo.
"I need some heat cuz." He sniffled again.
"Yeah cuz, something small and light."

Tre finally looked to the passenger side and he
calmly asked Duke why in a calm tone. They were
stopped at a red light and a box Chevy on big rims
pulled up next to them. Tre and the driver exchanged
nods and Tre waited for the light to turn green and the
car to gain some distance before he spoke again, because
of its loud music. The rain still crashed against his own
window.
"Why Duke? What the fuck you need a gun
for?"

"Protection," Duke shot back quickly and with agitation in his voice.

"I done got myself in some shit and I gotta get myself out of it."

"Look man," Tre said then reached in his pocket and came out with a small gun and held it in his hand with an open palm.

"You know I don't ever let my pistols leave my side, right?" It was more of a statement than a question. He let the words hang in the air for a moment then sat the pistol on the arm rest. Duke reached out quickly and grabbed it, but Tre placed a hand over Duke's before he had a chance to pull it away. Lightning flashed again.

"All I'm saying is be careful my nigga."
Duke pulled his hand and the gun away slowly and stuck them both in his coat pocket.

"Yeah, I got you cuz."
Tre gave Duke a once over and saw a lump in the sleeve of his coat. He looked up and him and Duke locked eyes.

"Is you good, Duke?"

"What you mean cuz?"

"I mean...with that monkey you was trying to get off of your back."
Of course, Duke reassured him that everything was fine. He said he'd been kicked the dope. They pulled up to Tre's house and Tre grabbed his umbrella from the back seat and stepped out into the rain. Duke stayed put for a moment then flipped his hood over his head and climbed out. Tre climbed the stairs to his house and inserted his key in the door's lock, but he noticed that Duke wasn't behind him. He looked back and Duke was standing in the middle of the sidewalk, in a puddle of water, and rain poured down on him.

"Yo Tre?"

Robert "Big Dee" Williams

Tre nodded his head acknowledging Duke, and Duke pointed behind him.

"I almost forgot cuz, but I got some shit I gotta go and handle."

Tre just stood on the steps with his key in the door and looked suspiciously at his cousin over his shoulder.

"Yeah, alright," Tre said, his tone unconvincing.

"Just make sure you bring my shit back how you got it. And don't do shit stupid either."

Without another word, Duke turned and walked away with Tre watching, until he was out of sight. Once out of sight, Tre opened the door and stepped onto his enclosed porch, but before he could even close the door his phone rang. It was his sister Felicia, and she was crying about her kids not having any food to eat and that she needed money for groceries. Tre sighed and looked through the porch's window at his wife. She was on the couch curled up and waiting for him. She looked at her watch, then at her phone, she was expecting him to walk in at any minute. Tre looked at his own watch. It was after nine pm and he'd planned to chill with her, order a movie and food, but he couldn't just leave his nieces and nephews hungry.

It took him 15 minutes to drive to his sister's house. When he walked in all of her kids were huddled around the youngest, a baby girl named Sky. They were trying to stop her from crying. Felicia had five kids and they all ranged in different ages, from her oldest PJ, down to Sky who was just a little over a year old. It seemed like her crying grew worse by the other kids gathering around her, whatever they were doing wasn't working. She was hungry and patty cake doesn't work for that.

Tre walked into the kitchen after looking at the kids and he opened the refrigerator, it was empty. Inside

Robert "Big Dee" Williams

there was only a box of baking soda and a pitcher of water.

Feeling Felicia's presence in the room, he turned and looked over his shoulder and gave her the screw face.

"Where the food Felicia?" he asked with his head still in the refrigerator and in shock from what he was seeing.

"Boy! You know my stamps don't come for another two weeks," she said, then fixed her bra strap.

"Well, then what happened to the stamps you got two weeks ago?"
Her eyes drifted off.

"Tre, now you know these kids got bottomless stomachs." She walked over to the cabinets and opened all of them, they were empty too.

"You don't remember how it was when we had to stay with momma before my section 8 kicked in?" She pulled out a pack of cigarettes and lit one. Tre watched the bright cherry as she inhaled the smoke and wondered how she could afford cigarettes and thinking that with the five dollars that she spent on them, she could have went and bought a twenty four pack of ramen noodles. Disappointed in his sister, Tre dug in his pocket and pulled out a roll of cash and peeled off three twenties and gave them to her. As soon as she stuck them in her bra, her son PJ walked into the room. PJ froze and stood eyeing his mother. He had his friend Chucky with him and both their coats were dripping wet from the rain.

"What up uncle Tre?" PJ said and his friend Chucky just nodded to Tre but spoke to Felicia politely.
PJ dripping water the whole way, walked over to the refrigerator and opened it. Then the freezer, they were both empty.

Robert "Big Dee" Williams

In the other room, Sky's cry grew louder and it reminded Tre of his purpose for being there.

"You got a ride to go and get these kids some food?"

Felicia butted her cigarette, then walked into the other room and snatched up Sky by one arm. Tre followed her. She turned and face Tre, then smacked her lips.

"Yeah, I got a ride."

"Who?"

"Eddie'll take me."

"Eddie?" Tre repeated with disgust.

"I wanna know why Eddie ain't put no food up in here, so you can get these kids fed."

"Cause," was all she said before she hesitated and rested Sky on her once thick hips.

"Cause what, Felicia?"

"Cause they cut his SSI off."

Frustrated, Tre kissed Felicia on the cheek, he'd seen enough.

"Aight man. I'm about to go. Make sure you get these kids something to eat. And make sure it's something that'll last you until your other stamps come."

Sky stopped crying for a moment and reached out to grab Tre's face with her small hands and Tre grabbed her hands. He kissed her fat cheeks, then looked around the room at the other kids, they all looked hungry. He turned back to Felicia and Sky.

"Look, I'm about to go, alright? Hurry up and feed these kids Felicia."

Outside in his car, Tre checked the time again and noticed he'd spent more time than expected dealing with Felicia. He knew that by the time he made it home, his wife would be asleep. He just sat parked on the curb outside of Felicia's house for a moment as he thought. He didn't want to go home just to watch his wife sleep. He opened his phone and called up his girlfriend's number and told her he was on his way over. First he stopped by the liquor store and grabbed a bottle, then he went to Liz's house. They sat, talked, and drank for a while, until they started getting physical and ended up in the bedroom.

4:30 AM

A loud noise outside of Liz's window woke Tre from his sleep. He paid it no attention and looked over at his phone that was sitting on the night stand. It was vibrating. He grabbed it and looked at his caller I.D., it was his wife. Just outside of the door, he heard footsteps, they were light, but he could tell that they were footsteps. The noise came closer, then stopped.

The door knob rattled lightly, then again, but this time harder. On the other side of the bed, Liz squirmed, then woke up when something rammed the door and it split down the middle with a loud cracking noise. Then Liz jumped up from her sleep with a scream and threw the covers back.

"Bitch!" a loud deep voice shouted from the other side of the split door.

"Open this god damn door!"

Liz screamed again, then curled into a ball and Tre grabbed his pants from off of the floor. Then the door flew off its hinges and Tre saw only the shadow of a huge man step into the room. The shadow stepped closer.

"Bitch!" the man's voice was cracking and it was easy to tell that he was on the verge of crying.

"You think you just can do what you wanna do? Huh?"

The shadow raised one of its arms, and in his hand he had a pistol. For Tre, it seemed as if time had stopped and froze as he held his pants in front of him and frantically searched his pockets for the gun he always carried, but it wasn't there. He dropped his pants and

Robert "Big Dee" Williams

they fell to the bed in slow motion, as he remembered that he'd loaned his gun to Duke.

Time restarted and fire shot out from the tip of the gun and Tre held his hands up in front of him in self-defense and tried to use them as a shield for the bullets, but it was useless, the first bullet entered Tre's flesh, four more followed.

THE VISIT

Tre woke up, yawning. He stretched out of bed and went to the bathroom. When he walked out and walked back to his bedroom, what he saw stopped him in his tracks. There was a big muscular dude with long French braids, a back full of tattoos, and no shirt on going through his dresser drawers. Tre rubbed his eyes, then looked around. He took another look, but was still unable to process what he was seeing.

"Who the fuck is you?!"

Startled, the shirtless man who was running through the dresser jumped and turned quickly, sending clothes flying in the air and over his shoulders. He regained his composure quickly, looked around the room, then pointed to his self.

"Who me?" he asked, then looked around and realized that Tre had to be talking to him.

"Damn, I guess you is talking to me."

With his hands made into fists, Tre stepped closer.

"Yeah, I'm talking to you! Now who the fuck is you and what you doing in my house?"

"I'm Ghost, but they call me G," when he said 'G', he made quote signs with his hands. "But you just call me G. Aight, son?"

Tre looked over at his bed. His wife was sleeping peacefully, but then he noticed that the bed wasn't his own, but a hospital bed that was fully equipped with side rails and all. He looked down at his lower body, he had on a hospital gown and only a pair of gray footies covered his feet. He looked back up at G, who was rummaging through the dresser again. G found a bag of weed and slipped it in the pocket of his baggy jeans.

"Oh, I get," Tre said with a wide smile. "I'm dreaming, ain't I?"

G turned around and faced Tre; he had on a pair of Tre's expensive glasses. "Naw son, you ain't dreaming. To be honest, you on your deathbed right now." He pulled a cell phone from his waist, flipped the screen up, then held it out in front of Tre. Tre could see a video playing, but at first he couldn't make out what it was. He turned his head sideways, and that's when he saw his self in a hospital room on a surgical table surrounded by doctors with blood covered scrubs on. G continued.

"Yeah, some fatal attraction cat gave you the business last night, and real talk yo, it ain't looking too good for you kid."

"Riiiigggghhhttt...."

Tre said, all sarcasm.

"Okay, so what you here for then? G, right?"

"Yeah, Ghost, G, it really doesn't matter. And I'm here to show you all the dumb ass decisions you made last night." He let the words soak before he continued.

"I've been on you for a long time now; I guess you can call me your guardian angel. I give it to you though, you a smooth dude and I ain't never had to intercede in your life, but last night, last night you fucked up bad and not just with shit involving you, but shit that affected a few other people as well son."

"Dog, what the hell you talking about?" Tre was shaken by his words.

"I can show you better than I can tell you Tre. There's one thing though..."

"And what's that?" Tre asked, playing along with the charade.

Robert "Big Dee" Williams

"You gotta agree to let me show you."

"And how I do that?"

G dropped his chin to his chest and laughed like Eddie Murphy. He pulled his head back up and now his facial expression was serious.

"All you gotta do my dude is say, 'I wanna see my fuck ups', and I got you."

Tre was still skeptical, but told himself it was a dream and said the words anyway.

G held up a finger.

Tre laughed.

Tre wiggled his shoulders and stepped back and forth from the left and right a couple of times.

"First stop," G said and held up his index finger, "the hospital."

He did his two steps again and both him and Tre dropped through the roof of the hospital and landed on the operating room's floor.

"You'll get used to that in a minute son."

"Where we at?" Tre asked then froze when he looked at the operating table where he saw his self lying on top, soaked in blood, cut open with doctors standing over him.

"Have a look for you yourself kid," G said then pointed to the horrific scene anyway.

Now the doctors were running around screaming out for tools and medicines, and Tre gasped deeply at the sight of his self on the cold steel table.

"You want a closer look," G asked.

Tre didn't respond, instead his eyes grew wide, as he watched his self flat line and the doctors began pumping his chest. He watched his body start to convulse as they tried to pump life back into him. One screamed out for the defribulator paddles. When they came he rubbed them together while a nurse smeared gel on his shaved chest. The doctor rubbed the paddles together, yelled out clear, and sent jolts of electricity through Tre's entire body.

Tre broke away from where he stood next to G and ran over and stood next to the doctor who had the paddles, then bent over his bullet riddled body and screamed for his self to get up. Embarrassed, G gripped his head with both hands. Tre had lost control, it was unusual, many did when they saw themselves on their death beds. He walked over to where Tre was.

The heart monitor beeped a few times and the room went silent just before the continuous flatline echoed throughout. After trying his hardest to save Tre, the doctor dropped the paddles and looked at all of the nurses that surrounded the bed. His face was full of grief and his voice came out gravelly when he spoke. He locked eyes with a nurse with a clip board and told her that Tre was gone.

Tre slowly turned and faced G.

"What the fuck he mean!"

"Bring it down a notch kid," G interrupted.

With a twisted face, Tre turned back toward the doctor who was now pulling the sheet over him. Tre lost control. He started screaming then reached out and tried to grab the paddle, but his hands didn't connect and passed right through them as if he wasn't there.

The doctors were all huddled in a corner discussing the time and cause of death when Tre walked over to them and pointing back at his lifeless body and screaming for them to help him. None of the doctors noticed him and Tre got mad and tried to grab one, but just like the shockers, he passed right through them too.

"Yo Tre?" G called out and waved for Tre to come over.

When Tre's attention was on G, G told him that seeing his self die wasn't even the worst part and there was more to come. Before Tre could respond, G did his two step and him and Tre landed in the waiting room. They were only feet away from where Tre's wife stood face to face with the doctor from the waiting room. He still had on his bloody scrubs and all. The doctor only spoke four words before Tre's wife collapsed and fell into her mother's arms crying.

G took one more look at Tre's wife and saw the pain and hurt that she was feeling and felt his heart cave in. He had a brief flashback from his past life before he died and could relate.

"Look Tre," G said, and then he swallowed hard.

"I ain't supposed to tell you this type of shit up front, but…but you killing me with this pity shit kid."
Sniffling, Tre lifted his head and the tears were coming out in steady streams.

"Tell me what?" he cried.

"That I got a little pull son."
Still sniffling, Tre silently watched as G pulled out the sack of weed he'd taken from his dresser, and then followed with his eyes as G broke a blunt down.
Tre rubbed his eyes, "pull?"

"Yep," G said, and then paused to lick and seal the perfectly rolled blunt. "I got enough pull to give one person another chance at life."

"What I gotta do?" he asked G desperately.
G smiled and looked at the blunt with lust before he spoke.

"It's simple. You just gotta understand your fuck ups."

"That's it?" Tre was confused, but a smile still flashed on his still moist face.

Robert "Big Dee" Williams

"Hold up," G warned, "it isn't that easy kid. First you gotta give me your word that you'll make better decisions and choices and shit." He lit the blunt, inhaled, and continued talking with smoke filled lungs.

"Because the shit that you do might seem small to you, but nine times out of ten kid, your decisions affect the life and future of all the people you deal with." He exhaled and the little smoke that was left in Tre's lungs clouded around Tre's face and stayed. He offered the blunt to Tre, but Tre declined and G shrugged.

"Aight, more for me. Just remember this; every action in the universe comes with a reaction. It's sort of like a package deal kid."

"I ain't following you," Tre moaned.

"It's simple, what ain't you following?"

"I just don't understand."

"Once again, I can show you way better than I can tell you." G said, then he did his two step and they were gone before Tre could open his mouth to speak again.

*****

They dropped through the roof of Tre's drug house and G struck the lighter and re-lit the blunt.

"Just watch," he whispered, then pointed to the door of Tre's drug house that was only feet away from where they stood.

"I told you it gets worse."

Robert "Big Dee" Williams

Both Tre and G watched, as Tre stepped out onto the enclosed porch and closed the door behind him. When he turned to walk to his car, he almost ran pregnant Angie over. She was only inches away.

Tre shook his head. "You know ain't shit up over here ma," he snapped, then looked down at her stomach. "Not with that seed up in you."

"Come on Tre baby, I been doing good. Today it's just my birthday....see!" She twirled in a half circle and modeled her outfit.

"I ain't fucking with you ma," Tre said sternly, then tried to walk around her, but she stepped to the side and blocked his exit.

"Please, please, please, please, please just give me this one pack," pregnant Angie pleaded. "I swear on my baby's life I'll go to rehab tomorrow." For added effect, she rubbed a hand over her huge stomach.

"How many months is you ma?"

"Six."

One of his major rules was to never sell drugs to a pregnant woman. He looked at her stomach again. She was big. His thoughts were shattered when she reached out and grabbed his hand.

"Come on baby," she begged. "Just this one pack, pleeeeaaasssee?"

"Come on Angie, you know how I feel about them babies." He grabbed her by the arm and swung her around like they were ball room dancing. His eyes went straight to her ass.

Robert "Big Dee" Williams

"But damn, you do look like you been taking care of yourself." Still holding her, he turned and with his free hand opened the door and called out for one of his workers.

Seconds later, the door opened. One of Tre's workers named Q, stuck his head out of the cracked door.

"Yeah, what up Tre?"

Tre held a hand out in front of Q, but he kept his eyes on Angie.

"Let me get a pack, Q."

Q hesitated.

"But --," Q said in an effort to protest, but was cut off by Tre.

"But nothing!" Tre barked. "Just give me a pack Q!"

Confused, Q reached in his pocket. He pulled out a pack and placed it in Tre's extended hand, then turned and went back into the house shaking his head.

Tre gave Angie the pack; she snatched him into a hug and kissed his cheek.

"Thank you Tre baby," she said seductively.

"Yeah, whatever," he shot back dryly, then broke her grip on his neck and pulled away from her.

"You just make sure you take your ass to rehab tomorrow."

Without another word, she spun on her heels and walked off into the dark night. She could feel Tre's eyes glued to her ass and picked up speed, hoping that he didn't notice that she didn't give him any money.

Tre and G followed her until she turned the corner and was out of sight. When the first rain drop crashed to the ground, G smiled and for Tre everything went blurry, as if the tape of his life was being fast forwarded. When it stopped, Tre and G stood two feet from Angie; she sat on the toilet in her bathroom. She had on a sports bra and her belly was sticking out, her panties were on the floor around her ankles. She was humming a song when she looked up at her cosmetic bag that sat on the sink and thought about the heroin inside. She grabbed and unzipped the bag, dug around, and came out with the small pack and a fresh syringe.

The process was simple, pour the heroin in a spoon, add a few drops of water, and heat. When the poison began to bubble in the spoon, Angie became excited and wiggled her toes, then sucked her teeth, as she drew the light brown liquid through the cotton ball and into the syringe.

Once every drop of liquid was inside, she held the syringe in the air and softly pressed it's plunger sending a squirt shooting from the tip and removing any deadly bubbles that were inside.

"Happy birthday, Angie," she mumbled to herself, before she pierced her skin with the needle and eased it into her vein. She pulled the plunger back slightly and drew blood into the syringe, then in one fluid motion, pressed down with her manicured hand and injected all of the warm liquid into her blood stream.

Moments later, she sat on the toilet with the needle still in her arm and nodding, as the heroin coursed through her veins.

Like a thief in the night, a sharp pain shot from her back and stomach, jerking her fragile body and sending her to her knees instantly. Falling to the floor, shaken, and trembling from the pain, she started to contract.

"Oh, God! Help me Lord!" she cried out.

"Help, somebody help me!" as the blood begin to trickle out of her vagina. Contractions hit her harder by the second as she screamed out for her friend and get high buddy Nikki.

Rushing in the bathroom, Nikki was overcome from the amount of blood on the floor. Frightened, Nikki ran out the house and flagged down the first police car she saw. Rushed to the hospital, Angie was admitted to intensive care.

Her right arm was cuffed to the rail of the hospital bed and two uniformed cops, one on both sides, stood over her.

When the doctor came and discharged her, the cops took her straight to the precinct and after taking her mug shot photo and finger printing her, they booked her on the charge of homicide in the first degree.

G turned and looked at Tre.

"Aight. After seeing all that now do you understand how you played a big part in that situation?"

Tre shook his head no.

Robert "Big Dee" Williams

"Aight, look kid, plain and simple," he put a hand on Tre's shoulder.

"Your choice to give Angie that pack, you created what you just watched."

"But she would've got it anyway from somewhere else." He shrugged.

"So it really didn't matter."

"Whoa, hold up son. That's some bullshit and you know it. You know wasn't nobody on the west side about to serve her. You know your rules stand around these parts. You the man Tre. Come on dog, you can keep it real with me." G raised an eyebrow and smiled. "You seen that fat ass, didn't you?"

"Okay, I understand," Tre said unconvincingly.

G held up both of his hands. "Hold up, son. I ain't finished."

"Give me my life back," Tre said pathetically, but G paid him no attention.

"Angie been sober for months now. And now you come along and go against your own rules and morals and give her some of that top side shit from your spot, and now babygirl done got bagged on a murder case. To make matters worse, yo, you just gave her the dope. And guess what? She ain't even have no money either."

G paused for a few seconds and watched Tre. "Her intention when she came to the spot wasn't to buy dope. She knew wasn't shit up, she knew that you

Robert "Big Dee" Williams

strict on that baby shit, but you let a fat ass and a smile cloud your judgment….and everything you stand for."

They were still in the holding cell and Angie was still in the corner when a group of women walked over to her. They surrounded her and one was at least three hundred pounds.

Horror crossed Tre's face.

"Okay!" he screamed. "I understand G!"

"Tre?" G called out calmly.

"She was just coming to kick it with the workers like she always does, and that's what Q was trying to tell you, but you cut him off boss man."

Tre reached out and grabbed the front of G's hoody. G just looked at his hands.

"I said I'm ready to get my life back!" Tre screamed and yanked on G's hoody front.

G grabbed Tre's wrist and applied pressure to his pressure points.

"It ain't that easy kid."

"But I said I understand," Tre said through clenched teeth.

G released him. "But that ain't all I gotta show you. Remember I said you fucked up way more lives than your own."

Tre opened his mouth to speak, but G did his two step and they landed in front of Tre's house. Tre had his key in the door knob and Duke stood on the side walk next to a puddle of water, and as the rain drops fell, they ran down his face. Every few seconds, lightning struck and illuminated his face. He pointed behind him.

"I almost forgot, cuz, but I got some shit I gotta handle."

Tre just stood on the steps with his key in the door and looked suspiciously over his shoulder at his cousin.

"Yeah, aight," Tre said, his tone unconvincing. "Just make sure you bring my shit back. And don't do shit stupid either."

Without another word, Duke walked away and Tre watched until he was out of sight. Once he was out of sight, that's when everything fast forwarded and stopped when Duke reappeared. He was getting drenched by the rain, as he walked the streets crying. People stopped and offered him rides. Duke declined everyone, but nobody noticed the tears running down his face, because of the rain. Every time he was offered a ride, he'd hide the despair in his voice and tell them that he was cool.

He turned into an alley, then into a back yard and removed the board from an abandoned house's back door, slid inside, and replaced the board behind him. After finding the darkest room in the house, he sat on the floor Indian style, pulled out the fifth of vodka from his shirt sleeves, took a long swallow, and sweat began to trickle down his face, as the liquor set in.

Duke had been happily married for ten years. His wife was beautiful, but lately their

Robert "Big Dee" Williams

relationship had fallen apart. First, it was the cocaine. Tre had gotten him some help, so when Tre asked him about the 'monkey' on his back, Duke didn't lie when he said no. It wasn't drugs. Drugs would be good compared to what he was dealing with now. A man had shown up at his and his wife's house and told his wife that Duke was gay or what they call on the 'down low'. Duke had done a few years in the joint and while he was locked up, he had formed a relationship with a homosexual. Before Duke went home, he'd made all kinds of promises and talked about how they were going to be together. But when Duke got out, he didn't so much as write his lover a letter, and when Duke's lover got released, he was set on destroying Duke's happy home.

Duke finished the entire bottle and sat rocking back and forth in the dark room, trying to build up the courage to do what he was about to do. He lost everything, his wife, his kids, his home, everything. He pulled Tre's gun from his coat pocket, took a long hard look at it, then pulled its hammer back, inserted it in his mouth and pulled the trigger.

Tre jumped from the explosion and the brightness, then watched as Duke's blood sprayed all over the wall. Then, Tre watched as the bottle and gun fell to the ground, followed by Duke a fraction of a second later.

Tre felt his chest tighten up and G took a step closer to him.

"Now do you see what I'm trying to show you?"

"Why you just show me that?" Tre asked pitifully.

G shrugged. "Why not? Everything I'm showing you, it's your fault."

He turned from Duke and pointed at Tre. "You probably ain't pull the trigger, or you probably ain't clip Angie either, but because of your actions, all of this shit happened."

Tre thought for a moment and that's when Felicia popped into his mind. Before he went over Liz's, Felicia was the last person he saw.

"What about Felicia?" asked Tre sincerely.

G smile and pressed his hands together. "See kid, now you catching on! But, I want you to figure this one out all by yourself son, and if you get stuck, I'll show you where and how you fucked up."

G walked over to where Duke was lying dead on the ground, then looked up at the ceiling and called Tre's name. When he had Tre's attention, he said, "I only get one chance to help somebody get their life back Tre, and if I'm successful, I get my wings son."

"Wings?" Tre repeated under his breath, then looked at the ceiling too.

G grabbed the bottle of vodka Duke dropped, put it to his lips, and then turned it up.

"A man! What the fuck is you doing!" Tre shouted, his voice high pitched and cracked.

G jumped and the bottle clanked against his teeth. "Damn kid, chill out." He said then turned the bottle upside down, showing Tre that it was bone dry.

Robert "Big Dee" Williams

"Do you know how long it's been since I had some liquor?"

Tre just looked at him with a blank expression.

"My point exactly, ain't none of this shit where I come from." G said, and then tossed the bottle. It landed just outside of the pool of blood that had formed around Duke's body.

"So, you come up with any ideas about your sister yet?"

"All, all I can think of is the money," Tre stuttered.

"Ding, ding, ding, ding, ding!" G exclaimed and held one of his hands to his mouth pretending it was a microphone and he was a game show host. He snapped his fingers and him and Tre dropped through Felicia's roof and into her kitchen.

Felicia walked over to the row of cabinets and opened them.

"Tre now you know these kids got bottomless stomachs. You don't remember how it was when we had to stay with momma before my section 8 kicked in?"

She pulled out a pack of cigarettes and lit one. Tre watched the bright cherry as she inhaled the smoke and he wondered how she could afford cigarettes, and thinking that with the five dollars she'd paid for them she could've bout a twenty four pack of ramen noodles. Disappointed in his sister, Tre dug in his pocket and pulled out a roll of cash, peeled off three twenties, and gave them to her.

As soon as she stuck the money in her bra, he son P.J. walked into the kitchen. Both him and Felicia froze and eyed each other. P.J. and Chucky's coats were dripping wet from the rain outside.

"What up uncle Tre?" P.J. said. Chucky nodded to Tre, but spoke to Felicia.

Dripping water the entire way, P.J. walked over to the refrigerator and opened it. Then opened the freezer. They were both empty.

In the other room, Sky's crying grew louder and it reminded Tre of his purpose for being there. After he questioned her about her ride, he looked around at all of Felicia's kids and they all looked hungry. He turned back to Felicia and even though frustrated, he kissed her on the cheek.

"Aight man. I'm about to go. Make sure you feed these kids."

Outside in his car, Tre watched Felicia's silhouette through the curtained window. She was talking on the phone and changing clothes at the same time. G snapped his fingers and the next thing he and Tre saw was Felicia running down the sidewalk and almost tripping in her high heels, she caught herself and climbed into a money green Cadillac.

Tre looked at G. "Why you ain't doing your two step no more?"

"Oh, that was just for show and effects kid," G said, then pointed to the green Cadillac. "Now be quiet and watch."

Robert "Big Dee" Williams

Felicia closed the door, then leaned over to the driver's side and kissed Eddie on the cheek. "Guess what daddy?" She said excitedly and pulled out the three twenty from her bra.

Eddie turned and looked at her. His face was hard as stone and menacing. Without body language or emotion, he plucked the bills from her hand, stuck them in his pocket and pulled off.

Once the Cadillac was out of sight, P.J. let the curtain close, then scanned the living room looking at this four brothers and sister. He knew that money he saw his momma sticking in her bra was for his brothers and sisters to eat.

He looked at Chucky, who was still sitting on the couch in his wet coat and told him to follow him. They went out the back door and into the back yard. P.J.'s pit bull jumped up on him, but P.J. pushed him off of him and crawled inside her dog house and seconds later came out with a small pistol in his hand. They walked around the corner and paced back and forth in front of the hood liquor store and waited for the right time to go in. At five minutes to closing, it was now or never. P.J. followed by Chucky ran inside of the store. The clerk after hearing the entrance bell looked up. There was one customer inside of the store and she was the first to see the gun in P.J.'s hand and held at his waist. She screamed and the clerk followed her eyes to the gun quickly, then he quickly drew the pistol he kept in his back pocket and squeezed off shots in P.J. and Chucky's direction. Terrified, P.J. pulled the trigger with this eyes closed.

Robert "Big Dee" Williams

The clerk fell to the ground and P.J. took a step closer and saw a tiny hole in the man's forehead.

P.J. called out for Chucky to help him with the cash register, but Chucky didn't answer. P.J. looked over where he had last saw chucky and saw a small pair of Air Jordan's sticking out from the chip aisle. He slowly stepped closer and heard gasping and gurgling, then saw that the feet were moving and shaking uncontrollably. He stepped closer and closer until he turned the corner completely and saw Chucky lying in a pool of blood and clutching his throat. He was whispering and blood seeped through his hands like a crack in a dam. His eyes darted back and forth and they said the words that his mouth could not speak. He was dying.

It took P.J. a minute to accept what he was seeing. He swallowed hard then sprinted to the counter. There was mostly singles and coins, but it didn't matter. He stuffed his small pockets, then ran through the store and loaded his arms with lunch meat, bread, and on his way out the door, he grabbed a can of baby formula for Sky and ran full speed from the store.

He ran home with his arms full of food, closed the door, and took a few minutes to catch his breath. When his lungs stopped stinging, he made his brother sisters sandwiches and Sky a warm bottle and fed her in his arms, rocking her back and forth. She finally stopped crying.

When the cops arrived at the crime scene, they watched the store's surveillance tap and took a statement from the witness who'd escaped and ran out after the first shot erupted. Thirty minutes later, the cops came to

Felicia's house and arrested P.J. and took the other four kids to child and protective services.

After Tre and G watched P.J. get placed in the back of a cop car, they dropped through the roof of a dark room with only a little light.

The light came from a lighter. It was a motel room. Felicia was lying on the bed, Eddie was next to her, and they had a saucer of crack on the bed in between them. Eddie struck the lighter again and raised it and the crack pipe to Felicia's lips and G snapped his fingers and they froze just like that.

G stepped in front of Tre, as the tears began streaming down his face again. G took a deep breath.

"Now this probably was the hardest shit you had to watch, but…"

"Naw – naw," Tre sobbed and tried to step around G to see his sister.

"Ain't none of this really happen. None of this happened." Tre was in shock. He shook his head in denial of what G was showing him.

"Oh, but it did Tre," G was sympathetic. He put a hand on Tre's shoulder.

"I just hope that what I'm showing you proves that your decisions affect everything around you. Do you understand now, kid?"

Tre looked at his sister, she was still frozen in time and lying on the bed with Eddie's hand between her legs and the pipe still in her mouth. Tre glanced at the

Robert "Big Dee" Williams

plate of crack, then P.J., Chucky, and the clerk at the liquor store, all flashed in his mind.

"I should've bought the food and took it over there myself, instead of giving her the money."

He put his hands on his head in frustration and continued. "But I never thought some shit like this would happen."

The G's entire facial expression changed and now anger was written on his face.

"P.J. fourteen, Tre!" G's words were filled with emotion and they cut through the air like a knife.

"What you think he was going to do? Come on Tre, he the man of the house and his siblings in there starving and can't do for themselves." He laughed, not from humor, but disgust, then he sized Tre up.

"Then he got this big uncle Tre telling everybody not to sell him dope so he can't get no money, what he do? He goes take that money to feed his sisters and brothers."

Tre's lips quivered and his voice barely was a whisper.

"But I don't want him out there in the streets G."

"It would've been better than this, he facing first-degree murder now!" Lightning struck just outside the window and illuminated the room through the motel's dingy curtains.

"Peep it kid. Even if nobody ever sold him drugs, he still got his hands on a gun, and that's worse. Tre you gotta understand that in life, everybody got free will and that most gotta do for themselves and take care of others. But those babies, them babies gotta be taken care of, and if a few rocks gotta be sold or couple packs of heroin need to be pushed to do that, then I'm sure the man upstairs will look the other way for a quick second. It' the lesser of the two evils. But now, look...lives done got took, and for what? A hundred dollars in coins and singles, some stale bread, old lunch meat, and some fuckin' baby formula? Chucky dead, the store clerk dead, your nieces and nephews stuck in the system, and P.J. going to jail for a long time. I ain't gotta explain no more, you get the message. It's the lesser of the two evils Tre. The lesser of the two evils."

G snapped his fingers and him and Tre dropped in Liz's bedroom.

"Our last stop," G said and pointed toward her bed, "your last breath and the demise that you brought upon yourself."

Duke grabbing the gun from the arm rest flashed in Tre's mind for a millisecond, then Liz's boyfriend raised the gun, as Tre tried to shield the shots, but again it didn't work and the gun fired.

"Do you see where you fucked up here?"

Tre dropped his head. "Yeah."

"You do? Well, then what?"

Tre's voice was lifeless. "I gave Duke my gun."

G shrugged. "That's one way to look at it, but look at this."

They were back at Tre's house and he had his key in the knob.

"Okay," G said and the scene froze.

"Before your phone rang, you had called it a wrap for the night to chill with wifey, but you had to go and fuck with Liz, since she was so close, didn't you? On top of that, you knew about her ex-boyfriend. You knew he had just come home from prison for manslaughter, and you knew that he was obsessed with that chick. But you still made the choice to put yourself in that fucked up situation."

"But back to your answer though." The scene switched back to Liz's room where Tre sat frozen with his hands in front of his face and his face twisted in horror at the sight of the gun.

"You see? Right there. You had enough time to grab your pistol out of your jeans and save your own life. You could have gotten dude before he got you, but Duke had your gun. Now look at you."

They dropped through the ceiling of the hospital's operating room, where Tre's lifeless body was still on the surgical table and under the sheet with one hand dangling over the side. G snapped his fingers and they were in the waiting room. The doctor had just delivered the news of Tre's death to his wife.

"You don't see that chick Liz out here nowhere, do you?" G asks and Tre thought silently, as he scratched his head. It was a damn good question. "I don't know what you were thinking."

Robert "Big Dee" Williams

G walked over and stood next to Tre's wife, she was crying in her mother's arms.

"She dead Tre. You wasn't the only person that got hit. She was D.O.A., and when he got her, dude turned the gun on his self. And guess what? I checked before I came down and neither one of them get a second chance kid. It's over for them. So when I give you your life back and they still gonna be gone, destiny just came early for them."

"I understand, G! I swear I understand!" Tre pleaded and looked at his wife wishing he could hold her and stop her tears.

"So that mean you ready, since you understand."

"Yeah, G, "Tre cried. "I'm ready."

G began to snap his fingers, but Tre stopped him. "But what about Angie, and Duke, and P.J., and my nieces, and nephews?"

A smile crossed G's face. "It's all on you, kid. It's all on you."

He snapped his fingers and was gone.

*****

Tre closed the door to his trap house and when he turned around, pregnant Angie was in front of him.

"What's good Angie?"

"Nothing," she said happily. "You know it's my birthday boo."

Robert "Big Dee" Williams

"And you already know how I feel about them –
"he let his words trail off and remembered the dream
he'd had and some of the things the G said ran through
his mind. "I mean happy birthday ma. So what you up
to?"

She smacked her lips. "Nothing. I just came to
come and chill with Q and them."

Tre smiled. Aight. You take it easy with that
seed up in you."

She wrapped her arms around his neck and
kissed him on the cheek. When she released him, he
started down the steps, but she called out his name. He
stopped and looked back up at her, as rain began to fall.

She was underneath the porch light.

"You like my outfit?" she asked and did a 360
turn.

"Looking good, ma. Looking good." Tre said
honestly and climbed in his car.

He stopped at the number house as usual, and
when he came out a bright light illuminated the inside of
his car. Tre jumped and reached for his gun, but when
he saw it was Duke, he let out a deep sigh of relief and
grabbed his heart. Tre could tell that Duke was nervous
and noticed that his conversation wasn't the same as
always. Duke had asked Tre a question that he'd never
before in his life had asked, he asked Tre to loan him a
gun. Tre reminded Duke that he never let people use his
guns. Duke kept asking, but Tre stood his ground and
kept to his rules.

"I know you don't let nobody use your guns," Duke said. "But cuz, I done got myself in some bullshit."

Tre laughed and threw a playful punch at him and his fist hit something hard in Duke's coat sleeve.

"Well, then I just gotta keep you by my side for a while then, don't I?" Tre asked and reached over and felt the lump in Duke's coat sleeve.

"What's that, Duke?"

Duke pulled up the bottle from his coat and held the cheap bottle of vodka in the air.

"It's vodka cuz."

Tre leaned back in his seat and got comfortable and Duke tossed the cigarette out of the window.

"Aight Duke," Tre said calmly. "So let me know what's going on."

Tre kept his eyes on his cousin and after a few moments of silence, then a few more with Duke stumbling over his words, he took a deep breath, then answered Tre's question.

"I lost my life, Tre."

His words were filled with pain and Tre looked at him in confusion.

"Vonda left me and she took the kids." He looked out of the window, so Tre wouldn't see the tears fall from his eyes.

Robert "Big Dee" Williams

Tre knew Duke was hurting and didn't force him to go on. He told him they'd talk about it later and climbed out of the car. Duke too. They stopped in the grass and Tre grabbed the bottle of vodka and poured the liquor in the grass. When Tre stuck his key in the door, his phone rang. It was Felicia and she was crying about her kids being hungry. They got right back into the car and fifteen minutes later, they were parked in front of her house. Tre looked at the house and saw the kid's shadows through the curtains and he restarted the car and drove to the grocery store. When he dropped the food off, he saw P.J. and his friend Chucky coming down the street and waited for him, before he pulled off. When P.J. was in front of the house, Tre climbed out and pulled his nephew to the side and asked him was he hustling. P.J. gave him an honest answer and told him no, and that even if he wanted to, he couldn't because nobody on the west side would sell him any dope. Tre didn't give him any, but he told him to meet him at his house in the morning and to wear his work clothes, he planned on showing P.J. how to earn an honest dollar by providing landscaping services. There was no way he was introducing him to the drug game.

When Tre made it home, it was still early, and he, his wife, and Duke ordered that movie that he'd promised her.

Duke slept on the couch and the next morning, was awakened by the news. There was a special update and it caught his attention. Duke recognized the bright skinned woman. He thought for a moment and figured out it was Liz. Tre walked in just as the reporter began explaining that Liz had been shot to death by her ex-boyfriend, who'd just gotten out of prison, and after

Robert "Big Dee" Williams

killing her he turned the gun on himself and blew his own head off.

The End

"The choices we make today affect our tomorrows. Think wisely out there in those streets. Make the right choices, value your family and your community and by all means, do your best to make your wrongs right."

– DC Bookdiva

Wrong Move

Nathan Welch

One

I'm out trappin' early because there ain't enough time in the day – time to stack some paper, I gotta do it quick before all deez bitches and police get on my line, thought Slick while reclining in the passenger seat, smoking a spliff of loud.

Slowly, Slick inhaled the chronic fumes. His chinky eyes were bloodshot red as he tried to remain focused on the task at hand. The first move he wanted to complete was dropping off four ounces and a half to a hustler named Ug that hailed from the 640-Lorton Morton projects. Whenever Ug called him, Slick knew it meant more money.

Making a detour was the last thing he wanted at that moment. His homie was already making a turn to go see a bootylicious dame he met at the T. C. B. White Party the night before. Slick knew that he would be wasting his breath by saying anything to Mozart to derail him from chasing some pussy.

All the home boys and girls from the hood near Kennedy Street was making moves in their own fashion. But Slick outshined them all. Being 6'1 and tipping the scale on the heavy obese side didn't deter him from pulling and fucking some of the baddest dime pieces in Washington, D.C. Slick let his money do all the talking. The boy was a certified boss who could pass for a younger looking Ricky Rozay.

Out of nowhere, Mozart made a dangerous left turn. Slick wanted to curse Mozart's ass out for driving crazy while they rode dirty, but Slick remained silent. He was silently kicking himself in the ass for getting in a car with Mozart's crazy –crash dummy-ass. Point back, Slick knew he made the wrong move today.

Slick knew the only way for him to possibly get through the sticky situation without arguing was to simply remain quiet and not confront Mozart.

"Damn Moe, why you so quiet and shit," Mozart spoke in an octave higher than the blaring sounds of Backyard Band. "I ain't seen your fat ass in three days and all you can do is give a nigga the silence treatment?" he said as he slammed on brakes, stopping in front of a house where three sexy women sat on the porch.

Slick gave Mozart a funny look. "Moe, I'm just tryna' get to my man and dump off this work," he muttered. He had love for Mozart, but he could be a pain in the ass sometimes. Slick couldn't figure out how he let Mozart convince him to ride shotgun with him in the first place.

"I got chu' Bob, soon as I holla at this bitch right fast," he said and honked the car horn.

Both men looked on as the exotic looking honey brown female stood up and started towards the car. As she got closer, Slick zoomed his bloodshot eyes on her.

Damn, I know that ain't Samone lil' fine ass, he wondered, remembering how good her pussy and head game was. Slick had met her at Howard U's Homecoming. A week later, he was slamming massive dick up in all of Samone's holes.

"He boo-boo, wassup wit'chu?" she greeted Mozart while leaning inside the driver's side window.

She possessed nice round breasts, prettier than a Barbie doll, and had an ass that men would die for.

"I'm tryna' see what that box hittin on?" Mozart cut straight to the point about having sex.

Slick played with his iPhone and eyed her out the corner of his eye. Once he peeped her up close Slick recognized her.

"Damn, why you gotta' come at me all crazy like that?" she sucked her teeth.

"What! Ay Samone, stop saying anything," Mozart snapped. "You know why I'm on your line, so cut the bullshit...what's up?"

"I'm on my period right now," she lied, eyeing Slick. She wondered if he already gave his homeboy the 411 on their sexcapade.

"So hit me up when you get off."

"Okay, you can't introduce me to your friend?" she smiled.

Slick recognized her play immediately.

"Moe, let's roll...I got shit to do," Slick blurted out and then looked at Samone. "No offense sweetheart, but I'm not in the habit of being buddy-buddy with my partner's dames...shit cause too much confusion," he said giving her a wink on the sly.

Samone bit her bottom lip seductively. "It's cool...my bad. Ay Moe, I'ma get a chu' soon boo-boo, but until then throw a bitch a bone. You know I gotta' keep my hair and nails looking good for you."

"Oh yeah you just gonna' try me like that huh?" he asked, and quickly pulled out his bank roll. He gave her $200 and pulled off without saying good bye.

After viewing Mozart's actions, Slick Pulla sensed that Mozart was nothing but a trick.

"I'ma tea bag that bitch the first chance I get," Mozart said, getting back on Georgia Avenue, heading southbound for 640 projects.

*Already been there and done tha*t, Slick thought, and decided to keep hush-hush about having sex with a woman that Mozart was chasing. Even though it wasn't nothing big to expose Samone, he felt that Mozart couldn't take the knowledge of chasing his sloppy seconds. Slick was heavy into reading and studying people. He'd read time and time again of how pussy led to destruction of empires and created war, jealousy and separation between the best of friends.

Slick had his sights on the almighty dollar and didn't need any petty drama in is life over a skirt who just going to spread her legs for the next contestant that appeals to her.

Two

When Mozart pulled to a stop on Morton Street, Slick looked outside the passenger window. Ug was already standing outside. Ug was one of those guys whose looks matched his nickname. The boy had a face that only his mother could love.

Slick had spent over two years doing time with Ug in a juvy prison somewhere in the mountains of Pennsylvania. At first he paid Ug no mind about hooking up and getting money on the streets. But when he came home, Ug called like clockwork. Wanting to do business, at the sound of all the cash amounts Ug wanted to spend, Slick couldn't resist.

After confirming the purchase of three -ounces of crack, Slick asked one of his homies to front him the work for a few hours. One of his homies gave Slick a funny stare like he didn't trust him.

"Moe, I'll be right back with your ink. You think I'ma do dirt or be cruddy to the home team? I just gotta come up, fuck!" he snapped.

Once Slick got his hands on the work, he slid off quickly and re-cooked the drugs, eliminating most of the cut and impurities. After selling Ug the work, Slick paid his homie in full and never looked back. Once Ug put the work out on the block, he sold out in record time – he had to call Slick for more work. By the time Ug made his fifth call to Slick, Slick was already flipping a half kilo and steady climbing.

Nathan Welch

Slick had developed quite a reputation because of his expertise in the kitchen and track record of having high quality cocaine. On the streets, Slick's work was referred to as "88".

As Ug approached Mozart's car, Slick eyed the hustler and admired him. Even though he surpassed Ug in the drug game, he felt he owed all his success to Ug.

Decked out in a black Hugo Boss tee shirt with blue Prada jeans and butter-hued Timberlands, Ug opened the back door of Mozart's Buick Regal Turbo and climbed in.

"What took you so long champ?" Ug asked after closing the back door on Slick's side. "Shit is jumpin out dis' bitch. The cluckers ready to kill me cause I got'em waiting on that 88!"

Slick looked over at Mozart then turned back to Ug. "I had to get a ride from my man who don't believe in money over bitches," he said in a calm voice. "But he gon learn one day."

"Alright! Alright! Alright!" Ug blurted, mimicking a skit from the Kevin Hart "Laugh At My Pain' comedy concert.

"Ay' Moe, you don't know me like that!" Mozart snapped, giving Ug a mean mug through the rearview mirror. After his statement, Mozart reached for the chrome plated Desert Eagle on his lap.

"Shit ain't that serious champ," Ug grinned nervously, trying to kill the tension and uncomfortable energy engulfing the car.

Ug decided that it wasn't worth it to go further with a guy who apparently had a chip on his shoulder.

At the sound of his plea, Mozart turned and quickly looked out the window. Although Ug played the timid/nervous role, he wasn't nowhere near those things. He was 640's most notorious head bussa'. Ug had developed a solid reputation for killing anyone who rubbed him the wrong way.

Mozart had no idea he'd just made the wrong move.

"My bad slim," Slick apologized. He felt bad for what just happened. "That's on me, so here's what I'ma do." He sighed. "Just gimme enough bread for three and a baby. The other one's on me."

Ug smiled like a killer who just got away with murder. The two men did business in the car, then Ug shot Mozart a serious look.

I'ma catch cho' bitch-ass later...trust me on that, Ug thought as he gave Slick some dap and got out the car.

"Ay big boy, I'ma hit you later on, cause I really need to breathe on you about the company you keep!"

Mozart's head swiveled in Ug's direction and he raised his gun so it rested on the steering wheel. At first sight of the huge cannon, Ug quickly raised his t-shirt and flashed his gun.

Ug tossed Mozart an air kiss, "Thank your man Slick for the fact that you still breathing."

Nathan Welch

With that said, Ug turned away and quickly headed inside a nearby building.

Mozart's expression resembled a scared child who just got caught with his hand in the cookie jar. Slick enjoyed a good laugh at that one.

"Mozart, you hafta' stop crashing…it's a rack of cowboys in the city that ain't seeing nuffin…and if you and I gonna keep fucking with each other, then some drastic things need to change. I mean if you tryna' really see some cash, then take heed to what I'm about to lay down to you."

Three

The northbound traffic seemed fairly light for a Wednesday morning. Mozart sped up Georgia Avenue in his metallic cobalt blue Buick Regal Turbo with a vengeance. He felt angry and he wanted Slick and the world to know it.

"Fuck dat' nigga god!" he said to Slick. "How the fuck you gonna take his side over mines?" Mozart was tired of Slick always talking down to him like he was a kid – like he couldn't handle B.I. like most nigga's do. For years he'd been hustling, beefing and surviving on the District streets without anyone's input and he felt like he damn sure didn't need any input now.

Mozart made up his mind that if Ug wanted some gun play, and decided to bring him a move, he and his family would literally be on Mozart's hit list.

"I'm just saying slim, you was wrong," Slick smirked. "Take it how you wanna take it...It's not up for debate...you jumped out there and could've got both of us smoked all cause you wanna perp."

Mozart made eye contact with Slick and gave him a mean mug. "Fuck dat nigga", he snarled as he sped through a yellow light. "I did what I did and I'ma stand on it, simple as that!"

Just as Slick tried to respond, a police cruiser appeared behind them out of nowhere.

Nathan Welch

"Fucking feds Moe, fuck!" Mozart said, looking in the rearview mirror at the red and white Metropolitan Police cruiser.

Slick looked back at the cop car following them then turned back to Mozart. "I still got dis' water on me Moe, damn," he said in a calm tone, referring to the 3 bottles of liquid P.C.P. tucked in his sweats.

Mozart glanced in the rearview again, ready to run the police. When he saw how close they were on his bumper, everything around him seemed to fade away. All the beefs and arguing he'd just had with Slick and Slick's customer disappeared as he sized up his escape vision.

"Moe, deez people's way on my line for no reason, like your man put em' on us!"

"How the fuck," Slick snapped, but quickly caught himself. "Just drive and don't do no stupid shit either."

Soon as the words rolled off Slick's tongue, the cruiser's sirens and lights came on. Instantly, both men's hearts began pounding rapidly as the officer's voice blared from an intercom, ordering Mozart to pull over.

Beads of sweat started forming on Slick's brow as he began stashing the liquid P.C.P. inside his underwear, under his nuts. Seconds later, he felt a burning sensation in his groin and knew the P.C.P. had leaked out somehow.

In a rush to hide the drugs, Slick accidentally cracked open one of the bottles – literally releasing enough liquid P.C.P. to kill an entire football team into his pores.

As the deadly toxins oozed into his pores, Slick told himself over and over not to panic.

Suddenly, Mozart flung open his door and dove out the moving vehicle. Slick reached for the steering a second before the Buick jumped the curb and crashed into a florist shop.

By the time Slick looked around, the two cops already had the car surrounded and aiming guns at him.

"I got him covered, go after that track star!" the cop told his partner.

All the chasing in the world wouldn't catch Mozart's ass who already was three blocks away and steady gaining insane Bolt speed with his fast – scary ass.

"Out of the car now fat boy!" the cop demanded.

Before getting out the Buick Regal, Slick spotted Mozart's Desert Eagle laying under the gas pedal. As Slick reluctantly obeyed the cop's demands, the only thing he thought about was prison and how he got caught up on a humbug. There was no way he could beat that case in court.

Mozart pulled a straight crud-ball move. Considered a cruddy type dude by most people in the hood, Mozart just showed his true colors. He was strictly for self and self only. If it came down to it, Mozart would've left his own mother with a gun beef to get away.

Mozart figured since Slick had a lot of money, he could get a high powered attorney to fight the case. Mozart knew he was wrong for bolting on Slick and leaving his gun, but he didn't care. He felt that since Slick chose to side with another guy outside the hood over him, all ties and loyalties were dead between them.

"Your fat ass couldn't run like your partner huh?" the cop pressed, keeping his gun locked in on Slick's chest. He told Slick to take a seat on the sidewalk as several pedestrians began crowding the area.

With each step he took, Slick felt a little dizzy. He grabbed at his chest, feeling a sense of panic come over him. Slick's lungs felt like high octane flames. His eyeballs felt like they were going to pop by the time he fell face first onto the concrete.

"Oh my God, someone call 9-1-1!" Slick heard a woman yelling out as his entire world went black.

Four

Moments later, the sounds of a speeding ambulance drew closer, two paramedics worked frantically to resuscitate Slick. The female paramedic rubbed two defibrillator pads together before placing them on Slick's chest.

"Clear!" she said, and sent jolts of electricity to his heart.

"I got a pulse," her colleague yelled, "It's weak, but he's still with us."

"Another day at the office huh Frank?" she sighed and smiled. She cradled Slick's bald head in her lap, watching his eyes flutter underneath his closed eyelids.

A doctor and medical team with a gurney were already waiting out on the sidewalk when the ambulance reached the emergency room of Howard University Hospital.

"What's the prognosis?" one of the doctors asked as two hospital attendants rushed Slick through the sliding glass doors towards the Trauma Room.

"He passed out on some cop during a traffic stop. It was kinda a weird call actually," one attendant replied as Slick was pushed through a hospital personnel only side door.

After attaching an IV drip to Slick's arm and oxygen mask to his face in the trauma room, the attendants sliced open his clothes and removed them. They attached leads of the heart monitor to his chest.

The doctor immediately saw the bottles of liquid P.C.P. He made an awful frown when he removed them and smelled the drugs.

"This man is suffering from a P.C.P. overdose!" the doctor yelled and put the electrified paddles to his chest.

The medical staff watched Slick's hairy chest surge upward with a pulse and the heart machine bleated out a gentle bloop bloop sound. A neon green scratch line spiked upward on the spooling readout – then another, showing the miraculous beat of Slick's heart.

Signs of relief and pats on the backs of gratitude had began happening in the room – when suddenly an awful beeeeeeeep sound erupted, signaling the patient had just flatlined.

The doctor and medial team went to work frantically trying to revive Slick, but the screeching monitor wouldn't change from that flatline tune.

****

Mozart felt dizzy for a second, after reaching the hood like the wind had been knocked right out of him. He blinked rapidly as he wiped sweat from his face, feeling stunned and elated. He had just sprinted close to

Nathan Welch

thirty blocks at full speed and didn't get caught by the police.

Mozart's adrenaline was pumping so hard that he didn't notice the long full speed run in the process of trying to escape capture. All types of thoughts raced through his mind – mostly cruddy ones.

He didn't bother stopping at his house for another weapon as he jogged down the block to Slick's mother's house. As he ran up the concrete steps, and reached the porch, he spotted an elderly looking , chubby woman dressed in a brown UPS uniform exiting the home.

"Excuse me, Miss Floyd?"

Ms. Floyd looked at him and smiled, "Yes baby."

"It's about your son, Slick"

From the way Mozart said that, Ms. Floyd sensed something bad had happened to her son. Worry and fear immediately overcame her. She felt like her 64 year old body couldn't take hearing the bad news about her baby.

Ms. Floyd quickly stepped back inside her home, and invited Mozart inside. Mozart looked her deep in the eyes, giving her a chance to see his regret for what he'd done to her baby.

"Ms. Floyd, I'm so sorry," he muttered as he suddenly embraced her.

"It's ok baby," Ms. Floyd said soothingly. "Just tell Mama Floyd what you so sorry about?"

"I...I uh...hate to tell you this but...uh..." he said.

By the time Ms. Floyd took her a step back, Mozart already had a shiny Harley Davidson knife in his hand.

"I just need the money in here. I know Slick stash his money here. Don't make me hurt you." He pointed the knife as her threateningly.

Left speechless and defenseless, the 64 –year-old woman got very upset and started crying. Mozart cringed slightly at Ms. Floyd's crying plea of not knowing about any money.

"I'm sorry Ms. Floyd. I believe you. Now what's Slick's fiance's name and cell phone number?"

"Oh, that girl's name is Anya or Ayanna...something like that. The number is 265-9314."

"Hold on for a second." Mozart pulled out his phone and called the number. He kept the knife pointing outward to keep Ms. Floyd in check.

When the female answered on the third ring, Mozart looked at Ms. Floyd with a happy expression. You could tell he made the connection he wanted.

"You Slick's woman right?"

"Yeah, why? Is he okay?" replied the woman on the other end.

"For real – for real, I don't give a fuck, but if you don't want his mother's death on your hands, you gonna do exactly what I – aaaarrrrghhhh fuck!" he winced as Ms. Floyd rushed him and raked her nails deep down the sides of his face.

After launching her attack, Ms. Floyd looked at Mozart with a sad expression. He could tell she wanted to do more, or at least try. Mozart sensed something was wrong. He looked down and noticed the shiny blade embedded in her chest. Apparently, Ms. Floyd impaled herself accidentally in her rush to protect herself.

"Oh shit…oh shit," Mozart yelled, looking on in horror.

"Hello! Hello! Who is dis?"

Mozart didn't waste any time in ending the call, pulling his knife out of Ms. Floyd's chest and getting as far away as possible from the scene. He never intended to hurt Ms. Floyd. She was only supposed to be a bargaining chip. He had no idea, the knife wound punctured Ms. Floyd's heart deeply.

As Mozart ran home to seek out an alibi, the butterflies, anxiety and fear began to build even more. He was a nervous wreck. He couldn't believe what had happened. He started talking to himself.

"How the fuck she run into the knife like that? I knew I shouldn't have went over there. And I called his girl on my phone? I'm going to jail for a body and didn't even mean to do the shit."

As reality began kicking in, Mozart shattered his cell phone to pieces and tossed it in the garbage can. While he cleaned his fresh wounds with peroxide, he silently prayed to God asking him to spare Ms. Floyd's life.

Those were prayers that God wouldn't answer. Therefore Mozart was responsible of negligent homicide - a secret he would take to his grave, all from making the wrong move.

Five

The very shapely hour-glass figured woman known to the world as Anya, hustled her high yellow butt out of the house soon as the mysterious caller hung up on her.

Fear and worry consumed her as she made it to her Mercedes Benz, sitting on shiny chrome 23' inch rims – a gift from her fiance Slick. A billion bad things raced through her mind. She shuddered, thinking of the danger Slick and his mom could be in.

"God, please let them be safe, please," she said, closing her car door.

She had her cell phone in her hand by the time she started the engine. The more Slick's phone rang, the scarier she became.

"Please pick up baby…c'mon." Tears began to stream down her cheeks. A quivering hand went to her mouth. She felt dizzy for a second, like the wind had been knocked right out her.

Anya was about to try to call him again, but then stopped herself. She decided to call him soon as she reached his mother's house.

Four years together, fighting to be wifey, she thought wistfully as she pulled off and headed to D.C. She felt like she'd been through too much and sacrificed even more to lose Slick – to lose all the luxuries his

criminal activities provided for her. Now she had to go
put up with his evil bitch of a mother just to look good in
Slick's eyes for just because purposes.

Anya shook her head in wonder at the things
she'd done and how she'd change just to get ahead in
life. She felt no different from a street prostitute – her
only difference, she had to fuck only one trick and got to
keep all the money. Not bad for a 19 year old who been
a runaway since age 14.

Only two years of stacking money, she thought
as she reached the Baltimore/Washington Parkway,
heading southbound. Now she had to hope and pray
Slick was still alive so she could finish milking her cow.
She wanted to have some money tucked away in order to
survive if anything bad happened to Slick.

Minutes later, Anya reached D.C. and headed
north up on Georgia Avenue in Northwest. She tried
calling Slick a couple of times and still got now answer.
She tossed her phone in her purse in frustration and sped
towards Ms. Floyd's house.

I know one motherfucking thing, let his ass be
dead or locked up, Anya thought as she turned on Ms.
Floyd's street and pushed her car up to the house. *That
old bitch ain't getting shit he left behind.*

As she got out the Benz and strutted her fine ass
up to Ms. Floyd's house, Anya noticed the door was
open a little. SAs she reached the door, Anya sensed
something bad had happened.

She nudged the door open with her open-toe
sandal. With her hand clutching her purse strap, she tip-
toed inside. As she entered the living room and

discovered Ms. Floyd's body, it took everything she had to contain her laughter and joy.

Finally, the evil bitch croaked and can't get in my business no more, she thought, kneeling beside the body.

When Anya saw the blood staining Ms. Floyd's brown shirt, she couldn't believe somebody actually killed her. Immediately she felt bad for thinking negative and feeling happy about Ms. Floyd's demise.

"Who did this to you Mama Floyd?" she muttered as she took a hard look at Ms. Floyd's ghastly expression in death. Anya made the sign of a cross and gently closed Ms. Floyd's open eyes. After doing that, Anya reached in her purse for her phone. As she dialed 9-1-1, Anya realized for the first time that the person who called her had to be the one who killed Ms. Floyd.

Anya looked around, noticing no forced entry or no turned over furniture. She knew what this was about – somebody wanted money from Slick.

But who?, she wondered as the 9-1-1 operator answered the phone.

"Yes, please help me! I just found my mother dead on the floor," Anya told the operator then gave her the address and hung up the phone.

Six

Anya got through the intense interrogation only fifteen minutes before the coroner's van arrived. She was still a little unsteady behind the hour long questioning the homicide detective threw her way.

At first Anya believed that the mean looking black detective would take her to the police precinct as soon as the interrogation ended. But he gave her a card and walked away, making it plain to her that he would not take her anywhere. Discovering Ms. Floyd's body weighed heavy on her. Now she'd have to be the bearer of bad news once she saw her man.

And so, with that burden, she waited on the sidewalk with a spaced out look until the coroner removed Ms. Floyd's corpse from the house.

****

That bitch could be my downfall!

Mozart faded away into the crowd of onlookers as Anya stood on the sidewalk. The expression on the woman's face had told it all. She was a wife, and radiated the tenderness, care and love that all wives possessed. The death of her mother in-law could move her to do almost anything.

Like inform the police about her phone call?

Nathan Welch

The thought sickened him. Mozart didn't ever kill a woman, til today. He didn't like it at all. It left a bad taste in his mouth. He leaned against a teal Dodge Durango on the other side of the street. He would do it again if push came to shove. He could do anything he had to do. He had proved that.

But maybe killing Slick's girl wasn't necessary. He had to clear his head and think. Would he have to put that work in? Would it even bring the result he wanted? The situation was serious, but he felt it would be better to explore other avenues? Everyone had secrets. Suppose he followed and pried until he knew every detail of the woman's life. He might be able to catch her slipping and motivate her into moving to his tune...

It would take time.

Not if he bent all his will and effort to the task. In only minutes of studying her, Mozart had come to admire Slick's wifey. She reminded him of the kind of woman he wanted to be in a serious relationship with. Surely, he could tail her for a few days.

A week at the most.

Taking any more time would be irresponsible. He could allow himself a week to decide her fate or rind another option. If things still seared him after seven days – then he would have to kill the sexy woman.

****

Anya watched in silence as Ms. Floyd's body disappeared into the rear of the white coroner van. Ms. Floyd was gone, and there wasn't anything Anya could do about it.

Unless, she thought almost immediately. She turned and rushed to her car. Ms. Floyd's sudden death disturbed her. As she thought about the mysterious call she'd received and Ms. Floyd's death by stabbing, she made up her mind to find out the son of a bitch responsible for the mysterious call and the murder.

Moments later, Anya reached a block on Georgia Avenue near the police precinct. Before she could make it to the next block, her cell phone rang. She answered on the second ring.

"Hello?"

"Mrs. Floyd?"

"Yes, who is this?"

"I'm Nurse Winslow, here at Howard University. I'm calling about your husband, ah…Mr. Nick Floyd." The nurse found Slick's wallet, and decided to notify his wife.

The agony was exploding inside her. "What's happened…I'm on my way," she whispered.

"That would be fine," the nurse's voice was soft with compassion. "I think its best you hear this news in person."

Anya raised a shaking hand to her lips as she thought of the worse. "My God, its it that bad?"

"Honestly ma'am, it is. I'll see you soon," the nurse was silent a moment before ending the call.

Anya shook her head and blinked her tears. She pulled over to the side of the road and leaned her head back on the head rest. She felt empty, knowing something terrible had happened to Slick. The call had drained everything out of her, leaving nothing but an aching hold. At that moment, Anya knew she loved Slick. She doubted if that could ever be replaced and that's what created most of the pain she was feeling.

She pulled off slowly, staring distantly as she headed to Howard University Hospital to see about her man.

■■■

At the same time, the lead homicide detective took a walk through of Ms. Floyd's entire home. Probing certain areas in search of a motive behind Ms. Floyd's murder. Det. Mitchell Irving stumbled across a cedar chest full of drugs and money. The 38 year old detective couldn't believe what sat in his range just waiting to be confiscated.

"Jackpot!" he whistled and looked around quickly, giving up that sneaky look like he was about to do a dirty deed.

Det. Mitchell began counting the money inside the chest. By the time he reached $275,000, he already made up his mind to only turn in $75,000 to the department. He felt that he could use the dirty money more – hell, he had a wife and five kids to feed. Not to mention the mortgage on the house and two car notes. He believed the money had been God's way of answering his prayers as far as helping him get ahead in life.

Once he reached $365,000, Det. Mitchell's hands began shaking. He closed his eyes. "Thank you God, you finally came through for me – Hallelujah!"

After cuffing $290,000, Det. Mitchell stuffed the money in a gym bag and left the cedar chest open. He rushed down the stairs and located a uniform cop.

"Hey, I need you to go upstairs and guard the first room on your left with your life until I call in what I've found," Det. Mitchell instructed the bright eyed uniform cop.

"Yes sir, will do," he said before rushing upstairs.

While the cop rushed to his task, Det. Mitchell exited the home in the midst of all the fingerprinting lab and technicians conducting their investigation. The cops were so busy doing their jobs, they never even noticed Det. Mitchell walking away from the scene with a gym bag full of dirty money.

Seven

Anya looked completely dazed with sorrow when she entered Slick's hospital room 35 minutes later. She knelt beside the bed and kissed his forehead. She feared the worst for Slick, the only person who made her feel loved like a queen and gave her the world.

The complete silence of the room made the beeping life-support machines seem louder than an alarm clock ringing in Jumua's service. She wanted to go to sleep and wake up just to start over as if everything happening had been a bad dream. She knew that wouldn't happen. Everything happening was real. She'd seen it with her own eyes. She'd just learned that Slick was in a very deep coma, after being brought back from the clutches of death two times.

From what she saw, Anya could tell Slick was barely making it. All she could do is remain by his side and hope and pray that God pulled him out of this.

The sight of her man lying unconscious and hooked up to so many machines was too painful for Anya to bear. For the first time since learning about Slick's plight, Anya let the tears stream down her face like a waterfall. Nurse Winslow did her best to console the disturbed young lady. She rubbed her back gently.

"Now baby, what you need to do is be strong for him. Although it may look bad right now, there's nothing that God can't do chile. Put your trust in God. He's very merciful."

Nathan Welch

"I will Ms. Winslow," She sniffed, "I will." She got off her knees and pulled a chair close to his bedside. She leaned over to Slick , held his hand in her soft palms, and gently planted a kiss on his lips.

"However long it takes baby, I swear I will always be by your side. I love you, Booby."

Anya looked over at Slick's life-support machine beeping. She then looked back at Slick and smiled faintly, remembering their wedding vows – through sickness and health – for richer or for poorer – she could do without the poorer part – until death do us apart.

"I do Booby...I do... I'ma hold you down...all I need you to do is fight through this... come back to me baby, I need you." She kissed his lips again, and rubbed his hand. She felt this was her duty. After all, she was his wife and it was mandatory in her eyes to be there for him through thick and thicker, until death do them apart.

****

Outside the hospital, Mozart sat in his other car, A maroon '78 Monte Carlo with dark tints and watched Anya's car. He parked his car only a car space from her luxury vehicle.

Every minute he had to wait on her return had been like little knives, tearing him apart. Not knowing what she was going to do about their phone call was tearing him apart.

He wished she'd hurry up, so he could stick it to her like a wet t-shirt. He wanted to know her every move.

Eight

Ug stepped into the vacant apartment and smiled when he noticed how packed the hallways were at the moment. This shit gonna' be gone in no time, he thought as he quickly cut up the last ounce and made his way back out into the hallway. Soon as he made an appearance , several crackheads swarmed him.

Ug pulled out his gun, which he knew would increase his chances to do business with a sense of safety and get the feenin' crackheads in order.

"Damn Ug why you always have us waiting like this? You be missing boo-coo money and shit," his best customer Claudette said.

Ug pulled out his product and went to work. "Y'all ma'fuckaz always complaining about nothing. Y'all can't get this yay' no where, so deal with the wait."

"Shit! Dealing with the wait, I've already missed out on making a buck fifty sell and they ain't coming back." Claudette rolled her honey brown eyes at him.

To be a crackhead, Claudette still had a banging body. She had an average face, but most guys were willing to overlook her looks because her 36 perky D-cups, 28 inch waist, and 44 inch wide ass and hips made up for whatever she lacked in the beauty department.

Claudette always seemed to demand the attention in every place she stepped foot in.

Nathan Welch

Ug kept serving fiends, disregarding Claudette's complaints.

"That's a'ight. I'ma wait until your black ass want some of this pussy, I bet chu' listen to what I have to say then." She said with a slick smile.

Ug walked up to Claudette and said, "You might want to stop feeling yourself cause your pussy ain't that good. Everybody round da' forty done fucked that beat up joint!"

"They keep coming back, so I guess it's good enough, and they pay good for it, you know how I go." Claudette didn't give a damn who knew their business. She'd been running the streets since the age of 13 and was still going strong at 42.

Ug wasn't the type of guy to argue back and forth with a woman – especially no crackhead woman. He knew she was a has been ho, looking to stay in the spotlight for some reason.

Suddenly Ug had an idea – a very wicked idea. He knew she wasn't built to lure him into tricking with her anymore, but she did have all the right assets to bait in the chump he wanted to kill. She had an enticing body that made guys drool in the hood, which was rare for a crackhead.

Ug would turn her craving for cocaine into his murderous plan. He'd use what she had to smoke the guy who disrespected him. Claudette was about to become his bait and didn't even know it. *I'll be killing that bitch nigga in no time if I can get Claudette to roll with the punches,* he thought.

"You right Claudette," he sighed. "Is this your slick way of asking me for the dick?"

She placed one hand on her hip and sucked her pouty lips. "You think you know everything, but see there, you don't know shit, cause I ain't fucking you no more." She said jokingly with a smile.

Ug smiled too. He could tell that she wanted to give him some sex in trade for his product.

"I'ma hold you to your word too." Ug turned on her, served several more customers and began to walk away.

"Hey Ug, you just gonna leave me geekin' huh!" She shouted after him as he continued walking down the hallway.

Ug stopped in his tracks. He turned around and looked at her for a long moment.

"If you trying to get something big to smoke then wait right here," he replied.

Claudette looked at him and wanted to respond, but she noticed him disappearing into an apartment and slamming the door. She looked back at Sharon, who was eagerly watching the entire encounter.

"Girl, I'll give you a bump until Ug hit chu' off. Just pay me back."

"What!" Claudette yelled. "Bitch, do you know how hard it is to get a bump outta' your petty ass? If you wasn't being so damn nosey, I wouldn't have been able to get shit out cho' funky ass, so just keep it moving bitch."

Nathan Welch

After telling the woman off, Claudette burst into laughter as she walked towards the apartment where she'd seen Ug go inside.

Claudette couldn't stop laughing because she knew Sharon felt small after getting screamed on. With her eyes glued on Sharon, Claudette lifted her hand in the air and knocked on the door

Sharon frowned evilly as she returned Claudette's stare. When the door opened, Claudette nodded to Sharon and entered the apartment.

Once inside, she smiled seductively as she rubbed Ug's chest.

"Ease up," Ug stopped her. "I got all the coke you can smoke, but I need you to do me a big favor."

"Boy what?"

As Ug told her a bullshit story to get her to hook-up with the Kennedy Street dude he wanted to kill, all Claudette thought about was all the free crack she had coming to her for doing something as easy as hooking up with a total stranger.

If she only knew!

Nine

The following day, Mozart could feel the butterflies fluttering in his stomach as he approached the hospital entrance where Anya was heading. He noticed her fly Louis Vuitton printed jacket that stopped just at her waist, revealing the skin tight business skirt she rocked. The skirt stopped at her mid-thigh to show her thick legs and designer open-toe heels.

Damn, shorty is a dime, he thought, giving her a quick smile while holding the door open for her.

"Thank you," she smiled weakly as she walked pass him.

"No problem sweetheart," he shrugged and followed her to the elevators.

Before the elevators could arrive, Mozart made his move. He looked at the sexy high-yellow amazon who possessed the beauty of a supermodel, and tapped her on the shoulder.

She turned on him and frowned, her perfectly arched eyebrow showing her mood. Mozart disregarded her evil demeanor as he went at her.

"What's up beautiful?" he looked her up and down, licking his lips in lust.

Anya didn't respond. She crossed her arms and looked at him with an attitude before turning her attention towards the elevator.

"Whoa! Whoa! ," he said, moving to face her. "Hold up, no disrespect I just wanted to compliment you on your beauty and body and see if I can take you out sometimes."

Look, this ain't the place or time for all that. I'm a married woman and not one of those hoodrat bitches you used to dealing with." She said as she walked away.

Mozart walked after her and grabbed her arm lightly. "Don't do that shorty. Believe me; I don't chase behind nothing ass hoodrats. I just saw one of the baddest women in the city, and wanted to get to know you, that's all."

"I'm going through something right now...and I just can't-

"Whoa! Hold up...all I asked for is something light. I'm not tryna' breakup a happy home. I know men and women can be friends without making things complicated...make sense?"

Anya picked up on the comment and said, "Yeah, it definitely makes sense, but I don't have the time. I'm dealing with my husband's health right now."

Anya could hear his frustrating sigh. She looked him over again, wondering what other reason than sex did he want to be her friend. Even though, she shot him down, his body language displayed confidence.

"That's understandable," he nodded. "Well it was a pleasure meeting you ah..." he said in a way to get her name.

"I'm Anya, and you are?" she asked while shifting all her weight on one leg, giving her hip an enticing shape.

A half-smile crossed Mozart's face as he observed her. "It shouldn't matter...you don't have time, remember." He took her hand and kissed it gently.

"Sometimes, you gotta' live honest." He smiled before turning on her and walking away slowly.

By the time Mozart reached the elevators, Anya caught up to him. She walked over to Moazart and circled him, eyeing him up and down.

"What's all that suppose to mean?"

"You're an intelligent woman. I'm pretty sure you can figure it out." He said, while looking up in the air at the glowing elevator display.

Anya got up in his face, standing so close to him that Mozart could smell the kiwi-mango scent on her breath. He backed up a step to avoid succumbing to the urge to kiss her.

Slick got a bad-ass bitch, he thought as she moved closer to him. Just the fact that she still hung around surprised him. He figured she were testing him to see how far he'd go to pursue her. He realized that if he fell for her games, things would be over before they started.

When the elevator arrived, Mozart and Anya along with three other people got on. Mozart softly bumped Anya into a corner and looked into her eyes.

Nathan Welch

Right before the elevator doors closed, Mozart kissed Anya softly on the lips and rushed off the elevator!

"Hey stop!" he heard her yelling as the doors closed.

Let the games begin, he thought as he bolted for the fire escape stairwell and ran up the stairs in hopes of reaching Slick's room before her.

****

Claudette couldn't wait to locate the truck for Ug. She knew that this was her chance to come up in a major way. Ug told her the guy had long money, but he loved tricking it off. Now that she was on the hunt, Claudette would hang around the Kennedy Street area until the hood-rich guy she'd heard about showed his face. And she hoped that he'd do it soon so she could make that fast money.

She knew that she couldn't really afford to hang in the area going unnoticed, but she figured that if she treated herself to some crack, none of the local dealers would pay her any attention.

She counted the money that Ug had given her-$150. She planned on using that to buy a couple outfits to help with her hunting. She currently wore some stretch pants and a pink I Love DC tee shirt, and some multicolored sauconeys track shoes. She knew her gear needed an upgrade, but she felt that could wait.

She wanted some cocaine and didn't care if she had to spend the clothes money Ug had given her. With that in mind and the crack monkey sitting on her back, Claudette headed over to the 1st –N-Kennedy drug strip.

Soon as she stepped on the block, several aggressive hustlers with dreads and colorful outfits surrounded her. They thought that she was a young woman in search of some P.C.P. or e-pills. They had no idea that she smoked cocaine faster than it could be produced.

Claudette had a trail of young men following behind her as she quickly searched the block for her trick with her eyes. Not wanting to waste anymore time, she walked directly to a dark skin guy with short dreads who smoked on a blunt.

"Hey Boo-Boo. You got that?"

The man glanced at her as the swarm of street corner hustlers watched her every move.

"Depends on what chu' looking for?" He answered, giving her a quick overall look. Her pants was so tight, he could see her chunky pussy print, looking fatter than a camel-toe.

"I need some coke. I'm tryna' get seven for fitty', straight money.

He raised an eyebrow at her. "The best I can do is six."

"No…I'm good." She said, and begin to walk away.

Hold up Shorty, damn." The man laughed and shook his head. "We should be able to work something out. You got something I want that could make up the difference, so what's up?" He asked, licking his lips in lust.

Claudette leaned in close to him and said, "If it's what I think you want, that's worth more than twenty dollars baby. My pussy pay my bills, so come better than that."

What she told him made the bulge in his cargo pants stiffened. He licked his lips again and asked her what she wanted. Soon as the question rolled off his tongue, Claudette rubbed her hand over his bulge and gave his dick a gentle squeeze.

"We can talk about it on the way to somewhere more private."

He grabbed her hand so fast and pulled her towards the nearest alley, Claudette thought he was going to yank her arm out of the socket.

Ten

As Anya emerged from the elevator, her blood was boiling. The strange man had a serious problem. Instead of giving her his name, his kissing exit left Anya infuriated, embarrassed and totally disturbed.

If I ever see his ass again, so help me God, I'ma, she quickly stopped talking to herself as she rounded the corner and spotted the same man standing by her husband's hospital room.

Anya eyed the man talking to a cop posted outside the room as her pace quickened. For some reason, she felt there was trouble up ahead. She thought it might have something to do with Slick's overdose on illegal drugs.

Moments later, Anya found herself standing between the cop and the stranger. Instead of going off and cursing him out for his earlier disrespectful actions, Anya focused her attention on the uniform cop.

The cop, a tall paper bag brown complexioned man with a thin mustache, average lips and an extra-wide long nose that seemed to belong to a cartoon character.

"Excuse me officer, why are you outside of my husband's room?"

The cop's eyes slid up and down Anya's body, attempting to undress her and intimidate her at the same time. "Just doing my job and following orders ma'am," he said sarcastically and tipped his hat at her in the process.

Anya glanced over her shoulder and frowned at Mozart. "Thanks for fucking up everything." She spoke with her back to him and then spoke to the officer.

"Do I need permission from you to go in and see him?" Her voice was dripping with bitter anger.

"Oh yeah," he coughed abnormally, "On that, well he's currently under arrest for something. I'm here to babysit and make sure he doesn't escape until he can be brought to stand before a court of law." He smiled before continuing.

"So your husband can no longer have any civilian visitors, no exceptions...no wife...no mother, no kids...nada."

His nasty response sent Anya over the edge. She whirled around on her heels and slapped Mozart with all her might.

"Damn!" The cop groaned as if she'd just smacked him, he reached for his Taser gun, preparing for whatever.

Her blow made an angry feeling sweep through Mozart like a powerful volcanic eruption. Anya tossed a mean mug at the sight of Mozart's angry expression and the pitiful way he rubbed his cheek.

"You better recognize MOTHERFUCKER!" She snarled. "I am not one to be disrespected! Don't fuck with me!"

Mozart had to take the blow on the chin due to the police presence, but at least he got her attention. Mozart stood there, plotting his next move as he watched the sexy woman turn and head back to the elevators like nothing happened.

The cop waited for Anya to get out of eavesdropping range before saying, "what a crazy bitch! Better you than me. You gonna be okay?"

Heaving with a sigh of relief, Mozart shrugged. "Hey, shit happens you dig." Mozart said and stepped off with a sense of urgency.

He knew he had to hustle to his car before she did, so he could continue stalking his prey.

****

The dark skin hustler shut the basement door of an abandoned house and jammed a wooden chair underneath the door knob. When he turned around, Claudette held her hand out.

"I'ma need ten dimes up front. Nothing personal Boo-Boo. It's just how I conduct business."

"Ten!" He gasped in shock. "Fuck no...I'm cool. Fuck I look like giving a clucker ten dimes to trick?"

Clauddette eased down her stretch pants and bent over. She stuck one finger in her pussy and then waved the finger close to his lips. "Cause once your dick dive's in this pussy, you gonna be happy I'll only charge you that."

He licked her wetness off her finger as he dropped his pants to his ankles, freeing his massive hard-on. She moved in closer and started grinding her pussy lips against his aching boner.

Her actions sent a jolting sensation of euphoria throughout his loins and balls. She knelt down on one knee and slid her tongue along the crooked vein on his rock hard dick.

"I need ten Daddy to take you to heaven," she moaned loudly; knowing he couldn't resist the urge to get his rocks off.

The sexually aroused man looked down at her and then quickly reached inside his pocket to give her what she wanted. It had been a long time since he had done something freaky with a crackhead. His girlfriend satisfied all of his sexual fantasies at will. Being a man had him chasing something different that looked good and her head game sent exciting tingles up his spine.

Once she got the drugs, Claudette went to work. She wrapped her lips around his dick and began sucking like a girl trying to keep her ice popsicle from melting.

"Aah yeeeaaah....damn bitch," he groaned, palming the back of her head as he urged her on to give him more oral pleasure. Up and down, she took him deep in her warm throat.

She gave him so much pleasure, he couldn't help but to fuck her mouth with hard thrusts. She extracted his glistening piston and licked all over the head and then snaked her tongue down to his balls and back up around the tip, before easing up on her feet and jerking him off. The look she gave him told him what she wanted.

He smoothly eased her body into a bent position and got behind her. He gripped both of her soft ass cheeks. He massaged them as he spread them apart and slid his dick inside her tight wet pussy.

Claudette bent lower to see his long hard shaft plowing in and out of her pussy. The sight of his pumping piston made her get into the act, working her juicy pussy back onto his thrusting power.

"Ssss...fuck me boo...fuck me...fuck me," she urged winding her hips in circles like a belly dancer. His dick game was more than official and she couldn't help but enjoy it.

He inserted a finger into her asshole as his dick filled her sugary walls with satisfaction. By the sounds he made, she could tell her pussy still did the job. There was no way he could tell she'd fucked over 150 men.

Even with him gripping her waist and slamming dick inside of her relentlessly, she put her hands around her ankles and took the dick fast and hard, turning them both on more and more.

"Aaah...Aaah...Aaaaah...fuck me boo...fuck meeee!" She shrieked, urging him to go faster and faster.

As his breathing grew louder and faster, his dick swelled harder and harder in her. The fullness Claudette felt, along with the fingering sensation in her asshole made her wetter and wetter until she skyrocketed over the edge into orgasmic bliss.

"Aah...Aahhhieeee...you motherfucka...I'm ca-ca...cuuuuummmmmiing...oooohhh   shit...I'm cuummmiiiinng..."she moaned, bucking forward.

"Ssss damn bitch...let me get mine too," he groaned and started fucking her hard as he could. Her juices poured out all over his invading jizz-rod.

"Hurry...up...I ca...can't take no more...it's toooo gooood...she moaned, throwing the pussy back on him to get him to hurry up and explode.

Damn, this clucker bitch can fuck, he thought and felt his whole body quivering.

"Ugh...ugh...uggggrrrraaaaaa! He bellowed and pushed her forward.

As his dick slipped from her pulsating canal, he jerked his dick and exploded all over the dirty concrete floor. Claudette turned quickly and sought out the remants of his warm sperm. She felt the warm nut hitting her tongue and loved it. After she drained him, Claudette got up to pull up her stretch pants.

The man wiped his dick off with some napkins and pulled up his pants. A few moments later, the guy ended up trying to fuck her again, but Claudette wasn't having it.

"So that's how you going?" He asked, while contemplating on robbing her for what he'd just gave her and whatever else she had.

"I can't boo…I don't want chu' stretching my shit all outta' wack," she stroked his ego on the sly. "I ain't spose' to give this pussy out to nobody but my nigga. I hope he can't tell this fresh outta jail pussy ain't fresh no more."

"Oh, I see. You got that. Whenever you get a chance just come back on through and holla at me. If I ain't around, just ask for Boogie, somebody will point chu' in my direction," he said, walking over to the door to leave.

Claudette followed him to the door. He removed the chair, opened the door and they left the abandoned house, heading in different directions. Claudette was pulling out her straight-shooter crack pipe as she rounded the corner. She dropped a whole dime rock in the burnt glass stem, lit it and caught the best high she had in week.

Eleven

Anya turned the corner and saw the strange man leaning on her car like he'd been waiting for her- no more like he's stalking me, she thought as she reached in her purse to grab her taser stun gun.

"What the fuck are you doing, stalking me?"

"Whoa! Fuck no. Look, let me explain and apologize. You know big Slicky Rozay's my man, and I swear to God I ain't know you was his wife," he lied "please don't tell him what I did, cause that'll be the end for me literally."

Anya changed before his eyes, her face took on a softer gentler and more vulnerable look-not the look of the killer that slapped fire out his face moments ago.

"See there, you crossed the line, and now you want me to keep it a secret from my man?" she mumbled softly. "Why couldn't you just tell me your name and leave well enough alone?"

"What can I say, your beauty made me crash ...I mean can you blame me now that chu' know?"

"Don't play with me boy," she barked. "What chu' did wasn't proper at all." She chided. "You know damn well you can't be going around putting your lips on people. That shit gonna' get chu' stabbed."

"Shiiid, Georgie Porgie did it, and made the girls cry. Ain't none of them wanna do him no harm." Mozart countered smoothly and made her laugh.

Anya smiled, showing a set of evenly pearly whites," you silly. So, how you knew Nick was in the hospital?"

The moment had arrived, and Mozart had to navigate the movie how he wanted it to play out. Mozart matched her stare as he slowly rose off her car.

"I think you should be sitting down when I tell you this."

She frowned and gripped the stun gun inside her purse as a million bad things he may possibly say danced around in her head. Her emotions were getting the best of her. But if she didn't sit down she would never learn what the stranger knew.

"No, tell me now," she demanded. " I'ma big girl. I can handle it."

"Naw," he said, trying to stall for time and come up with the perfect lie.

Suddenly, Mozart got an idea and figured it may just work if he maneuvered the V sooth enough.

"Listen shorty, just sit in the car, so I can give you the scoop on the nigga who set up your man to go down."

Instantly, Anya rushed to her car and unlocked all the doors. The thought of what the stranger had to say sent chills through her body.

After entering her car, Mozart took a moment to examine her demeanor. He took a deep breath, staring at the anxious interest springing from eyes and body language.

Nathan Welch

For Mozart, the lies he began telling Anya was a chance to see how good his manipulation skills were. He told himself if she accepted his lies for truth and acted on them, then he'll kill two birds with one stone – thus the wrong move he made would eventually turn out to be the best move he ever made in life.

Twelve

Ug had just arrived at the Stadium strip club when he got a phone call. He nodded his head to Nikki Minaj's hit single, "I beez in da' trap" as he answered the call.

"Yeah, talk to me," he said, sticking a finger in his other ear so he could hear.

"It's me Cluadette boy. You know that guy ain't been round' here all day." She told him about the guy he wanted to kill.

"Oh yeah?" He mumbled.

"Yeah, so what chu' wanna do? I can stay round here until whenever, but it's definitely gonna cost you."

Ug listened to her thirsty-ass, thinking she was pretty much guaranteed to locate his prey – If she didn't go on a crack binge. Or maybe that would speed up the process if she did.

Ug said, "You can chill round there if you want. I got chu' on the back end."

Claudette said, "Don't play Ug! You for real right?"

"What I just tell your thirsty-ass?"

Claudette said, "Thanks Boo-Boo, I won't let chu' down."

As she ended the call, Claudette quickly took a hit of crack. While getting high as a kite, she was thinking how it good it was to get a sweet job for once in a while to support her habit. Now she just had to keep her habit under control.

****

"What did you say?" Anya asked, stunned by Mozart's made up story.

"I know shit sounds fucked up, but that's how niggaz be going nowadays over they girls. I hate to be the bearer of bad news...I'm sorry to tell you, but Slick's in a coma all because of a bitch!" Mozart lied and went on to repeat the same lies he'd just told her, claiming that Slick's number one customer from 640 projects had been responsible for Slick's plight.

Slick's cheating ways was the last words Anya expected to hear from the stranger. Life was passing by in a blur. Agony numbed her senses. Anya felt paralyzed with a mixture of anger, pain, heartache, and regret. Thoughts of her man being out in the streets sticking his dick in other women repulsed her. It had been the focal point in her mind during the minutes she listened to all of Mozart's lies. She didn't want to have nothing else to do with Slick ever again.

Holding back her tears, Anya said, "You know I really appreciate your honesty and concerns for Nick," With his cheating – no good ass, she thought before continuing. "But if it's not too much, I'd appreciate it more if you allow me the chance to get a little revenge."

"Ca –come again?" He snapped like her reply had been all wrong.

Anya looked hard at him. "Look, I wanna do what I feel needs to be done far as cleaning up the mess Nick's so called friend made, and I need your help." She said and thought, *then get chu' to help me in doing something even more wicked to repay Nick's cheating-ass.*

Now that Slick's dirty secrets had been revealed in the form of a jealous snake, nothing else mattered to Anya but getting revenge. For a long moment, Anya sat frozen in the cockpit. She couldn't understand what she'd heard about her husband. It was a major blow to her self-esteem.

How could you cheat on me, you son-of-a-bitch?

Much as I bend over backwards for your fat – ass to fulfill all your kinky fantasies… I even engaged in a threesome a few times for your fat – bitch ass!

Why me?

How in God's name had this happen to me?

Mozart's eyes were focused on Anya, scanning her from head to toe as they entered her spacious home. When she asked him to come to her house, Mozart figured it was now the perfect time to eliminate her and take whatever riches Slick had stashed in the house.

"You jive living big," Mozart said, eyeing all the fly artwork on the walls and Italian leather furniture.

"You know what they say...pussy is power," she said, then stepped out of her high heel sandals, took off her blazer and pulled down her skirt.

"Make yourself at home," she ordered, standing in her bra and thongs. "I'll be back in a few minutes."

As Anya switched hard out of her living room, making her butt cheeks jiggle, Mozart's eyes were locked in on her every move. For the next 35 minutes, Mozart sat on the couch struggling with himself on whether he should kill Anya.

A few moments later, Anya walked into the living room with a towel wrapped around her body. She placed a hand on her wide hips, running her tongue across her slightly plump lips.

"Can you come and lotion my back for me?" She said with a smile.

Mozart smiled at the aggressive woman, allowing his little head to dictate his actions. He eased off the couch and followed Anya into her bedroom.

"The lotion's on the dresser over there," she pointed and Mozart went to grab it.

When he turned back around, Mozart's eyes were stuck on Anya's naked flesh, scanning her smooth back, plump behind and zoomed in on her trimmed pussy lips that peeked at him between her slightly closed thighs.

"Well...don't just stand there...do something," Anya said.

"You sure about this? I mean what about Slick?" He asked, not really caring one way or the other. Her bold offer just made it harder for him to take her out.

"What about Slick? He did him, so I'ma do me...what he don't know won't hurt right?"

"No bullshit," he muttered, feeling the aching bulge in his pants ready to explode. His eyes danced from her pretty looking cheeks to the exquisitely decorated bedroom. The platinum stained walls were filled with various shapes of mirrors, a barrel vaulted ceiling was overhead with a huge flat screen T.V. posted discretely over the double-wide king size bed. A crème suede sectional sofa made an L shape over in the corner near the fireplace, and tall platinum book shelves that sat on both sides of the fireplace. A small lake was right outside her huge bay style windows.

Mozart walked over to the bed as Anya turned over to reveal her perky breast and V-shape pussy. She leaned up and kissed Mozart on the lips, slipping her tongue deep into his mouth. Her intoxicating mango-wild cherry scent pushed his arousal into overdrive.

When they broke the tongue wrestling match a few moments later, Anya whispered, "Hurry up and get outta' those clothes, so you can help me feel what getting revenge is like."

Thirteen

Anya eyed Mozart mischievously as she helped him remove his shirt. She caressed his hard chest and put her lips on his nipples as she eased off the bed and down to her knees.

"Mmmm...I can't wait to feel that," she moaned kissing his crotch while undoing the buckle of his pants.

She helped him out of his pants and underwear, planting subtle kisses all over his granite joy stick. She stroked him gently, sending arousing tingles down his spine.

Mozart couldn't believe how easy it was to fuck Slick's woman. He was amazed at how eager and willing she was to set the head and pussy out.

Anya darted her tongue in and out of his pee-hole while she raked his nut sack between her manicured nails.

"Aaah...sss," he groaned, feeling his dick disappear into the wet heat of Anya's mouth.

Wrapping her small fist around his thick, stiffness, she spun her tongue around his dick head, tracing his vein with her lips. She deep throated him far as she could until she gagged and choked.

"Ease up shorty," he moaned, tapping her bobbing head, to stop her. She popped his hulking boner from her mouth and pushed him back onto the double-wide king size bed.

She climbed on the bed, kissing all over his body, until she eased her dripping pussy over his face. As they got into a 69 position, Anya's fresh pussy scent made Mozart's dick jump in anticipation. She quickly went back to work, sucking hard on his stiff wood and slurping even louder, blowing his mind.

"Damn guuurrll," he huffed before sliding his tongue between the wet lips of her pussy. The taste of her sweet wet nectar, the feel of her body grinding over his face and the feeling of his dick being gobbled up vigorously sent fireworks bursting through his body but he fought back the urge to explode.

"Oooh…yess…yeah, suck dis pussy – eat it good…mmmm…eat dis…pus…pussy!" She howled, as her pussy lips quivered onto his tongue.

"Aaah…oh   my…gawd…boy…I'm cummmming like shit!" She gasped, "hurry up and fuck me…hurry!" She begged for the dick.

Mozart pushed her over; she laid back, opened her legs and looked into his eyes while softly stroking his dick against her hard clitoris.

"You don't have nothing do you?" She asked, sliding his rock hard shaft along her slick slit.

"Hell no." He said, spreading her legs wider. He put one of her legs over his shoulder and pushed his aching boner deep inside her wet contracting love canal.

"Ssssss boy," she moaned. "You sooo big…ump…ump…ump…sssss…damn   boo…fuk me…don't stop," she urged before digging her ass into the bed and humping her pelvis upward to meet his churning strokes.

In an instant, he hit her G-spot, making her eyes roll into the back of her head. When her orgasm settled, her eyes open to the sight of his long, thick dick disappearing and reappearing inside her tight pussy.

"Ssss…fuck me…fuck me…yeah…right there," she moaned while he stretched her tight pussy to fit his plowing penetration.

"Aaah boy…Aaaah!" She yelped, feeling his full girth deep inside her, seeming like he was tapping her stomach.

"Damn, your pussy good," he moaned, slamming dick in and out of her with all his might.

When he saw tears in her eyes, Mozart did his best in trying to kill the pussy with his dick until it spurted his love juices deep inside her womb.

****

For close to an hour after having sex, Mozart and Anya talked in bed about everything under the sun. She was snuggled up in his armpit, softly jerking his dick up and down, Mozart slowly eased out of bed.

"Where you going?" she asked, stunned. She wanted to go a few more rounds with that monster between his legs.

Nathan Welch

"Bathroom." He said, heading into the master bathroom.

Black and white tile lined the floor, matching the black and white walls, ceilings and color scheme of the bathroom. The double toilets blew his mind. He had no idea one of them was a fancy French contraption that allowed you to wash your ass after defecating.

Damn, it's a lot of money in the streets, he thought while staring at the shiny onyx hued Jacuzzi styled tub. The glass door to the shower were in a light smoky black tint.

Unable to resist temptation, Mozart stepped inside the huge shower and turned the power jets on. A full stream of hot water blasted from six different nozzles, hitting his body from all angles.

"Man, what the fuck," he muttered, cracking up with laughter as he got lost in the shower.

"Big boy, always crying broke, but the whole time he living like a ma'fuckin Don! I knew his fat-ass had that bag."

Seconds later, Mozart felt a draft. Turning quickly when the door opened, Mozart released a relaxing sigh when he saw Anya stepping inside and tying her long hair into a ponytail.

"You can run, but chu' can't hide." She said to him before grabbing his inflated pole. Suddenly, she squatted down and started sucking all over his manmeat.

"Mmmm…that big ma'fucka tastes sooo good," she moaned between slurps.

Looking down at her sucking on his magic stick had him turned on. He backed away, but she held on like a pitbull. By the time Anya got turned on from sucking his dick, she slithered between his legs, came up and stuck her tongue between his ass cheeks as she gently jerked him off.

"Ssss...ha...ha...hold up shorty!" He huffed, slapping the shower wall from the overwhelming pleasure she inflicted on him. He couldn't believe how freaky she was. When he couldn't take it anymore, he pulled her up to her feet and took charge.

Mozart pulled Anya by her hair and bent her over. He slapped her hard on the ass, slid his dick deep inside her pussy, and hit the bottom.

"Oooo Daddy...I love it from the back...hit it hard...then fuck me in my ass...I love it hard and rough." She cooed, as he extracted his pulsing phallus and guided it towards her tight anal opening.

He spread her cheeks, pushed his dick inside her tight milky way and sunk in deep.

"Don't play with it nigga...punish my asshole," she demanded. He quickly obeyed, slamming in and out...in and out of her clenching asshole. He thrusted his hips and slid his fingers inside her pussy, penetrating both her holes at once.

"Aaah," she yelled. "Fuck me...harder...harder...harder...harder!" She shrieked while he used a finger to stroke her hard clitoris.

Nathan Welch

"Ugh...ugh...uggghhhhhh...ssssss boy...oh my fucking God!" She huffed, exploding all over his probing fingers.

Mozart quickly pulled out her tight ass, making a pop sound.

"Come here, with cho' nasty-ass," he said, turning her around to face him.

He lifted her up and slammed her against the shower wall. She wrapped her thick legs around his waist before feeling his thick dick slamming upward inside her oozing cuntal canal.

"Take dis dick...take it," he groaned, totally caught up in the good sex they were having.

"I...am...I am Daddy...sssss...shit boy!" she yelled when he hit her g-spot and fucked her viciously.

Mozart held her up in the air by her soft ass cheeks while plowing his stiff meat in and out of her. Anya's eyes connected with his, while she took his relentless fucking like a porn star.

"I'm ba...bout to nut," he groaned, slowing down his fucking to a easy grind, giving her a slow-motion plowing until he felt himself about to explode.

He extracted his jumping cock, lowered her to the ground and exploded all over her titties, and stomach. Anya quickly squatted to catch the rest of his warm semen in her mouth.

"Aa fuck," he groaned, shaking at the knees as she swallowed hard, moaning in pleasure as she milked the rest of his babies oozing from his spasming cock.

After their round in the shower, Mozart moved Anya to the Jacuzzi where he pampered her by soaping her body and pleasing her with an affectionate full body massage.

Anya's mind was completely blown. She couldn't help but to pull him from the Jacuzzi and back into the bedroom where she fucked him and made love to him in various ways that she'd never done with Slick.

For the remainder of that day and night, Mozart and Anya did their best trying to turn each other out with sex. They went at, licking, tasting, experimenting, and fucking in various positions until they fell out from exhaustion. Both of them slept in comfort knowing they brought their A-game to the bedroom.

After that experience, Mozart knew he made an error by having sex with her. It complicated things. Even if he wanted to do her in, he felt pretty sure that he could no longer pull the trigger.

At 5:30 A.M., Mozart sat up in bed. He stared at Anya snoring peacefully on her stomach. He remembered why he was here to kill her.

For Mozart, killing Anya was no good in his eyes. Her sex game was too good. She acted like a dick starved slave to his dick and he never wanted that feeling to end.

With that in mind, Mozart knew he had to find a way to slip inside Slick's hospital room and kill him so he and Anya could be together forever.

Fourteen

For the next two weeks, Mozart put his game plan and thug passion down. He had Anya climbing the walls and screaming out his name every time he made love to her. Anya never went a day without blowing up Mozart's phone, begging for the dick.

She just walked around the house in her thong and heels, and waited for Mozart to come over and tame all her freaky desires. The only gripe Mozart had with Anya, he had to spend the night every time he visited her, which was a disadvantage to his scheme mainly because he didn't have enough time to get at Slick and end his lease on life. Mozart wasn't good enough to sneak pass the police guard during the day. He tried it a few times, but always came up short, which enraged him. He, therefore, decided to try at night to kill Slick.

While Mozart spent most of his time fucking Slick's girl and plotting on Slick's demise, Slick was opening his eyes slowly, awakening from a 16-day long coma.

After glancing around, Slick realized for the first time that he was laying up in a hospital room.

How in the hell...fuck I'm doing in here? He wondered. It took a few seconds before everything that happened came oozing out of his memory bank.

He calculated that after fainting on the police, they somehow got him to the hospital. Soon as he tried to move out of bed, Slick heard and felt the iron handcuffs and shackles restraining his left ankle and wrist to the bed's metal guard railing.

Slick sighed, wanting to hurt Mozart really bad for the jam he'd gotten him into.

Damn look at cho' dumb-foolio ass now, Slick thought. You thought that you had all the sense huh? Guess you ain't so smart after all. Not only did you let an anything nigga work you, but you locked up and on top of that, you losing boo-coo money. I know my wife probably worried to death bout' me. I gotta' get the fuck outta' here, but the major answer to the puzzle is how?

Slick knew he couldn't move the whole bed outside the room. It would be impossible to escape without being detected, looking around, Slick scoped out the policeman on guard duty outside his door.

Fuck! I'm hit like good weed...unless, Slick got an idea and began easing over to the brown telephone near his bed. He licked his dry lips, and swallowed hard, trying to get the scratchy sandpaper feeling out of his throat. It enraged him that he had to go through so much bullshit because of Mozart. That alone made him want to kill him even more, but first things first. His plan to escape the hospital was way more important.

****

Kennedy Street was busy with traffic like last minute Christmas shoppers at the mall looking for gifts. A gang of hustlers huddle around a crap game, and when they dispersed, the ghetto gorilla, Black Doo-Doo stood victorious, counting his winnings. Doo-Doo did almost everything you could think of for that fast dollar. From robbery, murder, to kidnappings, extortion and gambling, Doo-Doo had no cut cards about hurting others to get that almighty dollar. Just picture a darker version of Debo from Friday with his go hard demeanor turned all the way up – yeah that would be Doo-Doo aka the Ghetto Gorilla.

He leaned against a black jaguar XJ Sedan, where he had extorted the owner for $2,000 a week to hustle around Kennedy St. several days ago. After counting up the $3,350 he'd just won, the ghetto gorilla headed toward the corner store, but instead of going all the way, on impulse he made a left and walked over to the next block to the other corner store. Just a necessary precaution he took having a bunch of people who feared and hated him, the ghetto gorilla knew anybody could try to kill him at any given moment to stop his reign of terror in the hood.

As he entered the store, Doo-Doo felt someone's eyes on him. When he looked up, an attractive woman at the soda machine was staring at him intently. She looked to be in her early twenties, strawberry blond dread locks tied back into a ponytail, the contours of her hour-glass frame were revealed by the spandex body dress that was too short for his taste and too skanky for her.

The woman looked familiar, but he didn't know her. He looked away, got a call on his Blackberry and answered on the second ring.

"Holla at me?" When he looked up during his call, the woman was gone.

Nathan Welch

"Ay Doo-Doo, it's me Slick...I need you big guy?"

"What's up?"

When Slick began telling him what he'll pay to have done, the ghetto gorilla hung up, thinking Slick was trying to set him up to take take a hard fall...

I'ma fool, but not a damn fool, he thought, realizing that there were lines even his crazy ass wouldn't think about crossing. What Slick just asked him to do was one of them.

Damn!

Slick had to face it! If the ghetto gorilla wasn't down to break law and rescue him then he was doomed. Had he turned over a new leaf already? Or had I called his bluff?

Slick thought back to the break that divided them for good. It happened when Doo-Doo and Slick were in the ninth grade, thirteen years old.

Gemeni was a year older.

He was a hustler, and always dressed fly, he could charm any girl and drove a different car everyday to school. He'd had a Versace wardrobe before anybody in school knew about Versace.

He liked to walk between Slick and Doo-Doo and make fun of them. He said he only played with them because he liked them. Doo-Doo wasn't too crazy about the idea of being made fun of. Doo-Doo got Slick to agree that they'll avoid Gemini at all cost. The terms were set. It never occurred to either of them that greed would destroy their bond.

The school dance was on for Saturday night, and a dozen kids showed up at the door to pay their way in. Gemini showed up and patted Slick on the back. He had on a rose gold chain and a fly sweat suit.

"You going in?"

"I can't, I'm broke," Slick sighed, lowering his head.

"Not no more…c'mon, you with Gemini," he smiled, and walked towards the gymnasium.

As Doo-Doo ran up with enough cash to pay for he and Slick to attend the dance, he saw Slick walking side by side with the enemy, Slick picked Gemini over him.

Doo-Doo didn't forgive Slick and he didn't forgive Gemini. Doo-Doo's bitterness escalated, resulting in physical fights with Slick and Gemini and lived on after they got older. Continued even after Doo-Doo's first trip to jail. Continued even after he got out and killed Gemini for his stash. Gemini was out of the picture, but not the bitterness between the two.

Slick knew they had bad history between them, but could Doo-Doo, would he, get revenge by leaving me hanging when I needed him the most?

Slick stared up at the ceiling, thinking Doo-Doo was capable of doing anything and he couldn't depend on nobody but himself to get out of the jam he was in.

Fifteen

Around one-thirty the following afternoon, Mozart and Anya were parked inside the big circle-style parking lot inside 640 projects. The parking lot sat smack-dab in the middle of the infamous projects. Cars, motor bikes, and other popular SUV's continually streamed in and coasted around the circle, waiting to meet someone or pick-up their favorite illegal drugs.

Mozart and Anya were watching one guy in particular: Ug – the same guy Mozart had beef with and somehow manipulated Anya into beefing with him as well. Ug hung out kicking the bull with three other guys who dressed too thuggish not to be in the streets in some form or fashion.

Glancing around the circle, Ug opened the door on his champagne colored Cadillac CTS-V coupe and grabbed a bottle of Moet Rose' out of a cooler. He called out to one of the other 640 hustlers. When he got their attention, Ug began stuntin'.

"Ay' stink, you know I'm poppin' champagne like I won a championship ring!" He shook the bottle a little before popping it, so the bubble could volcano out in the suds – all apart of his stuntivities for the day.

Stink laughed and said, "Stop swagger jackin' moe. That's Lil' Wayne, Baby and nem' song, champ!"

"Dem' niggaz hip to me!" He blurted, making the trio of hustlers crack up with uncontrollable laughter.

Watching them from inside the old school Monte' Carlo, Mozart pointed Ug out to Anya and repeated a bunch of lies he concocted about Ug and Slick.

"Yeah, that's his bitch-ass right dere'! Ug's da one in the Hugo Boss shit off da' Gucci hat and holding the bottle of Rozay'!"

Anya applied a thick coat of some glossy-fire-engine-red lipstick to her lips and looked at Mozart.

"You think he's going to take the bait?"

"I fell for you, didn't I? And I don't even be chasing no pussy like that," he lied. "You so bad, a nigga can't help but to holla at chu' and shoot his shot."

"I know that's right," she grinned. "Let's hope you're right, because I don't want his ass to be walking around out here like everything's cool!"

"Look Anya, you don't hafta' go through with this shit. I'll smoke his ass for you." He poured it on thick.

Anya gave Mozart an evil look.

Mozart grinned, adjusted his D&G shades. After positioning the frames to his liking, he said, "Excuse the hell outta' me then, Ms. Head bussa'...go head and do you, then."

When a cunning smile, Anya got out the car and walked over to where the four men stood near Ug's flashy ride. Two of the men, including Ug were tossing catcalls and whistles at Anya, vying for attention. The other two hustlers were shooting dice, in their own world.

They presented no challenge to Ug. But the hustler standing on Ug's left was a very handsome guy, ripped and bound to get chosen over Ug on his worst day. He looked like he'd done some modeling spreads before.

Anya stopped in front of Ug and said, "Ain't chu' Ug?"

All conversations and dice actions stopped abruptly.

Ug puffed himself up. "Yeah, dat be me. What's up beautiful? What chu' want?" He asked and took a sip of chilled bubbly.

Anya looked him up and down. "I gotta' message from Slick."

"Oh yeah? What's up with big boy?" He asked, taking another sip of the bubbly.

"I mean, you of all people should know being as though you put him there!" Anya said, while opening her jacket, flashing a gun on him – the gun she'd taken from Slick's safe in their bedroom.

As she went to direct Ug to get in Mozart's car, something strange happened, discombobulating her for a moment.

Soon as Ug caught sight of the shiny steel gun, he spat champagne in her face & eyes, pivot quickly and took off sprinting towards Georgia Avenue like an Olympic track star.

Anya wiped her face quickly and shouted, "Motherfucker! I'ma kill ya!"

By that time, Ug had got somewhere, and ran faster, and faster, picking up more speed with each stride.

"Aw, hell naw! Fuck!" Mozart complained, while starting the engine.

He pulled off with the quickness, pursuing his foe in hopes to make sure all of his scheming and plotting didn't backfire on him.

Weighing a little over 230 pounds, mostly flab, Ug moved quickly with the flair and grace of a professional track sprinter. He bolted past the small building at the Mouth's entrance of the circle and ran about sixty yards until he reached Georgia Avenue. Soon as he reached Georgia Avenue, Ug took a quick left and picked up more speed while running down the sidewalk.

Anya took off after Ug.

Anya was smaller and faster, but the red bottom heels she wore made her useless. She made her way to Georgia Avenue, seething behind the events that took place. She spotted Ug running south towards Harvard Street.

Anya held back her tears. The reality of what she was doing hit her right there. The death of Slick's mother, learning about Slick's infidelities, and the images of having sex with Slick's friend to get revenge passed through her mind. She felt heavy as sadness and regret invaded her senses causing her to let it all out.

Nathan Welch

The tears began flowing when she rounded the corner and heard some screeching car tires.

Scuuuuuuurrrrr! Were the sounds coming from Mozart's speeding car. Anya saw Mozart's car speeding past her and taking a hard left on Georgia Avenue.

She shouted, "Mozart stoooppp! STOP!" But Mozart sped right along, pursuing Ug with a vengeance.

Ug looked back once as he bolted down the sidewalk. Ug's heart raced in fear a moment later when he caught sight of the car chasing him down. Ug kept a steady pace for a few seconds, taking in everything at once. Vehicles of every size, shape and color were moving along Georgia Avenue, slowing down whoever pursued him in the Monte Carlo.

What the fuck is up with dis' luchin-ass joker, driving like that? Ug thought, peeping the driver's smooth nascar-esque moves as he swerved in and out and around the fast moving cars.

Ug knew if the driver kept up his speed and wreckless driving on the busy avenue, the end result was a car accident waiting to happen. Then Ug saw the traffic light changing up ahead. He just got across Harvard Street, reaching the mouth of the alley leading to Hobart Street. There was no way for the person in the Monte Carlo to catch him now once he got into the alley and hit a few cuts.

Slamming on brakes at the red traffic light, Mozart sprang from car after throwing it into the park gear. Running across the street, Mozart held up his gun like he was at the gun range for target practice.

Nathan Welch

Mozart got across Harvard Street just as Ug disappeared into the alley. Ug turned his head and saw Slick's buddy moving into the alley after him – and nearly had a heart attack. Ug grabbed the railing of a waist high chain-link fence and went over, hurting it sideways, giving Mozart the perfect chance he needed to shoot.

Soon as Mozart started shooting, Ug lost his footing and easily ducked the five bullets Mozart fired at his head. Ug rolled onto his back, drawing his gun in the blink of an eye. Ug locked eyes with his enemy and pulled the trigger rapidly, sending hot slugs in Mozart's direction.

While Mozart and Ug exchange thunderous gunfire in the alley, Mozart took up cover behind a blue DPW industrial trashcan in fear. With wide eyes, Mozart swept over the alley, looking scared to death. When he leaned his head outside the place of cover, Ug was standing in the middle of the alley making his trigger finger flex rapidly, sending more deadly shots at Mozart and into the steel trashcan.

Mozart had never been in a shoot-out, let alone had someone gunning at him to kill. Mozart refused to put himself in further danger, so he waited until his intuition told him the coast was clear.

Mozart released a burly sigh of relief once he looked up and noticed he was alone in the alley just like he hoped. Ug tucked his gun away before standing and running back to his car.

Mozart smirked after spotting Anya standing beside his car. He figured she must have got in and parked it on the side of the road while he went chasing behind Ug.

"Did you get his ass?"

"Yeah," he lied. Then Mozart told her, "I did that on the strength of you and Slick."

"Fuck Slick...with his cheating fat-ass...it's all about you and me now Boo-Boo." She smiled, stepping into his embrace. She kissed him passionately, then offered him a big house to live in and her over zealous sex drive to go with it.

That's when Mozart realized that his sex game and lies had shifted all of Anya's feelings away from Slick and over to him. He wanted to be her man. But he knew as long as Slick remained alive, he would never be able to live by her side in peace.

With that in mind, Mozart knew what had to be done.

Sixteen

By 3P.M., Slick was trying to call another goon to come break him out of the hospital when a 5'3" attractive female nurse walked in to check on his vital signs. Not wanting to be noticed by her, Slick quickly closed his eyes. In his rush to play possum, Slick forgot to put the phone back and the nurse noticed it immediately.

"Unngh…you need to stop pretending boy," she accused.

Damn, I'm busted! He thought, and slowly opened his eyes.

"Oh my God, boy you awake for real," she gasped, covering her mouth with both hands.

"Yeah, but I need your help."

"I have to tell the doc-"

"No!" He snapped, cutting her off. "You can't tell nobody nothing. Look, I'm in some serious trouble and I need some help."

"What kind of help?" she asked, putting her manicured hands on her wide hips.

Slick looked her 36DD, 32, 44 assets up and down and shook his head in lustful frustration. He wouldn't mind getting a taste of the burnt-caramel woman standing before him in a bedroom all night.

"Listen, I got money...a lotta' money. You can get paid. All you gotta' do is help me get outta' here," He whispered with wide eyes.

Peeping into his eyes, the nurse whispered, "By helping you outta' here, do you mean outta' bed or helping you to escape?" She already knew the answer. She just wanted to be sure that he wanted her to break the law.

"What chu' think? I ain't gonna pay your ass to go to no bathroom," he blurted in angst.

"Boy, is you crazy!" she yelled.

"Shhhh." He warned her.

She looked over her shoulder to spy the cop who paid them no attention. She turned back on him and whispered, "sorry, but boy is you crazy?" sarcasm dripped in her tone.

"Fuck no," he whispered, grabbing her wrist to get her full attention. "Name your price and I got chu'. I can't go out like this...I just can't do jail right now."

Her face turned into a grimace as she yanked her wrist from his grasp.

"Boy don't get fucked up in here," she snarled. "You need to keep your paws to yourself."

"You right. So you gonna' help me out?"

"I need a million dollars." She said quickly, letting all the ghettoness ooze out in her tone. Slick glanced at her multi-colored designer nails, her fly hot pink hairdo and several gold chains that peeked from her

Nathan Welch

V-neck nurse's smock. From his evaluation, Slick gathered the nurse was a girl from the hood. With that assumption in mind, Slick spoke a language he felt she'd understand.

"Look Shory, I ain't got no motherfuckin' million dollars! That's why I'm tryna' get da' fuck up outta' here so I don't lose out on that milli' I'm chasing," he griped.

"Then how much you gonna' give me for my help?" She asked with a little attitude while visualizing herself putting away some cash in the bank and catching up on a few overdue bills. If he offered the right price, she felt pretty sure that all her financial problems would be solved.

"Cause, I'm saying what chu' want me to do is totally inappropriate and very illegal. I can lose my job and go to jail on top of that for helping your ass. Now you need to come correct or I'm leaving to get the doctor," she bluffed.

"Got damn Shorty," he complained. "Look, the best I can do is three stacks." He said, referring to $3,000 in hood lingo.

"Okay, so you telling me that your freedom is only worth three stacks to you?" She asked sarcastically, shaking her head. "Tsk...tsk...tsk...boy, you petty as shit!"

Slick sighed with rage seeping through him. All his plans were falling apart, but his mind was made up to put them back together. Slick partially understood the nurse's position. If someone asked for his help in escaping police custody, he'd try to get the most cash he could get for his aid and assistance.

"All I got is eight stacks to my name," he lied. "I need some bread to get back on my feet."

The nurse saw through him. She felt he wasn't telling the truth, so she sighed and threw out a fee she knew he could handle.

"I'll take five thousand of that, thank you," she said with hope as he exhaled in frustration.

After expressing what she wanted, the nurse revealed her greed by holding out her hand for payment. Slick's mind raced after hearing her price, he had no other choice but to pay her price.

"While you thinking hard about paying for your freedom, just know this I got head nurse in charge privileges. No one and I mean nobody in this hospital is gonna' question anything that I do on my shift." She winked and added, "For five measly stacks, your secret will be safe with me."

Leaning up in bed, Slick nodded yes to her. He stuck out his fist so she could touch it with hers to seal the deal. When she did it, Slick said, "I got chu', just have some patience and just listen to me very carefully...first, I need for you to..." Slick began plotting his escape off the freestyle, knowing he was about to do something that he'd never imagined doing until today. It didn't matter that the nurse wanted $5,000. For Slick it was a small price to pay for freedom.

Seventeen

After persuading Kendra, the nurse to help him escape, Slick felt pretty sure that all of his problems would be solved. After Kendra left with his precise instructions, Slick called a few numbers to get some financial help until he could get to his stash. Nobody answered their phones. Even his wife's phone went unanswered which was unusual, She always picked up the phone.

Slick wondered why his wife wasn't at his bedside right now. The nurse told him that Anya had showed up a few times until the police blocked her visitation privileges. Slick felt that Anya was supposed to fight through tooth and nail to be by his side.

After racking his brain on finding a dependable person to call, Slick tried one more cell phone number.

"Yeah, who is dis?" Ug sounded out of breath on the other end.

"It's me, Slick."

"Oh shit! What's up Moses? I need to holla at cha' ASAP too." Ug paused, shuffled with his gun before continuing. "I had a helluva' surprise today...and damn near lost my head over it."

"Ay' slim, you gonna' hafta tell me about that shit when you come scoop me up toight." He said, then gave Ug a quick rundown of the events that led up to their current phone call.

"Damn big boy!" He sighed, feeling bad for Slick. "Gimme the time and I'm there ASAP!"

"When you come through, bring some cash and wait for me. I should be getting outta' here sometime after midnight."

"That's a bet. I'm there homez. Ay, what if you late or something comes up, what chu' want me to do?"

Ug sounded genuine and willing to assist him. Slick would never forget it. "Nothing but stay put and wait. More than likely I'ma be there. Just bring some money. Lots of it!"

"How much you ne----"

Slick hung up the phone before Ug could ask how much money to bring. Ug reasoned that if Slick was in on the ambush, then would've never called begging for help.

Ug tried to stay one step ahead of his enemies, but his newest foe seemed to get the jump on him first – for a second time.

"I bet chu' it won't be a third time, you can believe that." Ug muttered, his voice trembling with anger as he scanned his phone and called Claudette.

"Hello?" Claudette answered, sounding like she was choking.

"Claudette!" He yelled into the phone. "Bitc –"

"Click!" Was all Ug heard before the dial tone followed. He quickly called back and got her voicemail.

Nathan Welch

"Low life, stanky, cum drinking, clucker-ass bitch," Ug cursed Claudette out, exhaling in frustration. He knew he should have never trusted a crackhead to do anything for him. There wasn't a damn thing he could do to get his money back either. Chalking up the loss, Ug slapped himself in the face.

"You's a dumb nigga, you know dat?" He scolded himself like he knew he'd fucked up and would never see Claudette again.

Eighteen

The following night, Slick heard a knock. His intuition told him to wake up. He didn't even remember falling asleep. Opening his eyes and scanning the room, Slick saw big booty Kendra. She waved at him with a smile on her face and went to work. She quickly unlocked the restraints with the handcuff key she'd bought yesterday.

"It's time to move...hurry up boy...move," she said with caution while helping him out of bed.

Kendra knew the date rape drug she had slipped into the flirtatious cop's soft drink would have him out for the count for a few hours. But now her paranoia was starting to set in. Then she remembered that only one nurse manned an entire floor on the graveyard shift. Nurse Kendra signed up for a little overtime, claiming she wanted to stack some cash for a rainy day. During her politicking for overtime, Kendra slipped in a request to work her usual post. Having no idea what she had planned, Kendra's supervisor granted the request with no questions asked.

Slick looked away from nurse Kendra and looked outside the glass in front of his room. "Where's the fed nigga at?"

"Oh, he's out like a light...now c'mon."

"I'm coming," he whispered while rubbing his left wrist and ankle. "Ay', you know I can only pay you after I get all the way outside the hospital."

Kendra looked at him and frowned. "What if you get out there and then forget about the bitch who helped you?" She asked the same question she had asked during the entire time they went over the escape plans.

"I feel all your concerns Shorty. You can never be to careful or trusting nowadays," Slick said while easing his feet inside some cheap foamy hospital slippers. "On my soul, and God can strike me down where I stand right now, you gonna' get paid Shorty, I swear." He quickly removed all the wires and IV tubes from his body.

Kendra's eyes closed to slits as she looked at Slick. She studied his face as he talked, looking for any signs of deception. When she saw none, her face slowly spread into a wide cheerful smile as she took a few steps back away from him.

"Even though I believe you, it's better to be safe than sorry. Ain't no sense in both of us getting struck by lightening," she joked.

"Oh yeah?" He smirked. "That's how you feel huh?"

"Boy, I'm just playing...now let's get chu' outta' here so I can get my money." Kendra said, hurrying to get slick safely outside the hospital.

As nurse Kendra lead him outside the room, she shook her head wondering how long it would take for him to make good on his promises.

Moments later, Slick stepped into the hallway slightly paranoid. His heart raced in fear as he tip-toed past the unconscious police guard. Fear choked Slick as he looked down at the cop with every step he took. But he couldn't turn back now. He couldn't make it easy for the feds and just go to jail freely, if they wanted him bad enough, then let them come searching, he thought while holding his gown close together, that barely covered his wide backside.

Impulsively, Slick took off running with Kendra on his heels. His foam slippers slapped the linoleum floor silently while he sprinted towards the nearest stairwell. Nurse Kendra caught up to Slick just as he reached the exit. She grabbed his arm and put a cell phone in his hand.

"Here, this is a prepaid burn-out. It has my number in there on all the speed dials, so there's no excuse for you not getting in touch with me...so there, I guess you're all set now." She sighed. "Just make sure you don't forget about me boy. You know I can go to jail for all the shit I just did for you." She looked over her shoulder cautiously, forgetting that no one else but her worked the floor at night.

As Slick took off, jumping the stairs three at a time, his heart sent an erratic pulse through his entire body. The thought of escaping capture removed the idea of slowing down and stopping.

Slick didn't know what to expect, but he prayed that his last resort didn't disappoint him. Slick plowed through the fire escape door on the ground floor, nearly out of breath. The humming engine of the dark colored Chevy Tahoe was the only thing Slick heard when he made it into the parking lot. When he reached the passenger door, Slick yanked open the door and smiled appreciatively at Ug.

"Slim, you a life savor for real…how much cake you got on you?" He asked with excitement. He could feel his lungs burning from the run he just made. He wished he had an oxygen mask and most of all something to calm down his nerves and paranoia. He just made himself an official fugitive on the run from the law.

"Why what's up?" Ug leaned his head around Slick's body, looking side to side. "Somebody extorting you for that bread?" He asked playfully.

"Naw…never that. I just need to keep my word to this lil' Dame that's all." Slick said, making his eyes grow inside. "I thought I could count on you to come through for me, so that's why I called you."

Ug smiled and asked, "How much you need?"

"Like five stacks…I'll get it back to you tonight."

"Save that shit," Ug said, while reaching into his pocket. "We'll talk business later on."

Slick looked at Ug and shrugged his shoulders in confusion as Ug gave him $5,000 in mostly hundred and fifty dollar bills.

"It ain't nothing to talk about. You getting this business back soon as you make this quick run." Without another word, Slick lifted the pre-paid cell phone to call Kendra.

"When she answered on the second ring, Slick said, "You know I can never thank you enough for your help and I owe you big time so if you can get away for a few seconds, come out front to the parking lot. Your money is waiting for you to pick it up. I'm in a dark SUV." Slick said, feeling grateful that she had come into his life when she did.

Without saying another word, nurse Kendra hung up and rushed off her floor to get paid.

Slick took a deep breath and memorized Kendra's cell phone number. Then he broke up the cell phone into little pieces before hopping in Ug's Tahoe. He folded the money in a knot and stared anxiously at the hospital's front entrance until Kendra walked out, looking around frantically.

Spotting her, Slick tapped Ug's leg and said, "Hit the horn five times for me."

Slick watched carefully as Kendra's neck swiveled over in his direction. He studied her walk as her thick legs glided one before the other like she had some good pussy between them. He then looked up at her shiny lips spreading into a warm smile as their eyes connected on a level that made them feel the attraction.

Slick rolled down the window and gave her the money. "Thanks Shorty…see, I told you I'ma man of my word." He smiled, noticing her deep dimples.

Kendra cleared her throat and put on her best sexiest tone. "So now that our business is straight, I think you should keep my number just in case you need my help again." She winked.

Slick felt good about Kendra's realness and sincerity. He smiled and said, "If I ever need some help, you'll be the first person I call."

She smiled. "Now I'ma hold you to that, mister man of your word. I'ma tell you now that I'm down for whatever." She gave him a devilish grin before rushing off to return to work. Kendra put an extra twist in her strut, glancing back over shoulder at Slick, enticing just the right amount of lust from his eyes and loins.

For Slick, everything changed. It would be hard to return to life as he knew it. He realized all his old habits and ways of living had to cease. He thought about all the things he wanted to do in life and all the places he wanted to see. He thought about Anya, the woman he loved. He tingled inside, anticipating what the rest of the night held in store for them.

As Slick told Ug to pull off, he knew handling business while being on the run from the law would be his newest and most important mission.

Nineteen

Slick's plan came off without any drama. He sat in the passenger seat and gave Ug directions to his mother's house. Slick didn't know if they were being followed so soon, but to be on the safe side, Slick directed Ug to circle his mother's quiet block a few times When he felt certain nobody had followed them, Slick told Ug to pull up and park in front of his mother's house.

Slick's heart sank when he reached the front door and saw the yellow police crime scene tape blocking entry in a huge X shape fashion. Against his better judgment, Slick tore down the tape and found the door unlocked. He opened the front door, stepped inside and hit the light switch.

"No...No...naw Ma...Naw...Fuck Naw," Slick said sadly, dropping to his knees to study the white chalk outline of a body.

"Naw...Fuck naw Ma," he cried, completely devastated. As his eyes and fingers traced the chalk outline, he noticed what looked like dried up blood in the center where the chest would be.

Slick assumed right then that somebody had killed his mother because of the things he'd been doing in the streets. Frantically, he raced upstairs, being careful not to touch nothing. He entered his old bedroom, and then cautiously opened the cedar chest at the foot of his bed. Once he saw it had been emptied of its contents, Slick's heart dropped into the pit of his belly.

"Arrrgghh, bitch motherfuckaz!" He bellowed in agony. Not only did they take his mother from him – they took out his stach – well one of them.

The feeling of defeat and sadness consumed his body. His breathing came in small ragged burst as if he was having an asthma attack. Anger pulsated through his cranium. The reality of his life turning from sugar to shit hit him right there.

Slick felt a breeze up the crack of his ass, and remembered the gown he still had on. He moved to his closet and found some diesel jeans and an old pair of Timberlands construction boots. After putting on the jeans and boots, Slick helped himself into an old Ed-Hardy tee shirt and matching Ed- Hardy zip up sweat hoody. He squatted down, and pulled up the carpeting inside the closet. He lifted the gun from the small hole in the floor, tucked it in the small of his back and made his way back downstairs.

"Aaaaaaaaaaaaaaarrghhhhh!" Slick yelled in frustration upon seeing the chalk body outline on his way out the house.

He took several deep breaths to calm down all the rage inside. It didn't work. As he left his mother's house, Slick felt somebody had to pay for the death of his mother and right then Slick's thirst for revenge began eating at him like a pack of lion's devouring some fresh meat that had been tossed into the lion's den

Slick walked fast towards Ug's Tahoe, hoping nobody saw him. Before he could reach the Tahoe, Slick saw Boogie and a very curvaceous woman heading in his direction from a mile away. He shot Boogie a glare that told him he wasn't in the mood for nothing.

Nathan Welch

Boogie eased up on Slick, until they were only inches apart from each other's faces.

"Slim, my deepest condolences goes out to you. That's fucked up what happened to Mama Floyd."

Slick's eyes closed to slits as he slowly mumbled, "Wha...What happened?"

"Damn...you don't know huh?" Boogie snooped.

Once Slick nodded no, Boogie told Slick everything he knew, learned and heard around the hood pertaining to Ms. Floyd's murder. By the time Boogie finished talking, Slick's tear-filled eyes flooded over like a busted dam.

Ug stared and listened in as the duo talked. Once he spotted that scandalous bitch, Claudette hanging onto the strange guy arm, Ug wanted to jump out the Tahoe and beat her ass to a no count, but he checked his anger, staying cool.

Ug shot Claudette a glare through his rearview mirror that expressed his anger. Ug pulled out his cell phone and called Claudette. Once her phone began ringing, Claudette excused herself to answer the call.

"Hello?"

"Don't play with me bitch!" Ug snapped, watching her every move in the rearview mirror. "And if you hang up on me, I'ma jump out this motherfuckin' truck, beat cho' motherfuckin' ass and then kill your stupid ass. Bitch, you thought you could beat me?"

"Na...no," she stammered, lying throught her teeth.

"Yes you did...yeah bitch, I'm onto your games. Just keep on playin', and see if I don't fuck up your pretty little face and body...bitch you better find that nigga or else." Ug said in a threatening tone before hanging up on her.

Claudette's eyes grew wide in fear as she zoomed in on the Tahoe and saw Ug. She quickly dipped off into the shadows of the night, leaving Boogie with her body trembling from Ug's threats. She wanted to get as far away from Ug as possible to keep her health in tact. She tossed a final glance at Ug's Tahoe before disappearing into a nearby alley.

Claudette quickly jumped two waist high fences and ran fast as hell as if her life depended on it.

Once Ug saw Claudette take off in a hurry, he turned on the ignition and hit the horn, getting Slick's attention.

"You ready to go Moses?" He yelled from the cockpit.

"Yeah...yeah. I'm coming right now!" Slick said before giving Boogie some dap and a manly one arm hug. Slick jumped in the Tahoe and closed the door.

Before Ug could pull off, he and Slick heard Boogie complaining, "Damn, dat' good dick sucking bitch done slid off on me again."

Nathan Welch

Ug laughed inside, totally agreeing with Boogie about Claudette's blowfessional skills. He wondered how many times the stranger and Claudette tricked together as he looked over at Slick.

"Where to now big guy?"

Slick leaned his head back on the headrest, allowing his tears to flow freely. He closed his eyes and said, "Take me out Fort Washington. Wake me up when we get there, so I can give you the directions."

Hearing Slick's voice cracking up and seeing tears sliding down his face, Ug figured that Slick was stressing hard about something. That's the only reason Ug hesitated on telling Slick about the assassination attempt on his life earlier and who was responsible.

At the same time, Anya giggled as she straddled Mozart's lap while he sat on the couch.

"I love this dick Booby," she panted as she kissed and slobbered all over his face, neck, and ear lobes.

Mozart helped her off of his lap and stood up. He smacked her soft behind as he grabbed her hand and pulled her towards the bedroom. Soon as they reached the bedroom, Mozart stripped out of his clothes and tucked his gun underneath a pillow while Anya wiggled out her tight jeans like a snake. After pulling her shirt over her head, Anya unclasped her lavender Vicky Secret bra and threw it on the floor. Her big, very firm titties made Mozart's dick swell instantly.

Nathan Welch

She hooked her thumbs in her thongs waistband and slid them down until she stood in her birthday suit. Bending over to climb up on the double wide king size bed, Mozart's nose picked up the scent of her moistness and he couldn't wait to stick his pipe into it.

C'mere girl," he huffed, grabbing her soft ass cheeks and pressing himself against her body, slow grinding his wood on her budding clitoris.

"Mmmm," she moaned, nibbling up his neck and he parted his lips, sucking her tongue. Mozart gripped her soft ass cheeks, spreading them as wide as he could as she hooked her left thigh over his waist.

Anya moved her wet pussy along his throbbing boner without inserting it. She bit her bottom lip in anticipation, feeling his juicy dick grinding against her pussy, which made her clitoris get very wet and hard.

"Stick it in baby," she cooed, as his hands cupped the mounds of her ass cheeks and he pushed his hardness against the mouth of her pulsating pleasure palace.

"I need to feel you deep inside me," she whispered, positioning herself just at the right angle to guide his thick dick deep inside her wet gush.

"Aauugh…sss…uunhh…ooooohh," she moaned on his tongue as he stroked her tight pussy with deep churning thrusts.

As he started really laying dick up in her, Anya pinched tightly on his nipples and clamped her pussy muscled down on him. She hooked her calves under his calf muscles and then rode him hard and fast like he was a real live bull.

"Aaah…don't stop…don't….sss…stop!" She howled as her pussy muscled spasmed uncontrollably to accept all the dick he slammed up into her guts.

Heat and the scent of sex rose between their bodies as they got lost in another lustful and mind-blowing sexcapade.

Twenty

Ug drove out to Fort Washington, Maryland with Slick laying back in deep thought and grieving over his mother's murder. When he reached a red light, Ug tapped Slick, waking him.

Slick looked up like he was lost. The reality of his mother being dead hit him like a ton of bricks. The knowledge of never being able to see her smile, spend time with her, eat her delicious cooking and listen to her fuss at him about leaving the streets alone again passed through his mind. He felt crushed and let the tears flow out.

"You aight champ?" Ug asked with concern

Slick sniffled and quickly pulled himself together. "Yeah, I'm...I'm straight, just going through some shit that's all, don't trip."

"Okay Moses...okay now...where we going?"

"Make a right turn down this street," Slick pointed out for Ug. "Then go down two more blocks and hit another left."

"Gotcha!" Ug said and followed Slick's directions.

Ug looked very impressed and astonished by all the huge houses and mini mansions he drove past. Slick instructed Ug to go through a maze of several roads that led to his home.

"Damn slim," Ug exclaimed, looking at the huge home that could easily be showcased on an episode of MTV Cribs. "You doing it like that?"

"Ease up big guy. Ease up." Slick warned before opening the passenger door.

Both men exited the Tahoe at the same time and walked towards Slick's immaculate home. Ug looked at the 20ft" mahogany doors in awe, and then looked at Slick. Ug couldn't believe Slick owned a home that could accommodate king kong entering through the front door with ease.

Ug checked to see if anybody was in the vicinity. Feeling certain that they were alone, Ug grabbed Slick by the arm, stopping him.

"Ay' looka' here Moses. I know you may be going through some shit right now, but I can't keep dis' shit inside no longer."

Slick nodded, "Spit it out then, nigga."

"You know that bitch-ass nigga that chu' brought round my hood that time we had words in his car and he whipped out a hammer on me off his geekin' – perpin – out shit? Anyway, to make a long story short, you know his bitch-ass tried to kill me earlier today by putting a bitch on my line."

"Oh yeah?" Slick asked, stunned by Ug's revelation, Slick always knew Mozart's bark to be louder than his bite so the news was very surprising.

"Yeah, and the only reason I peeped the move cause da' bitch was way too fly and sexy…Moe, dis phat mafucka ain't had no business to be tryna' holler at me like I'm da' shit of da' party ...I know I'm ugly and I know da' type of bitches who will fuck an ugly nigga like...moe, she wasn't one of them...then what really fucked me up was her saying she had a message to give me that came from you." Ug said, staring hard at Slick, trying to see any signs of deception.

"A message from me?" Slick asked, completely confused. "I don't know why she'd say that."

"Yeah, me either...but shit ain't nothing," Ug dismissed the slight accusation. "But ay', after I got outta' there on they ass, that's when you hit me up on the cell phone, and talking all that wild shit, bout dat wild nigga leaving you to take his beef...dat's top of da line cruddy dog for real. Slim, I fucks witchu' and all that, but I can't even begin to think about how to swallow this one champ I just..." He sighed, shaking his head, "Fuck it, your man just gotta' see me slim...however, whenever on sight...he gotta' see me!"

"Look slim, I mean I can't tell you how to rock out when a nigga tried to exterminate cho' shit, but for me slim...give 'em a –"

"Naw champ...don't go there on no peaceaholic shit big boy. Your man chose dis work call, so I gotta' finish it plain and simple. Ain't no more room for discussions or debates. It is what it is"

Slick said nothing and walked over to the chest high flower pot beside the door. Ug followed, still not believing a guy from the same city streets was living so good out Maryland without a legal 9-to-5 gig. While looking around the area, Ug never saw Slick snatch up the spare key out the flower pot.l; Seeing Slick's home have up new ambition and motivation to stop bullshitting and really get on the grind.

In a few more years, I'ma have something like this if not bigger, he thought, watching Slick open the front door. As they entered the dark home, faint melodic sounds of Jodeci's classic: "Lady I, will cry for you, tonight," could be heard coming from upstairs.

Slick walked into his study and went to his safe, hidden behind a book shelf. After opening the safe, Slick removed $5,000 and some drugs to pay Ug for helping him on such short notice.

Returning to the living room to pay Ug, Slick and Ug heard a woman's erotic moaning and yelling, "Harder baby! Harder!"

Slick stared hard at Ug who just shrugged and whipped out his gun. On instinct, Slick pulled out his strap. Fast and lethal like cynanide pills, Slick silently made his way upstairs with Ug on his tail.

While walking to his master bedroom, Slick was afraid to think what or who Anya could be doing on the other side of the door. As he got closer and closer to the bedroom, the womanly moaning and screams got louder and louder, infuriating him. Slick remained silent, knowing his assumptions and thoughts were certain to bring about death.

Slick knew it was Anya's voice behind the pornographic sounds. He gripped his gun tighter as he got closer to the bedroom door.

I know this bitch better be fucking a dildo, cause if she ain't I'ma do – all Slick's thoughts ceased when he opened the bedroom door and moved in quickly, getting the shock of his life.

Twenty -One

Stepping inside the master bedroom, Slick's attention was immediately drawn to the two naked bodies sprawled out on his bed. The painful sight looming inside crushed Slick, making him stop in his tracks.

Ug tip-toed towards the bed with his desert eagle held down by his leg. Suddenly the scent of sex in the air invaded Slick's nostrils, inflaming his appetite for destruction. Slick's heart dropped to the pit of his stomach while witnessing the ultimate disrespect and betrayal from his wife and his so called buddy. Slick was amazed at how Mozart and Anya were fucking like two porn stars in his bed – his home that he threw bricks at the penitentiary to pay for. He got lost in his thoughts about the options he had.

He had a chance to walk away from all the pain, heartache, and drama and not put himself at risk.

Fuck that, he thought, boiling with rage. Slick rushed to the bed and cocked his weapon. Ug raised his gun and rushed to the bed to back Slick's play.

When Mozart and Anya heard the sounds of automatic weapons cocking, all their sexual movements came to an abrupt halt, looking over his shoulder; the nervous Mozart spotted Slick and the guy he couldn't kill earlier in the day aiming guns at him.

"Whoa! Whoa! Whoa big boy! It ain't what chu' thinking!" Mozart yelled, rolling quickly to put Anya in their sights, and use her as a human shield.

Nathan Welch

Without hesitation, Anya quickly turned her head. Her eyes ballooned in fear and surprise when she saw her husband standing next to the guy she thought had set him up.

What the hell's going on? She thought, attempting to cover up her nakedness.

"Bitch, don't move!" Slick warned. "It's funny Mozart how you seem to know what I'm thinking these days?" He gripped the gun tighter while staring at Anya's naked frame. The more he stared at her, the more he felt like she stabbed him straight through his heart.

"Baby please…I can explai –"she cried in fear.

"Bitch, stay in a slut's place. I'll get to you later." Slick raged, cutting her off.

"Here I am laying up damn near dead because of this bitch nigga and you got the nerve to be in here fucking him in my bed?" He had caught them in the act – now he planned on unleashing all his fury. He squeezed his eyes shut knowing death was the only answer for their betrayal.

In the seconds the heated exchange took place between Slick and Anya, Mozart had managed to slip his hand underneath the pillow to grab his gun.

"Slim…big guy, she's the broad I was telling you about!" Ug blurted. "She's the one who tried to get my noodles pushed back!" Ug's eyes looked like they were thirsty for revenge.

"Yeah, because I thought you had set up Slick to go to jail because he fucked your girlfriend!" Anya snapped, her eyes were slits of anger with tears streaming down her high cheek bones.

"What!" Slick and Ug bellowed at the same damn time, stunned by Anya's reply.

"Who da' fuck told you that shit –" before the whole question could roll off Slick's tongue, Mozart intuition told him to move. He leaned up quickly, pushing his gun through Anya's armpit.

"GUN!" Ug yelled, eyeing the weapon and reacting quickly to pull the trigger of his cannon.

In the next moment – gunshots rang out in the bedroom, spraying death everywhere and changing four lives forever all over the wrong moves they made.

Valentine's Day Massacre

Pinky Dior

The Beginning

Carla moved around her secluded office with the phone pressed to her ear using her shoulder to hold it in place as she flipped through the gun metal grey file cabinet with a sense of urgency; she was searching for one of her client's phone files. After finding the file, she told her client that she would get back to them in a week or so.

Carla took a seat in her plush leather office chair and breathed a sigh of relief as she reclined her head against it and closed her eyes. The busy week had been brutal for her. For six nights straight, she'd been up all night working on file after file for her clients and emailing sponsors. As Carla sat back with her eyes closed enjoying the brief moment of peace and quiet, her Blackberry began vibrating across her marble desk. She sighed before opening her eyes and moving to reach for her phone. Carla noticed she had just received an urgent text from her best friend, Amina.

Pinky Dior

Hey Girl,

I'm down here at the Café on 125th, you know the spot where you and your husband met. I need you to come down here and see this for yourself. I know you're probably busy at work, but I think this will be worth seeing and knowing.

Love ya,

Amina

Carla's eyebrows arched up as she read the text. Baffled by the message, Carla began wondering what was worth seeing. Curiosity got the best of her forcing Carla out of her seat to go see what Amina was texting her about. It was a nice day and she decided she didn't need her blazer. She wore a pretty short sleeve-collar shirt with ruffles at the shoulder and a dip in the shirt. It showed off a little bit of cleavage, but not too much. She paired it with a tight grey pencil skirt that showed off her voluptuous curves and smooth caramel skin complexion.

Carla wasn't like a model type thick; she was petite, but thick in all the right places. She rocked a short honey blonde Chinese bob that brought out her facial features. She was plain Jane only when she wanted to be.

Pinky Dior

Her four inch black heels clicked across the marble floor as she emerged from her office and walked toward the front where her secretary was.

"Hey Marcia, I'm going to the Café for my break. Just take any calls and let them know that I will return their calls as soon as I get back in the office."

"Alright Ms. Smith, don't forget to take your meds, remember you told me to remind you." Marcia smiled as Carla headed out the office.

After stepping outside the building and into the sweltering eighty-five degree weather, Carla turned around and smiled. She felt good about leaving the blazer behind inside the office because she was already burning up with what she had on.

Thank God I didn't wear any stockings, Carla thought while rushing to her car. She reached inside her purse pulled out the keys to her 2008 Honda Accord and got in. She couldn't wait to turn on the AC; it was too hot to be driving around with the windows down. She desperately wanted a Bentley and told her husband, Derrick. He told her that he would work on it. Knowing how expensive the luxury automobile was, Carla felt in her heart that he would never buy it for her since she had her own money from the business she owned. She decided she would buy the car herself one of these days.

Pulling up in front of the Café on 125th Street, Carla parked and stepped out of her car. She placed on her Chanel shades to block out the sun. She then grabbed two quarters from her purse and put them in the meter. That gave her thirty minutes; that was enough time to drop in on Amina and find out what was going on. A smile appeared across Carla's face as she walked down the sidewalk and saw her best friend waving her hand side to side in the air.

Carla rushed over to Amina's table as she stood up. Amina hugged Carla and began rocking side to side. Carla stepped back from the embrace, pulled out a chair, and sat down.

"What's up Girl?" Carla cooed.

"Nothing much, I was just down here doing a little shopping on my day off, as you can see." Amina chuckled as Carla looked over and saw all the shopping bags that Amina had on the ground from Bebe, BCBG, Express, and Banana republic.

Carla shook her head, "Girl, you got a shopping disorder." She chuckled.

You know me, Carla. I love shopping and plus I love to look good." Amina smiled as she grabbed a compact mirror from inside her purse and checked her lipstick.

Carla playfully rolled her eyes. At twenty-three years old, Amina was much younger then Carla who was thirty-two. Amina's pretty brown skin meshed nicely with her light brown hair that reached down a little past her shoulders. Amina looked like she was mixed with some Asian genes because her eyes were chinky. Every time she laughed hard, her eyes were so low they appeared to be closed shut. Carla thought Amina was pretty just like the rest of the men in the city chasing behind her.

"You're a mess girl," Carla smirked while grabbing the menu and scanning over it looking for something to eat. In the meanwhile, she ordered an ice water with lemon.

"So what did you want me to see?" Carla asked as she dabbed the straw on the table breaking the wrapping paper from it. "What was so important that I needed to know; this should be interesting," Carla said with a smirk while placing the straw in the water. She stirred it around a few times before placing her small lips on it. Amina didn't have such a bright smile on her face, so Carla knew something was up.

"Well, I invited you here to show you something."

"What? Show me what?"

"Don't turn around now," Amina warned her. "Do you see the guy over there wearing the suit?" Amina said as she secretly pointed her finger to where the guy was sitting.

Carla placed her hand on her neck, slowly turned around, and got the shock of her life. She had to do a double take after seeing her husband; Derrick was sitting down at the table with another woman. She couldn't see who the female was, but Carla noticed the woman had long black hair and was light skinned. She couldn't believe it, and she didn't want to believe it. Carla quickly turned around, shaking her head from side to side, and pursing her lips together.

"No, that's not my husband with another woman," Carla said hovering in a state of denial. I mean the guy does look exactly like Derrick, but my husband is in the office," Carla said assuming.

"Carla, I know you're upset," Amina could see the tears forming in her eyes. "If you don't believe what you see, why don't you just call the office to see if he's there," Amina suggested.

Carla looked up and nodded her head, "You know what; that's a good idea." She said and went inside her purse for her Blackberry. After retrieving the phone, she began dialing the numbers. Her fingers were shaking as she dialed the office number. The secretary answered on the second ring.

"Hello Denise, is my husband there?"

"Oh hey Carla, I didn't recognize your voice." She giggled. "He's not here right now; he stepped out of the office like an hour ago," Denise sounded unsure.

"Do you know where he went?" Carla asked eagerly.

Pinky Dior

"I think he mentioned something about he was going to the Café down on 125th. I told him to bring me something back. I love their food." She kept running her mouth.

"Oh really," Carla stared at Amina who was mouthing. "What happened?"

Carla turned around took another look at her husband and said, "Thank you Denise, just let him know that his wife was looking for him." Carla said sarcastically before hanging up and turning around. She tried to stop the tears from falling. Although Amina was her best friend, she was also shiesty in a way; not towards her, but towards other people.

"So do you believe what you see or do you believe…"

Carla cut her off, "Amina, it's my husband okay! I just didn't think that I would see him here with another woman." Carla shook her head and then blurted, "That bastard!" She was boiling inside while Amina was laughing inside.

"Well girl; we can just hit the club or something tonight, fuck him!" Amina shouted, "You don't need no nigga like that! Apparently he's seeing other people, so do you." She suggested waving her finger around as she talked.

"He's my husband Amina," Carla informed her. "He's been my husband for almost eight years."

"Well, Yo' dog ass husband for seven years now is over there in some other bitch's face," Amina stressed as she rolled her head and neck around with a ghetto attitude.

"You're right, fuck him!" Carla shouted, letting her anger talk for her. "I'm about to go over there and tell him he can kiss my ass goodbye," Carla sang as she started to get up, causing Amina to grab her arm gently.

"No girl, don't make a big scene here! Amina motioned for Carla to sit back down.

After sitting down, Carla ran her fingers through her short hair. "What am I going to do," she asked as her voice cracked on the verge of crying.

"Leave his ass Carla; you're a beautiful woman. You don't need no cheating ass man!" Amina stated with much attitude.

I'm just going to go home and think about this one, Carla pondered. "Thanks Amina," Carla got up and walked away.

As soon as she got into her car, she broke down and cried. She was thinking about how happy he looked enjoying lunch with another woman. She started the car and sped off like a mad woman. Carla pulled up in front of her job and rushed inside with tears streaming down her face. She didn't care who saw her.

"Are you okay Mrs. Smith?" Marcia, the secretary asked watching in awe as Carla stormed right past her.

"I'm fine," she said.

Carla walked into her office and slammed the door behind her so hard, a few pictures and plaques rattled in their hanging positions on the walls. She walked over to her desk, flopped down in her chair, and broke down crying. She couldn't believe after seven years that her husband was cheating on her after all she had done for him. Several times she picked up her cell phone contemplating; if she should just call him or not. Carla decided to go home; she couldn't work like this. It just wasn't going to work.

When she arrived home, Derrick wasn't there. She walked upstairs, entered their bedroom while dropping her keys and purse on the bed. She took off her blazer with the rest of her work clothes and decided to hop in the shower. Whenever she got angry, she loved taking long steamy hot showers to calm her down. Tears streamed down her face as the hot water cascaded down her body. She hopped out the shower and wiped off her body with a terry cloth towel. After wrapping her body in the towel, she emerged from the bathroom and grabbed some scented lotion to apply over her body.

Carla slipped into a silk gown and pulled her short bob back into a ponytail. She walked across the room and sat on the edge of the bed and tried hard not to think about seeing Derrick earlier, but seeing him laughing and having a good time with another woman irked her.

It was so quiet in the bedroom that she could hear her husband entering the house. She heard him walking up the stairs. His keys made music as they clinked with the other keys on his key chain. Carla didn't bother wiping her tears away; there was no point in hiding them. She wanted to show him that he hurt her.

Derrick walked into the bedroom and wondered why his wife was sitting in the dark. He could hear her crying a little bit. He turned on the lights and before he could even talk, Carla beat him to it.

"I saw you today," she said in a low tone. "Down at 125th with that woman, laughing and talking." She snapped sounding very jealous and angry.

"Baby it's not like that."

"DON'T BABY ME!" Carla shouted as she turned around. Tears were excessively streaming down her cheeks. Her face looked like she had splashed water on it. "I saw you today, Derrick! I can't believe you have the fucking audacity to tell me it's not like that; what the fuck would you think if you saw me with another man, and I said it's not like that! W-what would you think," she stammered.

"Baby, did you take your medicine today?" He asked.

"Do you think I'm fucking joking," Carla cocked back her head. "I took my medicine today. I'm not bugging. I know what the fuck I saw!" She barked, but she was clearly lying. Every time she took her medicine she was calm but when she didn't she was ready to rash and create a full blown storm.

"Baby, listen to me."

"Stop fucking babying me; I'm not your fucking baby alright? That bitch you was with today, you can make her your boo, baby, and your wife. I don't give a fuck," Carla snapped. "I don't want you sleeping with me; go sleep on the couch," she demanded. "Matter of fact, no you can sleep right here." She laughed as she got up and snatched the covers off the bed and two pillows. "I will sleep on the couch," She said as she brushed roughly pass him on her way out of the bedroom.

Derrick stared her down while she made her way through the bedroom door and slammed it. "Damn!" he mumbled while looking back at the bed where she left him with just sheets and one pillow.

The Perfect Lie

Derrick sat in his office playing with the stress ball. He had been squeezing it for about an hour with his left hand propped up on the desk. He couldn't believe his wife spotted him with another female. If she knew who he was with; she would kill her and him. What really surprised him was the fact that she never pressed him about the woman's name. He assumed that she didn't see the female's face. He inhaled deeply as he squeezed the stress ball while reclining his head against the head rest of the chair.

It had only been a day, and he couldn't get his wife off of his mind. He loved her so much and didn't want to lose her but her bipolar disorder was getting to him. Deep down Derrick knew she was a good woman and if he didn't stop his infidelity that she would leave him. There was a knock at his door. He sat up, opened the desk drawer, and dropped the stress ball inside it.

"Come in," Derrick said.

In walked his colleague and friend, Jerome. He was freshly dressed in a dark suit and tie with some papers in his hand. Jerome walked over to him and placed the papers on his desk.

"That's the information for the case about Carla's sister," Jerome said before stepping back from the desk. "Why do you want to know so much about her?"

"Because Jerome, I'm trying to help her. She has a few cases that I'm trying to get dismissed that's all." Derrick cleared his throat as he grabbed his stress ball from the drawer and started squeezing it again.

"What's really going on, Derrick? Not only am I like your Bro, but I'm your right hand as well as the best man at your wedding. If don't nobody else know, I know when something's bothering you, plus the way you're squeezing that stress ball tells me a lot," Jerome chuckled.

Derrick cracked a smile, looked up at Jerome, and sighed, "Alright bro, I got a problem."

"What happened?" Jerome said, walking back over towards Derrick's desk and taking a seat in one of the plush wing back chairs sitting directly across from him.

"Carla caught me."

"Caught you doing what?"

"I guess she saw me at the restaurant with another woman."

"What do you mean you guess?" Jerome was baffled.

"Well, I came home and found her in the dark crying," Derrick recalled the thoughts of seeing his wife crying. He hated when she cried and felt bad that he was the cause of her tears. "She told me she saw me, but the weird thing is that she didn't even come up to me. I don't know why, but thank God she didn't. She would have killed me and the chick," Derrick said shaking his head.

"Damn Derrick!"

"What should I do? I know she's on the verge of leaving me."

"Well, I mean if you think with your head and not your dick; you wouldn't have to worry about that."

"Alright Jerome, what's done is done," Derrick said angrily. "Now I need your help Bro; I know you're the ladies man and know how to handle a situation like this."

"You know Carla ain't taking your shit no more, don't you?" Jerome shook his head.

"I know, I know; I mean I can play it off, but I just don't know how to."

"Didn't you say that she wanted that new Bentley?"

"Yeah, what are you trying to get at?" Derrick asked eagerly, wanting to know how that would get him out of the sticky situation.

"Well, why don't you buy it for her then?" Jerome said easily, as it was nothing.

"A fucking Bentley; that shit cost a lot of money!"

"It's not like you don't have the money."

"Okay, but I don't understand how the fuck that's going to get me out of this situation. She's going to love the car if I buy it for her, but she will probably take the car and dip!" Derrick said, shaking his head. "Nah, fuck that idea; she aint' about to play me," He said arrogantly.

"Derrick, Derrick, Derrick," Jerome chuckled. "Listen Bro all you gotta do is buy the fucking Bentley, put a fucking bow on top, and just tell her that the woman you met up with was a sales rep lady who works for the dealership. Simple!" Jerome said sitting back in the chair.

"I'm telling you Bro, once you buy her that fucking car; she's going to give you the best pussy ever." He added in an excited tone, causing Derrick to smile at the thought. He hadn't gotten any pussy from his wife in a couple of weeks, well good pussy to be exact.

"That's a perfect idea!" Derrick exclaimed. "Thanks Jerome, thanks dawg! He said excitedly as he got up and grabbed his coat off the back of the chair.

"Where you going," Jerome asked looking back over his shoulders making Derrick stop in his tracks. "It's not four-thirty yet."

"I'm going out to buy my wife a Bentley and get me some good pussy." Derrick smiled at his plans of getting out of the dog house with Carla. "Thanks again Jerome, you're the best!" Derrick said before walking out the front door.

As Derrick rushed to the Bentley car dealership, he prayed that the plan worked. If not; he was going to lose his wife for just a piece of pussy, and he wouldn't be able to live with that.

Jerome smiled as he got up and walked around Derrick's desk. He took a seat in Derrick's throne grabbed his stress ball and began squeezing it as tight as he could. He had problems of his own that weighed heavy on his mind.

*****

Derrick entered the house with a smile on his face while tossing his keys on the couch. After taking off his coat, he placed it on the coat hanger hook. He slid his hand inside his pocket and produced the key to Carla's brand new, all silver Bentley Continental GT. Derrick walked up the stairs wearing a Cheshire cat like smile. He opened the bedroom door, catching his wife ass naked. She quickly grabbed the white towel from off the bed and wrapped it around her body.

"Don't you know how to knock?" Carla snapped as she tugged the towel under her arm pits. "Matter of fact, you're not even suppose to be in here," she said while rolling her eyes.

Derrick walked over to her and wrapped his arms around her waist. She tried so hard to pull away from him, but her attempts were futile. Derrick had a tight grip around her hips making sure that she didn't go anywhere.

He chuckled, "You ain't going anywhere so stop fighting it."

"Get your hands off of me; you filthy bastard!" Carla said and punched him in the chest as he looked over at the nightstand and noticed that she had her Lithium pills laid out with a cup of water next to them. *No wonder*, he thought eyeing the pills.

"Alright, you know what; I'm going to leave you alone."

"Yeah, you do that," She said with her back to him with her hands folded across her breasts.

Derrick rubbed his hands together while looking at her hips that stuck out the towel. Her ass was nice and round. He couldn't wait until he got a piece of that ass; he knew it was only a matter of time.

He smiled and said, I just want you to know that the chick you saw me with the other day is the owner of the Bentley dealership. I wanted her to help me choose the perfect car for you for a gift for our anniversary that's coming up this week, but if you want I'll be back later. Here are the keys."

She didn't even hear, "I'll be back later; all Carla heard was keys. After a few seconds, Carla didn't know what to think and she didn't know if she should believe him or not. She turned around and Derrick was nowhere in sight. She noticed a pair of new keys on her nightstand. She looked on the tag, and it said the new Continental GT. She didn't have time to get dressed.

"DERRICK!"

"DERRICK!" She yelled out his name repeatedly, but he was already gone.

She picked up the car keys and headed downstairs in her towel and slippers. Once Carla opened the front door, she saw her new silver Bentley with a red bow on top parked in front of their condo. She started screaming and jumping up and down joyously.

"OH MY GOD I CAN'T BELIEVE IT!" Carla shouted placing her hand over her mouth in a surprised manner before running down the steps.

"Shut up! No he didn't, no he didn't. My baby loves me, my baby loves me!" She sung while admiring the luxury car's beauty.

Pinky Dior

She ran her short, French manicured nails along the smooth car. She got inside and began inhaling. She loved the aroma of the new car smell. The leather seats were all black and everything from the wood grain dash boards to the fly stereo system was top of the line. Carla was smiling from ear to ear as she got out of her new ride.

She headed back inside the house and picked up the cordless phone. She called Derrick, but he didn't answer his cell phone. She left him a message on his voice mail, saying that she had a surprise for him later on. After finishing her message to Derrick; Carla hung up and quickly dialed another cell phone number so she could share the good news about her latest and very expensive gift.

The caller picked up on the third ring, and Carla cooed, "Hey Amina! Girl you're not going to believe this one."

"What the hell are you sounding so damn happy for?" Amina asked rudely.

"What, am I supposed to be mad or something? Carla questioned with a questionable brow.

Yes, you are supposed to be mad; Very mad! Amina thought. "No, I mean I just thought you'd be miserable crying over Derrick," Amina smiled. "I know you left that nigga; please tell me you did!" Amina hoped and prayed her best friend did leave him.

"No, I did not leave him," Carla smiled. "Why would I do a stupid thing like that when he just bought me a Bentley," She blurted in a giddy tone.

Amina cocked her head back, removed the phone from her ear, and stared at it like an infectious disease. She placed the phone back to her ear. "The Bentley; the brand new fucking Bentley; are you serious? Amina asked as she dropped her jaw.

"Yup, the brand new Bentley baby; he got me a Continental GT! My baby loves me; Aaahh! Carla sang.

"Wow!"

"What?" Carla asked, slightly confused by Amina's reaction. "You ain't happy for me?"

"No, I'm not saying that," Amina lied. "I just thought that you would leave his ass after catching him cheating on you. If I found out J..... Oh never mind. I'm happy for you, but I got to go; I'll talk to you later." CLICK!

Carla removed the cordless from her ear and stared at the phone with a confused look, wondering what the hell was wrong with Amina. She got up from the couch and placed the cordless back on the hook before heading back upstairs to get ready. She began planning out a wild night of sex for her husband since it had been a while since she put it on him.

*****

Carla was looking like a million bucks. She wore her hair pinned up with a curly strand hanging in front of her face and some pieces of curly strands left out in the back. Fourteen karat diamond earrings glistened in the dark, but shined when the candles caught them. She wore a white flowy baby gown from Victoria's Secret with kinky hells. Carla sat on the edge of the bed as the candles flickered on her pretty caramel skin. She placed Sweet Temptation lotion all over her body and then sprayed the perfume to make the aroma last longer. The room was filled with vanilla scented candles that lit it up leaving the room smelling like it was edible.

She could hear Derrick walking up the stairs as his keys jingled which gave him away. If she was a killer waiting for him; he would have died at point blank range. Carla hopped in bed as she stared at the bedroom door waiting to see his silhouette.

"Hey baby," Carla said in a low seductive tone.

"Hey honey," Derrick said as he walked in through the door and got undressed. "What's all this for?" He asked referring to the vanilla scented candles.

Carla got out of the bed and walked over to him. After wrapping her arms around his neck; she sang, "I wanna thank you for the new car, and I want to say sorry for acting like a bitch. I should have believed you." She bit down on her bottom lip hoping that he would accept her apology.

"It's alright babe; I understand," He said wrapping his arms around her waist while noticing that her medication was still on the night stand. "It's my fault. I should have told you the day it happened. He played along with the guilt trip she was going through.

"No, it's not your fault, it's mine. I should have never assumed." Carla suddenly reached over and grabbed her pill and water and downed them both before Derrick could finish.

"Anyways ma, it's all good; you look beautiful, he said paying attention to her lips while anticipating them being on his lips at any given moment.

Carla winked in reply and began running her tongue across her lips as she grabbed his hard rock dick that bulged out of his boxers.

"Mhm, I think you want some," she said flirting as she felt all over him.

"I think you want some of this good dick," Derrick said grabbing his dick.

"Well, give it to me."

Within seconds, Carla jumped on him and wrapped her arms around his waist as she tongued him down. He gently laid her on the bed as he stepped out of his boxers. He was hard as a rock. Carla backed up on the bed as Derrick adjusted his face in between her legs and started licking her clit up and down. He was licking so fast; she felt like she hardly came.

"Mhmmmm, Ssssss, Baby, Mhm Shit, she moaned while grabbing the sheets as she bit down on her lips grinding her pussy into his face.

After she came in his mouth, Derrick licked his lips savoring the taste of her sweet juices that tasted like peaches. He got up and started to insert himself inside her, but she stopped him and pushed him on the bed.

She got on top and guided his throbbing hard dick inside her tight pussy. She slid up and down his pole as she pulled out her bobby pins and tossed them to the floor. She rode him until she lost total control and began screaming like he was killing her. Derrick bust three times before Carla collapsed onto his chest and began rubbing it lovingly. His heart was beating so fast. She smiled knowing she did well.

Carla laid her head on his chest and pulled the covers over them. Within minutes after making love, she looked up and saw that Derrick was knocked out. She knew she hadn't put it on him in a long time, but he purchased the dream car she always wanted, so why not give him a taste of heaven on earth.

Business Trip

Carla grabbed a couple of outfits to stay a few days in Washington D.C. She hated the fact that she had a business meeting during her wedding anniversary. She stuffed the clothes into her Louis Vuitton luggage and grabbed the necessities she needed for her trip.

Derrick walked in the room and smiled. He'd been smiling for the last three mornings after waking up and remembering the mind blowing sex they'd been having every since he bought her the Bentley.

Carla walked over to him, wrapped her arms around his neck, and kissed him on the lips.

"I'm so sorry babe," Carla apologized.

"Sorry for what?" Derrick asked with a baffled expression.

"Well, I know our anniversary is this week and I feel bad that I'm going to miss it, since I have to go to this stupid meeting." Carla had her head down, and Derrick lifted her chin back up with his index finger.

"Carla, don't worry about it; I know you would never miss any of our anniversaries, but this is big for you, so go ahead. I support you."

"Aww, thanks babe," Carla hugged him and held him for a few seconds before letting go. "Alright, my plane leaves in an hour so I have to get going."

"I'll take you."

"Don't you have to go to work?" Carla asked. "I was going to call a cab."

"No need for all that. That's what you have your husband here for." Derrick kissed her forehead before going to grab her luggage and exiting the room.

Carla stood there for a second smiling, thinking about how her husband was perfect. After they got in the car, Derrick rushed to the airport pressing his sneakers against the pedal accelerating the gas. Once they arrived at the airport, Derrick quickly got out of the car, rushed over toward his wife's door, and opened it for her.

Carla was thrilled with Derrick's attentiveness, but something seemed fishy. Like when he bought her the dream car she'd always wanted after she confronted him about catching him in the act of cheating on her. She stood on the sidewalk staring into Derrick's eyes.

"Be good," she smiled.

"Why wouldn't I?" Carla didn't bother answering that question. "I love you."

She kissed him before walking off. "I love you too!" Carla shouted.

Pinky Dior

"And Sabrina," he mumbled biting down on his bottom lip as he watched his wife enter the airport and disappear within seconds. Derrick got into the car and drove straight to Sabrina's house. The two had been secretly fucking ever since he met his sister-in-law at Carla's grandmother's house; there was something about Sabrina that Derrick couldn't get off his mind.

*****

It had been two days, and Carla was having a blast in D.C., just realizing that she left her medication at home, she promised herself that she would do better when she returned home. Although she was there for a business meeting, she had gone out to a bar with a few of her co-workers and got a little shopping in also. Walking past the jewelry store in Georgetown Mall, Carla stopped in her tracks after a few pieces caught her eyes.

Since Derrick bought her the Bentley, she had no choice but to get him something in return. She had all her shopping bags hanging onto her left arm, weighing it down as she opened the door with her right hand. A white salesman was behind the desk with blonde hair and pale blue eyes.

"Hi, what can I help you with today," He asked with gritted teeth.

"Yes, my eight year anniversary is coming up in two more days."

"Congratulations," he said excitedly, cutting Carla off.

"Thank you," she smirked. "I was looking for a nice anniversary present for my husband, and I don't know what to get him."

"What kind of jewelry does he prefer?" The salesman asked.

"I don't know. He's not a jewelry type of man." Carla said. "But, he's always talking about getting a Rolex. I mean he has a few, but they look cheap if you ask me." She said pursing her lips together as he took the joke and cracked up laughing. She gave him a glare letting him know nothing she said was that funny, and he stopped laughing.

"Well, I have just the right Rolex for him," he said as he walked over a few paces and unlocked the glass display case.

After opening it up, he pulled out a diamond Rolex watch that had so much bling in it, it blinded her eyes. Carla held in her laughter thinking that the salesman's face was full of Botox, because he had no type of lip movement when he talked.

"That's gorgeous," Carla said taking the Rolex in her hand and examining the diamonds that were encrusted inside the watch. "I'll take it."

"Well the price is $6,483."

"Did I ask you for a price?" Carla snapped.

The salesman quickly cocked his head back as he held his hand over his chest and let out a little chuckle, "I was just letting you know Ma'am, just in case."

"Just in case what? Just in case what?" Carla barked.

He tried to explain, but Carla held up her hand in his face and rolled her neck around. "I said I will take it!"

She said in a feisty tone as she handed him her black card and smiled pleasantly.

He swiped the card and handed it back to her, "Thank You Ma'am."

"No thank you Ma'am!" Carla chuckled at her comment as she placed her black card back inside her wallet.

He didn't bother saying anything because he had started to realize that this customer may be a bit mental.

"Also make sure you wrap that shit up real nice with a bow and all that," Carla said as she watched him carefully, making sure he wasn't sloppy with the gift wrapping

Carla was getting impatient and began tapping her heel on the marble floor, making a loud noise. "Would you hurry the fuck up? I have to go and take my medicine, shit!" She rolled her eyes as the guy turned around and handed her the gift bag. She quickly snatched it from him and exited the jewelry store. The fact that she left them at home had become an afterthought.

*****

The night club in Harlem was packed for a Tuesday night. Every Tuesday they had a special occasion, but never before had it been so jammed packed. Amina was inside checking out a few prospective ballers when she spotted Derrick. She found him to look even sexier than the other day when he was all suited up. Derrick was a very handsome man, dark skinned with light brown eyes and always sported a freshly cut low fade.

Derrick wore a pair of Red Monkey jeans with a red, long sleeved shirt. Amina bopped her head, and danced to the Hip-Hop music as she wrapped her lips around the tiny straw and sipped on her margarita; she decided to walk over to Derrick, who was only a short distance away from her. She tried to walk over to him in a seductive manner but apparently the liquor had taken full control of her body causing her to stumble a few times.

Amina wasn't embarrassed because she knew she looked good. She rocked a short mini skirt that exposed the under curves of her plump ass cheeks every time she bent over. The white top she wore dipped low in the front and exposed even more cleavage every time she made a move. She walked over to Derrick, and didn't care who was watching. She pressed her body up against his and stared into his eyes. As she bit down on her bottom lip for a few seconds, Amina then licked her full lips.

"So when are you going to stop playing and get with a real woman like me?" Amina smiled seductively.

Her eyes never left his as she rubbed her hand up and down his massive hard chest. From the touch alone she could tell that he worked out. She could also tell that he was getting a little nervous by the sight of sweat forming on his forehead and sliding down his eyebrow.

"Look Amina, I got a real woman." He informed her. "Don't you have a man? I can't get caught up with all this drama." Derrick shook his head, "So just keep it moving with all that." He said dismissively looking away from her like she wasn't even present. He continued bobbing his head to the music making Amina laugh at his attempts to ignore her.

Amina chuckled as she grabbed his dick through his pants and held it firmly. He looked at her like she'd lost her mind.

Derrick chuckled nervously, "Girl, you know if Carla found out what you were doing right now she would kill us both." He said as he removed her hand from his dick but not really wanting to. The way she massaged him was making him horny. She grabbed his crotch again and tilted her head to the side.

"So," Amina said bluntly.

"Look, you know how crazy Carla can get when she doesn't take her medicine," Derrick informed her.

"She's not going to find out about us, babe." Amina smiled as she kissed him passionately on his full luscious lips, "I promise," she said with a twinkle in her eye. "But, of course she knows about you and Sabrina," Amina lied, testing him.

"What?" He yelled over the blaring music. "She doesn't know shit about Sabrina. That's not if you don't want her to." Amina smiled while throwing him a devious look. "So, it's either you take me home with you tonight or your wife will find out sooner than later," Amina said as she started to walk away.

Derrick pulled her by the arm and stared in her eyes. "Whatever Amina," Derrick said. My wife can't find out about this." His eyes widened in fear.

"Well then, she won't find out about what's going on with us neither." Amina winked as she led him by the hand out the crowded club. He walked over to his car, unlocked the doors, and got inside.

"Let's go back to your house," Amina suggested.

"Nah, I'm not ready to go home," Derrick lied. "We can do it right here in my car."

That's a better position for me anyway." Amina looked at him as she licked her lips. "I love being on top and in charge." She winked at him as she let out a little giggle.

Amina didn't need to take off her skirt. She just pulled it up, took off her blouse, and tossed it in the back seat. Derrick stared at her breasts and licked his lips. He just wanted to bite them and suck on them all night. He hit a button and the sexy sounds of R. Kelly engulfed the car. Amina unbuckled his jeans, and he helped her slide them down a little past his thighs. *It's unbelievable how your body is calling for me.* He hummed the song in his head, watching Amina spring into action.

She quickly hooked her right leg over, hopping onto the driver's lap. She grabbed his rock hard dick and guided it inside her wet kitty kat. As soon as she slid down on his dick, Amina wrapped her arms around his neck and began bouncing up and down. He watched as her breast bounced rapidly while she rode him. He placed both his hands on her hips as he threw his head back and bit down on his lip.

Amina never looked away from him. She wanted to see all the erotic faces that he was making while she fucked him and made her inner muscles contract on his penetrating shaft. She got a kick out of fucking her best friends' man. She'd been waiting for this day forever, ever since Carla first introduced them. She had her eyes set on him first, but Derrick chose to talk to Carla leaving Amina stuck with Jerome. She loved Jerome, but she played him all the time for other niggas. He never found out because he was too busy working so he could shower her with gifts.

"Oh Shit!" Derrick moaned. Amina smiled as she slowed down the pace and rotated her hips in circles. "I'm about to nut Ma! Derrick shouted as he thought she would go faster, but she didn't'.

Amina could feel his throbbing tool about to explode inside of her and she continued going slower and slower. She wanted to feel all nine inches expanding inside her as he pumped in and out, in and out. She didn't want to miss one stroke. As soon as Derrick exploded, Amina kept twirling her hips in a slow motion as she felt herself about to cum. He grabbed one of her breast and slowly started kissing it passionately, as if he was making love to her breasts.

"Mhm," Amina moaned. She loved the way he kissed and licked all over her nipples. That made her wetter and made her reach her climax. Amina tossed her head back as she panted while trying to catch her breath.

She got off of him and pulled down her skirt. She grabbed her blouse from the back seat and pulled it over her head. She flipped down the visor and fixed herself before exiting the car. Derrick wiped himself off with a napkin before pulling up his pants and zipping them. He then checked the mirror and removed a piece of hair that was out of placed and fixed it with the rest of his hair.

"When will I see you again?" Derrick asked.

"Whenever you're ready for a real woman like me," Amina said bluntly as she grabbed her purse, exited the car, and walked away.

Derrick watched as she switched her hips enticingly. *Damn that bitch is bad!* Derrick said to himself. *I can't believe I just fucked my wife's best friend.* Derrick rubbed his face as he started up the car and pulled off.

*****

Once Carla got settled in, she heard her cell phone ringing. She thought it would be her husband Derrick calling, but it wasn't. She screwed up her face at the caller ID; it was Amina. Carla rolled her eyes, pressed the answer button and placed the phone up to her ear.

"Hey Amina," Carla said dryly.

"Damn girl," Amina cooed. "What you not happy to hear my voice?"

"No it's not that," Carla said. "I had a long day. I'm tired, and I left my meds at home so right now I'm on the borderline of Miss Nice or Miss Naughty," Carla cracked a smile.

"Yeah, I know that's right." Amina eyes widened. "Well, I know you probably down there fucking some fine ass man. Girl I heard those D.C. niggas be looking right!"

"Amina please, I maybe bipolar, but I don't fuck around with other niggas." Carla assured her. "I'm married now." She waved her finger in the air, admiring her huge diamond ring that displayed the testament of Derrick's love for her and vice-versa.

"Yeah, whatever bitch; I don't know who you think you fooling." She laughed.

"Right, anyway what do you want?" Carla asked arrogantly as she rolled her eyes. *This bitch sure does know how to push my buttons. She's only doing that because she knows how I get if I don't have my meds,* Carla said to herself.

"Well, I just wanted to let you know that I saw Derrick with another girl at the club tonight."

"What! When," Carla snapped becoming outraged.

"I went to the club in Harlem and saw Derrick there smiling up in some bitch's face and when I was leaving I saw some bitch in his car." Amina said referring to herself and leaving out all the details as far as the unprotected sex she had with Derrick.

Carla didn't know what to say, but last time she assumed the worst about her husband; it wasn't even like that.

"Well, I will just have to see for myself," Carla hung up the phone and immediately called Derrick to see what he'd been up to. Once he answered, he sounded like he just woke up.

"Hey honey," Carla switched up her tone.

Derrick moaned, "What's up babe?"

"Nothing, just thinking about you; I miss you," Carla smiled. "What you doing?"

"I miss you too babe." Derrick faked yawned. "I just woke up; I have been asleep for like six hours. I had a long day at the office and when I came home; I went out like a light. I'm talking knocked out." He said lying through his teeth.

"Are you sure? Oh, never mind," Carla chuckled.

"Why, what happened?" Derrick sat up in bed curious to know.

"Oh nothing Derrick; Amina said she spotted you down at the club. I don't know," She said dismissively, knowing it wasn't true. *Why would Amina say such a thing?* She wondered.

"Man, Amina is a hating ass bitch, Carla!" Derrick said while raising his tone. "She always adored and admired everything you ever had and she wants to be in your shoes."

"Maybe so, but she can't!" Carla smirked.

"You damn right she can't. That's right baby," Derrick said amping her up. "Honey, look I'm tired. I have to wake up extra early to go to the work in the AM. When will you be back?" He asked eagerly.

"I'll be home on Saturday."

"Good, I can't wait to see you. I miss you," Derrick cooed.

"Derrick," Carla's voice got real sad. "I'm really sorry that I can't make it on Friday. It's our anniversary, and I should be there. She said getting teary eyed.

"It's okay honey."

Carla cut him off. "No it's not okay!" Carla responded, raising her tone. "I never missed one anniversary. Those are special moments nobody is ever supposed to miss. Why did I leave you?" She said with her voice cracking. "Why did I come to this stupid meeting?"

"Babe listen to me; listen to me," he said soothingly. You can make it up to me when you come home on Saturday, okay," he suggested.

"Alright, I got you babe and it's going to be so much better than the night you gave me the keys to my Bentley." Carla smiled and began thinking about all the freaky things she wanted to do with her husband when she returned home. "Alright, well have a good night honey."

"Alright babe; love you."

"Love you too Derrick," Carla said before hanging up the phone.

She rested her back against the fluffy pillows as she folded her arms across her breasts. She thought about Amina. Sometimes deep down inside Carla felt as if Amina secretly envied her and wanted her husband, but she could never prove it. Carla shrugged her shoulders as she cuddled up in the covers, reached over, and turned out the lights.

Caught

Carla wrapped up her meeting, gathered her suitcase, and exited the hotel suite. She was thankful that they decided to change the date for the meeting to the thirteenth instead of the fourteenth. Carla had a gracious smirk on her face as she thought about calling her husband with the good news. After giving it some thought, Carla decided not to call because she wanted to surprise him. Carla took a cab back to the airport and headed back to New York City.

She noticed when the cab driver pulled up in front of her house that Derrick's car wasn't there. Her Bentley was parked right there in the driveway looking absolutely stunning. After exiting the cab, she headed up the stairs, removing the keys from her purse. Opening the door, she rolled her luggage inside and left them in the living room.

"DERRICK! DERRICK! HONEY, I'M HOME!" She called out while rushing up the stairs.

Maybe he's at work. He did tell me that he had to go to work early today; Carla thought as she sat down on the bed and removed her cell phone from her pocket. She was about to call Derrick, but she noticed she had a few missed calls from Amina as well as a voice mail.

Dialing up her voice mail, Carla learned that it was Amina's sister Ty calling and stressing the fact that she needed to come over to Amina's to see something. Carla heard Amina's name in the message, but Ty failed to say what happened specifically. Carla didn't know what was going on, but she knew Ty didn't sound right because her voice was shaky.

Carla grabbed her keys and purse then she headed down the stairs. She exited the house, hopped in the Bentley, and quickly rushed over to Amina's house. She arrived within ten minutes. She was about to pull in the driveway when she noticed her husband's car.

"What the fuck is he doing here?" Carla said out loud as she parked the Bentley. She got out of the car and banged on the front door, waiting for a response. Ty slowly opened the door seconds later with a sad look plastered all over her face.

Carla barged in the house looking for Derrick. She noticed that he wasn't sitting on the couch. She wondered why he was there. She ran upstairs assuming that he was playing Xbox with Amina's boyfriend Jerome. Carla looked in the entertainment room and they weren't in there. She closed the door, walked down the hall, and was about to head downstairs to ask Ty why Derrick's car was parked outside but she had disappeared. She heard moaning coming from Amina's bedroom. Carla smiled as she shook her head. *This bitch is always fucking with her nasty ass*, Carla thought as she began to walk away.

Pinky Dior

Carla stopped in her tracks when she heard Amina screaming, "Ohhhh Derrick, faster babe; faster! Carla's jaw dropped as she slowly walked to the door. Every muscle in her body tensed up as she listened to the moaning and screaming of the sexual activity going on the other side.

God Please, don't let this be happening; please let me be wrong about this. Please. She silently prayed as she opened the door. The lights were off, but she could see her best friend riding her husband while bouncing up and down on his dick as he grabbed her hair.

"Oh my God," Carla's trembling hand covered her mouth as the tears formed in her eyes. She felt like her heart shattered into tiny bits of pieces. She backed up without saying anything and closed the door as they continued sexing and bluntly betraying her.

Carla ran downstairs with her hands over her mouth as tears freely poured from her eyes.

I tried to tell you," Ty cried. She knew how much Carla loved Amina and her husband. "I'm so sorry."

Carla ran out of the house and headed straight to her car. She was speechless and felt like she was sick to her stomach. She hopped in her car and sped off. She picked up her phone and called her sister, Sabrina. Although they weren't close as she was to Amina; they were blood. Carla felt like she was the only person she could trust and talk to at a time like this.

"Hello?"

"I, I na-need to come ta-talk to you right now," Carla cried. Tears blurred her vision as she drove through the streets of New York like a mad woman.

"Okay, I'll be here waiting on you," Sabrina said before hanging up. She wondered what made her so upset that she wanted to talk to her all of a sudden.

Carla pulled up in front of Sabrina's apartment building and saw her sitting on the stoop waiting for her arrival. Carla slammed the door and walked down the path where Sabrina stood to greet her with a warm hug. She wrapped her arms around Carla's neck and began rubbing her back with a devilish smirk on her face. It quickly disappeared when Carla pulled back from the embrace, walked past Sabrina, and sat down.

"I should have listened to you," Carla sniffed as Sabrina wrapped her arms around her neck.

"Carla everything happens for a reason," Sabrina said. "The first time his ass cheated, you should have left his ass. Now this time, you have to leave him. He fucked your best friend; well so called best friend. That shit is so fucked up!" Sabrina said instigating the matter, while trying to sound concerned and sad at the same time. Deep down inside, Sabrina was smiling and laughing hysterically over her sister's pain and heartache. *This will make Derrick and me much closer, once I get her to leave him,* Sabrina thought.

Pinky Dior

"Why couldn't I see the signs; why," Carla asked with tears streaming down her face and snot creeping down her nose.

Sabrina screwed up her face as she removed a Kleenex tissue from her purse and gave it to Carla.

"Carla, don't worry about that or him. What's done is done." Sabrina talked with her hands. "All you can do now is move forward." She rubbed her back. "So what are you going to do?" Sabrina pressed wanting to know if Carla was going to leave him, so she and Derrick could move on and be together without any problems.

"Oh don't worry; I got something for his ass," Carla said as she got up.

"Just don't kill him," Sabrina said while joking around, but she meant every word. She couldn't see herself living life without having sex with Derrick.

Carla turned around and shot Sabrina a nasty glare causing Sabrina to just laugh nervously.

Anniversary Day Surprise

February 14th was the day that Carla and Derrick met; a year later Derrick used that day to get down on one knee and proposed to Carla, asking her to be his wife forever. Carla could never forget that day. She even remembered the exact time he proposed to her; it was at eight-thirty p.m. while they were eating dinner at Justin's restaurant. That was eight years ago, but today would be different. It would be the day that Derrick would regret everything he'd ever done and was still doing to his wife.

Carla was dressed in an all white strapless gown and sexy white stilettos. She wore her hair down in a full bob. She had a sexy red bra and panty set on underneath. She stayed up all night waiting for her husband to return home, but he didn't. Carla knew he'd eventually come home today. She filled the room with tall red candles on the dresser and placed a few heart shaped candles on both night stands. Carla layed in bed with her knees curled up resting on her back and elbows, waiting for Derrick to enter the room.

When he came through the bedroom door, all he could say was, "Wha-what are you doing here?"

"What, you surprised to see me home so soon," Carla said seductively as she crawled across the bed like a cat. She got up on him, wrapped her arms around his neck, and began kissing him all over his face.

"You didn't miss me baby," She asked in between kisses. "I missed you."

"Yeah, I did miss you. I just didn't know you were coming home today," Derrick gulped down his spit as he loosened his tie. He felt the bedroom was getting much hotter than it already was when he first walked in.

"I came to the office yesterday, but you weren't there," she lied.

"I-I was"

Carla cut him off by placing her hand up to his lips. "I don't even want to hear it. I just want to make love to you, because it's our anniversary." She sang her rendition of the Tony, Toni, Tone classic. She ran her fingers across the bottom of his lips. "Take off your clothes."

Derrick didn't know where all the demands were coming from, but he liked it. He quickly stepped out of his pants, pulled his shirt over his head, and tossed it to the floor. Carla was horny as hell and wanted a piece of her husband one last time. Derrick's dick stood straight out and was hard as a rock. Carla grabbed his dick and yanked it hard, making him grunt.

"What are you doing?" He said through gritted teeth.

"I got this baby, relax," Carla said with her head cocked to the side. "You're too tense," she snickered as she kept stroking his dick.

She then pushed him onto the bed. She didn't take off her dress. She just pulled it up, crawled on the bed, and started kissing all over his body while biting at his skin. Derrick looked up at his wife like she was crazy. She then placed her legs on both sides of him, straddling his groin area. Sliding her panties to the side; she gripped his hardness and slid down on his pole. She began bouncing up and down like a wild woman. Derrick's eye brows shot up wondering what was the matter with his wife.

She probably didn't take her damn pills yet, he thought as he shrugged it off, going with the flow of the rough sex. He tried to pound a new hole in her sugary walls with his massive boner as she rode him, contracting her pussy muscles with each violent and relentless stroke.

"Fuck me, you bastard! I said FUCK MEEE! HARDER DAMMIT; HARDER!" She demanded turning him on even more as she ran her fingers through her short bob. She clawed at his chest, making a few stinging incisions with her nails as she rode him hard like a woman trying to stay on a mechanical bull in a western themed sports bar.

"Harder, damn you, give it to me; I said FUCK MEEEE!" She shrieked, sliding back and forth on his upstanding beef log, loving the way he filled up her insides.

She had already climaxed and wondered when Amina would arrive. She texted Amina and told her that she wanted her to come over for dinner. Carla rolled her eyes because she couldn't wait until Amina burst through the bedroom door. Once she did minutes later, Carla turned around while riding Derrick's throbbing pole as Amina turned on the lights.

"It's so nice of you to join us," Carla smiled as she moved from the reverse cowgirl position and off of Derrick's throbbing boner.

Carla crawled off the bed making sure to lower her dress and pull her panties back in place as she stood in front of Amina, her back stabbing best friend.

"WHAT THE FUCK?" Derrick yelled grabbing the covers in an attempt to cover up his nude body and aching hard on that began deflating quickly at the sight of Amina.

"Oh please Derrick," Carla said. "I know she's seen all of that before, so it's no need for you to hide it now."

"What the hell is going on here? Is this what you invited me over here for," Amina said getting uptight.

"Yes, I invited you over here because apparently, you two were fucking behind my back," Carla yelled while shooting an icy look at Amina. "You fucked my husband, and you fucked my best friend!" Carla snapped as she walked over to the dresser and opened the drawer.

Before Amina or Derrick could react to being busted, Carla pulled out a loaded gun and cocked it back. She turned and pointed the gun at Amina because she was the closest one to the bedroom door. Carla didn't want her to run; not for what she had planned. She wanted Amina to hang around.

"Bitch don't even think about running," Carla warned, looking directly at her so called best friend who was eyeing the door like she wanted to make a dash for it.

"What the fuck are you doing with that?" Derrick asked as Amina contemplated if she should run or stick around. "Where did you get that from?"

"Enough with the questions; don't fucking worry about where I got the gun from," Carla said with an attitude. "Just know that I will use it on both of you if I have to, but nah; I'd rather torture you two. No, getting shot is too easy for you two sneaky motherfuckers!" Carla snickered.

"Carla please don't do this," Amina cried.

"Shut the fuck up bitch," Carla barked. "You weren't crying when you were fucking my man, so don't

Pinky Dior

cry now. The dick was good to you right? Good enough for you to betray our friendship, huh? Now let's go. Get your ass up, Derrick! We're going downstairs to have a nice fucking Valentine's Day dinner; my no good cheating ass husband, my so called back stabbing best friend, and me.

Carla waited until Derrick crawled out of the bed and walked over to Amina in the nude. Carla pointed the gun at the both of them and demanded for them to walk downstairs slowly. As soon as they got downstairs, Carla pushed them into the kitchen and demanded for them to sit down. They both sat down nervously looking at Carla. They wondered what she was going to do to them. They noticed two roses at the dinner table with two pieces of Carla's best china plates. There was also rope, duct tape, and all types of silver tools that looked like something a doctor would use for surgery.

Carla grabbed the rope and smiled before tossing it to Amina. "Tie his ass up to the chair and leave his hands free," She ordered. Once Amina completed the task, Carla told her to sit down in the chair then she instructed Derrick to tie up Amina.

"Why are you doing this?" Amina cried as Derrick did as he was told. Tears fell freely from Amina's eyes as Derrick tied her limbs to the wooden chair.

Carla walked over to Derrick and slapped him hard as she could with the gun. His head snapped back violently from the blow. Before he could feel the pain, Carla slapped a pair of handcuffs on him. She quickly bound him to the chair with the rest of the rope on the table.

"Isn't this lovely; we're just one big happy couple enjoying dinner on our anniversary," Carla snickered while walking over to Amina. She slapped a pair of handcuffs on Amina and kissed her on the forehead.

"Please Carla, I'm sorr...."

"Bitch shut the fuck up!" Carla exploded and smacked her in the face with the gun making blood trickle down her lip. "Now, when I say speak, then you can fucking speak!" She was so close to Amina's face that Amina could feel every sprinkle of saliva that hit her face when Carla shouted.

"Matter of fact," Carla placed her hand on her chin as she looked up at the ceiling like she was in deep thought. "You don't get to speak at all. You two got your last words upstairs, now I get the last motherfucking word." With that being said, Carla didn't waste any time. She placed the rose inside Amina's mouth and grabbed the duct tape. Amina spat the rose out of her mouth.

"The longer you fight it, the longer it's going to take babe," Carla bit off another long strip of duct tape and slowly turned and moved over to Derrick. She eyed him intensely with a devilish smirk on her face. "Now it's your turn lover boy!"

"Another thing, I damn sure don't love you," Carla said bluntly as she placed the rose across his lips. Carla traced the rose across the outline of his lips several times, before shoving it in his mouth with brute force. She then grabbed the roll of duct tape and wrapped it all the way from his mouth to the back of his head several times causing his eyes to bulge in fear.

Carla walked back over to Amina and did the same thing with the tape. She didn't want the neighbors to call the cops. She knew that there was going to be a lot of screaming and blood popping off at the dinner table. After duct taping their mouths, Carla picked up a shiny silver tool off the kitchen table, a scalpel! Both of their eyes widened in horror as they noticed the light reflecting off the sharp tool. They didn't know what Carla was capable of doing, but they knew Carl had snapped for sure. Without saying anything, Carla plunged the scalpel deeply in Amina's chest and then began cutting through skin tissues and muscle to get to their heart.

"MMMMMMMHHHHMMM! MMHHMMMM! MMMMMMMHHH!!!!!!!!!!!!!"

Amina's muffled screams made Derrick cringe while watching his wife cut up her best friend.

It took Carla no time to cut out Amina's heart. She used to go to school to be a heart surgeon but stopped going so that she could start her own media consulting business. Still, she knew enough to make this an effortless feat and successfully accomplished the task at hand. Carla looked at Amina; she was watching the dark blood seep through her shirt as she extracted Amina's heart from her chest and placed it on the fine white china plate.

Carla turned and looked at Derrick who was crying like a little bitch. As tears streamed down his cheeks, the look of 'PUSSY' was written all over his face. Carla started laughing and couldn't stop. She slowly walked over to him, and Derrick began hopping around in his' seat, trying to get away from her.

"Why you running babe; y'all two wanted to be together right?" Carla laughed.

He shook his head vigorously from side to side as she stalked him with the scalpel. "Well, that's not what it looked like when she was riding your dick at her house the other day now was it? Mhm Hmm, I seen the whole thing Derrick; every little stroke," she told him and added how Amina's sister called her on the phone and let her in the house while he was having sex with Amina.

After hearing that information, Derrick slumped in his seat looking defeated. "Now, now don't look so sad babe; here's what I'm going to do for you. Since you love her so much, y'all can finally be together;

Forever. Y'all can have each other's heart." Carla laughed hysterically as she slapped her knee.

She got a kick out of the sick look plastered all over his face. She suddenly stopped laughing and jammed the scalpel in his chest!

"MMMMMMMHHHHMMM! GRRRRHHMMMMMM!" He screamed bloody murder as she started cutting around his skin and muscle tissues. During the brutal operation, he felt every slice and screamed as loud as he could but not loud enough where the neighbors could hear.

"Aww, Shh, Shh I'm almost there babe," Carla giggled as she ripped out his heart with her bare hands.

Carla smiled as a misty spray of blood hit her face. She placed his heart on the other china plate on the table and moved it in front of Amina's body. After placing Amina's heart in front of Derrick, Carla smiled at her handiwork.

"Mhm, revenge is sweet, isn't it?" Carla stared him in the eyes as she watched him die.

"Happy Anniversary babe; now eat your heart out," Carla blew him a kiss and began feeding him and Amina portions of each other's heart.

Carla headed upstairs to the bathroom and washed off the blood that was all over her face, hands, and arms. She stared in the mirror at the blood stained dress she wore and laughed at herself. Proud at what she'd just done; Carla headed back into the bedroom and grabbed her car keys. Right before she was leaving, she heard Derrick's cell phone vibrating.

Carla turned around and looked around the room to see where the noise was coming from. She bent down and pulled his cell phone from his pants pocket. When she saw the name on the text message her heart dropped. She opened the text and scanned through several of them. Derrick was supposed to be meeting her sister, Sabrina tonight.

Looking at the clock, Carla noticed that it was ten-forty-five, she texted Sabrina back pretending to be Derrick and told her to expect him around eleven thirty. Carla didn't think to change out of her bloody dress as she exited the bedroom and rushed down the steps. She walked over to the kitchen table, grabbed all the tools she needed, put them in her purse, and was on her way.

*****

Carla stood at Sabrina's apartment door as she rang the doorbell. A few seconds later, Sabrina opened the door wearing some sheer Victoria's Secret lingerie. Once she saw all the blood splattered over the front of Carla's white dress. She swallowed heard wondering what happened.

"What, are you expecting company?" Carla asked barging right in.

"Yeah, in fact he'll be over here shortly." Sabrina rolled her eyes as Carla headed into the living room. She closed the door behind her and placed her hands on her hips. "Didn't you hear me? I said I'm having company over."

"Oh, I'm aware," Carla smiled. "Very aware," she said sarcastically as she sat down and grabbed some grapes from the bowl that was sitting on the table.

"What's that supposed to mean?" Sabrina asked with a questionable brown. The blood on her dress was an afterthought. She just thought it was some new designer clothing that Carla was trying out.

"Well, I mean I'm aware that you're having company over." Carla said sarcastically. It's obvious the way you're looking like a fucking whore in that lingerie. I know he must have dicked you down real good to make you dress up like that," Carla said bluntly before popping another grape in her mouth.

Sabrina raised her brows as she walked over and poured herself a glass of red wine.

"So tell me, how's the dick?" Carla asked bluntly, catching Sabrina off guard. She spit out her wine.

"What?" Sabrina cleared her throat as she patted her chest.

"Well, let me be more specific; how can I put this? Carla looked up at the ceiling and looked back at Sabrina and said, "How's Derrick's dick? I mean, I know it's extra big, but how is it to you? Does it taste good?

"Carla, I don't know what the hell you're talking about," Sabrina lied wondering how she found out about them.

"Oh, you know exactly what I'm talking about," Carla said. "Is that your final answer?"

Sabrina looked at her sister, wondering if she was just fishing for an answer or did she really know about her sleeping with her husband. Carla walked over to Sabrina and showed her Derrick's cell phone. Next she showed Sabrina all of their ongoing text messages. Carla didn't replay the voice messages she heard with Sabrina confessing her undying love for her husband.

"You had everything to do with this," Carla said pointing to the blood stains on her dress. "You knew that my own fucking best friend was having an affair with my husband, and you didn't have the audacity to tell me?"

"Look sis, I had no idea. Honestly," Sabrina was lying through her teeth.

"Sabrina, Sabrina, Sabrina you're such a bad fucking liar!" Carla yelled unable to hold back the tears welling up in her eyes. "You were my fucking sister;

my blood Sabrina, and you turn around and go fuck my husband! My Husband!" Carla raged shaking her head in disbelief.

"Ever since I met Derrick; you always wanted him for yourself, so you wanted us to break up so you could go after him. You're such a slick bitch, and I have to give it to you." Carla smiled while clapping her hands and applauding Sabrina.

"Bravo! Bravo! You played this one good. On my way over here I realized something, and it didn't dawn on me until your little text gave you away. You were the bitch who I caught laughing all up in my husband's face at the restaurant. You have been fucking him my entire marriage!" As soon as the words left her mouth, Carla whipped the gun from her purse with lightening speed.

"Now sit the fuck down!" Carla demanded pointing the gun at Sabrina's head.

Sabrina sat down quickly, keeping her eyes on the derange look in her sister's eyes.

"Do you know how it feels to be broken hearted?" Carla asked, and Sabrina shook her head no.

"Do you know how it feels having no heart?

"I don't know, Carla. I'm sorry, but I do have a heart. I really do, and I'm so sorry." Sabrina kept apologizing.

"Well, guess what bitch?" Carla barked, moving quickly from her spot on the couch. She bent over and stared directly into Sabrina eyes. "Not any more you don't." Carla said referring to her heart.

Carla forced Sabrina around the house at gun point, making her snatch all the telephone wires from the sockets. Once she was done, Carla took her into the kitchen. After making Sabrina sit down at the kitchen table, Carla began tying her up to the chair.

"HELP; SOMEBODY HEL---"

Carla silenced her with a swift blow to the face. She quickly grabbed the duct tape from her bag and started unrolling it. Carla stopped in her tracks and chuckled.

"You know what, I'm not going to duct tape your mouth because I want to hear you scream and cry. I want you to feel the same pain that I felt after learning about you and my best friend fucking my husband. Now it's my turn to be on some 'fuck you' shit and do some crazy shit that I see in my mind."

Carla laughed wiping the rest of the blood away on her white dress and grabbed her gun. As she proceeded to the front door to leave the scene, Carla stopped in her tracks as she heard the front door opening.

Once the door opened, Carla locked eyes with Amina's boyfriend, Jerome and Derrick's right hand partner. He immediately stopped in his tracks after seeing all the blood on her dress, next he shifted his glaze over to Sabrina. Spotting Sabrina sitting at the table with her eyes wide open in a deathly gaze with her jaws dropped open and her heart ripped out, Jerome flinched a few times as if he was weaving several invisible blows coming at him. He looked at Carla and then back at Sabrina's corpse.

"Oh my God," Jerome yelled over his covered mouth. "Oh Shit! What the fuck did you do?"

"I'm sorry Jerome, she slept with my husband, and I assume she was sleeping with you too!" Carla broke down with tears streaming down her face.

Jerome made his way over to her with his hands held high in surrender. His eyes widened in caution and fear, never leaving the gun as he got closer and closer to her.

"Don't shoot me Carla," he warned her while slowly inching towards her. "I just want to help you, Carla. You need some serious help." *You crazy bitch!* He thought getting up on her. Carla shook her head up and down fast as the tears streamed down her face. Jerome quickly grabbed the gun from her hand. He wrapped his arms around her and held her. Carla placed her chin on his shoulder as a wicked smile appeared across her face.

"Happy Valentine's Day Jerome," Carla took the scalpel and stabbed Jerome in the stomach several times.

"Why?" He mouthed in apparent shock as she pushed the weapon deeper into his bleeding chest.

Jerome looked at her with his mouth hanging open, trying to utter some words but only blood poured from his mouth. Looking down, Jerome saw the sharp tool embedded in his chest and collapsed. Carla walked over, stood over his prone body, and stepped on the scalpel crushing it into his chest further.

"Grrrgggh!" He gasped looking up at Carla's evil leer.

Carla's maniacal laughter filled the apartment and chilled Jerome to the bone as his life slowly slipped away. He had no idea he'd get stabbed to death for creeping out to answer a Valentine's Day booty call.

February 14th always was a special day in Carla Smith's life. Carla remembered meeting Derrick on that lovely day. A day of loving, caring, and cupid playing match maker; February 14th would always stir loving emotions in Carla because it was her wedding anniversary, but not today.

No, she'd never forget this particular February 14th; the day she allowed her hate to boil over into a murdering rampage that left four people dead. Carla couldn't believe she went from loving her husband and giving him the wildest sex of her life to hating him enough to literally rip his heart out.

Pinky Dior

All Carla pictured was Derrick in bed with her best friend, Amina having wild sex. By the time the murderous veil fell from her eyes, Carla had reached her sister's front door. As she turned the door knob and opened the door all she heard was, *Boom! Boom! Boom!*

Lying on the carpet Jerome rose up just a tad bit. Using all the strength he could muster, Jerome's trembling finger managed to squeeze the trigger and let off three rounds into Carla's back. Carla felt her chest jerk up three times, and she panicked. She touched her chest, looked down at her hands, and saw they were filled with blood.

Blood trickled out of her mouth as her knees buckled. As Carla dropped to the carpet taking her last breathe; a lone bloody tear dropped from her right eye. A combination of feelings raced through her; gaseousness, anxiety, rage, hate, love, regret, and fear. Carla's heart ached as she saw her life flashing before her eyes. All thirty-two years of it, playing out like a movie set on fast forward up until it slowed down to the present.

The way Carla Smith looked off into the distance and gasped, it seemed as if she knew that death was inevitable. Her eyes were red with blood and grief as she stared at the man who shattered her vengeful happy ending. Bloody tears stung Carla's eyes as the will to live oozed rapidly from her troubled soul.

All Carla Smith ever wanted was to be loved and treated well by her husband. She thought coming home early to surprise her man on their anniversary would achieve that. That mistake had cost her dearly. If she could have done it differently; Carla would have let everybody live and walked away from all the pain they caused her, but the hands of fate had already been dealt and played out. She inhaled deeply to embrace her fate and the fact that she wouldn't live to see another Valentine's Day.

The End

THE CROSS

Eyone Williams

CHAPTER 1

Pistol in hand, Donald James, known in the streets and in prison as Dee, laid across the bed in his small hotel room in Silver Spring, MD, staring at the ceiling. He was stressing and had a thousand things on his mind. He hadn't seen his parole officer in weeks which was a sure ticket back to prison where he'd already spent twelve years of his life. Niggaz in the streets wanted him dead, but he didn't give a fuck about that; the way he carried shit in life always had him facing death in one way or another. However, what was bothering him the most was what he'd just agreed to. *Fuck it, it is what it is,* he thought, tapping the pistol on his leg.

The TV was on A&E, The First 48 was in Dallas, TX, where a body had been found in the trunk of a gold Lexus. Murder was a part of life in Dee's world, murder, robbery, and everything else that came with that way of life. He felt that watching such shows helped him think like the police did when they were investigating crimes.

A sexy little broad by the name of Fantasy was in the shower. Dee met her a few months back and had been fucking her on and off since, but he had no girlfriend. He didn't have time for that. In his world, he couldn't let anyone get too close to him.

Eyone Williams

Fantasy came out of the bathroom a short time later in nothing but a towel. Her sexy brown skin was still damp. She walked over to the nightstand and picked up a Don Diva magazine with a small pile of loud on it. "Ain't no more blunts?" she asked.

"Yeah, look on the other side of the TV." Dee said, still staring at the ceiling.

Fantasy grabbed a grape cigarillo and sat on the bed. Breaking up the weed, she said, "You still ain't hear from your man yet?"

"Yeah, he'll be here in a little while." Dee got up and walked to the window. "You need to get dressed so we can get out of here."

"Damn, can a bitch smoke real quick?" She sucked her teeth.

Dee gave her a vicious look and said, "Do what I said, I ain't in the mood for no questions, I got shit to do."

She rolled her eyes and did as she was told. She didn't play with Dee.

The cell phone at the foot of the bed went off with a Rick Ross ringtone: *Blowin' Money Fast.*

"Hand me my phone." Dee said, looking out the window. She handed him the phone. It was his partner in crime, Sean.

Dee and Sean were both from Northwest, D.C.—uptown. Dee was from 14th Street. Sean was from Kennedy Street. They'd done time together in the feds where they got close. At first they couldn't stand each other, mostly because they were so much alike. They were both cut-throat niggaz that had never had shit. Over time, they put their heads together and applied their cut-throat ways to getting money in prison. From extortion to drug dealing, they made it happen and stacked thousands of dollars in their prison accounts. Sean made parole a few months before Dee, but as soon as Dee hit the streets he and Sean hooked back up and got right back on their bullshit together in the free world.

"What's up, slim?" Dee answered the phone.

"You ready, slim? I'm like five minutes away." Sean said. Music was playing in the background, Scarface was rapping about how niggaz weren't to be trusted in the streets.

"Yeah, I'm ready. Shit straight on your end?"

"You know it, you don't even have to ask me that, homie. I told you the shit sweet."

Dee nodded. "Cool."

Sean said, "Shit straight on your end, is the bitch down?"

"Yeah, she wit' it." Dee cut his eyes at Fantasy to see if she was paying attention to the conversation. She was acting like she wasn't but she was. Dee was sure of it.

"Cool then, see you in a minute."

"Bet." Dee ended the call and tossed the phone on the bed.

It took Fantasy no time to get dressed in a white wife-beater and a pair of tight-ass jean shorts. Her wavy hair was pulled back in a ponytail. Nevertheless, she could get any nigga's attention. Once she was dressed she rolled the weed and put it in the air.

Blowing smoke in the air, Fantasy said, "So how long its gon' be before you and your man come inside? I ain't trying to be up in there with that nigga too long."

"Don't worry, we won't be long." Dee said, sliding his .40 cal. in his waistband. "Just keep the nigga at ease. Cool?"

With a sexy smile, Fantasy said, "I got you."

****

A black Chevy Tahoe with black tints pulled up in the hotel parking lot and parked in the back. It was summer time and the sun was blazing so all the windows were up with the AC pumping. Scarface's *Dopeman's* music could be heard outside of the truck. Sean was leaning back behind the wheel with a Glock laying across his lap. Like Dee, Sean was a wanted man, but not by the law. He was wanted dead by niggaz he'd taken bad over the years, not to mention that he'd smoked a big nigga in the streets when he first got out of prison. So what the nigga he'd smoked was a rat that had testified against the First and Kennedy Crew years back. Nevertheless, the rat nigga was connected in the streets and for that reason alone his crew had money on Sean's head. When the topic came up Sean's only response was: "Ask me if I care. You know how many niggaz want me dead? If a nigga think he gon' kill me he gon' have to get in line and that muthafucka wrap all the way around the corner."

Sean's cell phone went off. He looked at the name sighed. "Yeah." he answered.

"You gon' have that tonight. Half now and the other half when it's done. Got it?" a deep voice said.

"Nuff said, we don't need to keep talkin' on the phone. I got it. Shit gon' take some time. You know how serious shit is out here." Sean said.

"If you can't do it let me know."

"It's gon' get done!" Sean snapped, ending the call.

A tap on the passenger's side window grabbed his attention and made him grab his pistol. It was Dee and Fantasy. Sean hit the unlock button. Dee and Fantasy jumped in the truck to get out of the heat. Dee jumped up front while Fantasy jumped in the back right behind him.

Dee gave Sean five and said, "What's good, slim?"

"You." Sean said, still thinking about the conversation he'd just had. He backed the truck out of the parking spot and headed for Georgia Avenue. "Where the nigga gon' be?"

Fantasy spoke up, "Comfort Inn on New York Avenue." she said, texting the joker she was going to meet. "He just text me and said he in room 406. Want me to come right up."

Fantasy had set up a couple of niggaz for Dee since she'd met him. He'd always broke her off real good. At 25 she'd had a rough life in the streets but had learned at an early age that only the strong survive. To her, surviving was doing whatever it took to make ends meet and she did just that. The joker she was setting up this go round was D.C. drug figure by the name of Raymond Moore. Raymond was doing something nice in the drug game, but he was nothing compared to his uncle, Dexter Moore, who was doing life in the feds on RICO charges. Raymond was a vicious freak that loved to spend money on broads, most of which he met in strip clubs. Fantasy was one of the baddest broads to slide through any strip club in the D.C. area. She was one of those broads that brought her own crowd when she came to strip.

Dee looked back at Fantasy and said, "Get in there and do what you gotta' do, don't worry about shit. I'ma take care of everything else."

"Okay," she said. She didn't feel comfortable about the move. She knew how serious Raymond and his people were, however, she didn't want to tell Dee no when he asked her to set the nigga up. Dee was crazy and had instilled some fear in her.

Sean looked back and saw the nervousness in Fantasy's eyes. He could tell she didn't really want to go through with the move. That rubbed him the wrong way. He was a firm believer that if a person's heart wasn't in it then they shouldn't do it. However, he knew that Fantasy had came through many times for Dee in the past few months so he didn't have much to say about the situation. Besides, with all that was going on, Fantasy was the least of his stresses and worries.

Dee could tell what Sean was thinking by the way he looked at Fantasy. Dee said, "Slim, don't worry about her she's a big girl, she gon' take care of business. Trust that."

With a slight sigh and shrug, Sean said, "I'm cool wit' it." *I plan on smokin' the nigga anyway when it's all said and done, she can get it too*, he thought. That thought alone took his mind somewhere else, to something else he had to do.

Dee looked back at Fantasy once again. He could tell she was nervous, but he really didn't care. It was all about him. All that mattered was getting the money up off Raymond by any means. If that meant that Fantasy was to get fucked around in some kind of way then so be it, but he wouldn't let anything happen to her if he could help it. Reaching back, he rubbed her face and said, "Don't worry, I got you."

Yeah, right, muthafucka, she thought, with a quick smile. "I know."

Dee looked at Sean who seemed to be in a daze. "What's on your mind?"

As if Dee could read his thoughts, Sean pushed his thoughts to the back of his mind and said, "Just going over this shit in my head. We gotta make sure we do this shit right, slim."

"Don't we always." Dee smirked. He turned and looked out the window as they made their way down

Georgia Avenue. To be alive and free was a great feeling. At times, Dee wondered why he risked his life and freedom so much, however, at this point in his life those thoughts were too late. He was committed to the streets for life. Nothing was going to change that, except death, as far as he was concerned.

As they rode by Rittenhouse Street, Dee spotted a dude that he and Sean had been locked up with. He tapped Sean on the arm and said, "Ay, slim, ain't that that nigga, Fred right there coming out the liquor store?"

Sean looked back over his shoulder as they flew through the intersection and got a quick glimpse of Fred. "Yeah, that's him."

Fred was a big dope boy they'd done time with in Lee County, Va. He was getting money in the streets as well, moving heroin. While in prison Dee and Sean had extorted Fred for a few thousand dollars.

Dee said, "I heard that nigga told on his connect to give all that time back. What he was workin' wit'? Somethin' like 65?"

"Sixty-six, plus had a case down south somewhere." Sean said. "He getting' it now."

"Yeah, well, we need to see what's good wit' his ass too. He hip to us, he gon' give that change up wit' no problem." Dee said, lighting an Al Capone cigarillo.

As soon as Dee lit the Al Capone Sean cracked the window. "Them joints strong as shit, slim. I don't see how you smoke them joints. I remember when we was in you wouldn't smoke shit."

Dee laughed. "Got a lot on my mind. You know how that goes when everybody wants you dead."

Sean laughed, "You know what they say right ... you're nobody til' somebody kills you."

Dee and Fantasy laughed.

Dee said, "I'm cool wit' bein' a nobody then."

Fantasy said, "Yall niggaz crazy as shit, no bullshit."

Sean said, "That's the way it is, that's the way it's gon' always be in these streets."

Fantasy's phone vibrated. It was a text from Raymond.

Ray: Where u at girl? My dick hard as shit and I need you here to look out for the ole boy.

Fantasy looked around to make sure Dee and Sean weren't paying attention and then hit Raymond back.

Fantasy: I'm on my way, daddy. Don't worry, just have that muthafucka hard when I get there.

She slid the phone back in her purse and looked out the window, still feeling nervous.

Little did she know that Dee was clockin' all of her text messages, every one she sent out and every one that came in went right to his phone. He ain't trust a soul. Looking down at his phone, he nodded. *That's right, baby girl, stroke that nigga for me*, he thought.

Eyone Williams

A short while later, the trio pulled up in the Shell gas station on New York Avenue, right across from the Comfort Inn hotel. Fantasy's heart began to beat faster than normal, her palms began to sweat. As always, Dee and Sean began looking around for anything out of place. They couldn't afford to get caught slippin' in the streets. For them, slippin' was a one-way ticket to that box that got dropped six-feet deep in the dirt.

Dee turned to face Fantasy and said, "You good, right?"

She sighed, "Yeah, I'm good. Just be on top of shit on your end, you know this nigga ain't to be fucked wit'."

"Don't worry, I ain't to be fucked wit', you just do what you do best." Dee said.

"Okay." Fantasy got out the car and headed across New York Avenue, shaking her ass like a stripper.

Sean watched her every step of the way. He wanted to fuck her but had stayed away cause he felt that it was playing it too close even though he knew Dee didn't give a fuck. "Ay, slim, we might as well pull up in the parking lot over there and go up the steps. It's day time, we gon' have to walk the nigga out at gunpoint anyway."

Dee thought about it for a second. He'd been thinking the same thing. They were going to have to go in and take control of the situation as fast and as aggressive as possible in order to pull the move off. If not, shit would get out of hand. Nodding his head, Dee said, "Yeah, you right, slim. Go 'head and pull into the parking lot, we gon' do it that way."

Although Sean was older than Dee by two years, at 33, Dee somehow seemed to be the one who called the shots. It wasn't planned that way it had just evolved into such a situation being as though Dee seemed to always be the one to put their moves together. It was like that even in prison. Nevertheless, Sean was no fool and could think for himself as well. He was no yes-man, if he didn't agree with a move he spoke his mind.

Sean pulled out of the gas station and set the rest of the move in motion.

CHAPTER 2

Fantasy's heart was pounding in her chest. Her mind was racing a mile a minute. Nervously she looked around the hotel lobby as she walked through the sliding doors. Two rough looking dudes passed her on their way out. They had to be in their twenties; they were clearly street niggaz. She wondered if they were down with Raymond. Shaking her head in disbelief as she headed for the elevator, she put her game-face on. *What the fuck am I doing*, she thought, *I'ma fuck around and get myself killed doin' this dumb shit.*

Just as Fantasy got to the elevator the doors opened. She couldn't believe her eye. *Fuck!* She thought. *Now this bitch done seen me here.*

"Girl, what the hell you up to?" Ashley said, smiling at Fantasy as she stepped off the elevator. She and Fantasy stripped at the same clubs from time to time, but they weren't really close, just cool. Ashley was a sexy-ass light-skinned girl that thought she was the shit. "Somebody up in this bitch must got some paper if you up in here."

With a fake smile, Fantasy said, "I'm on a mission, I'm sure you are too, girl. Let me go I'm late. Talk to you later." She stepped on the elevator not waiting for Ashely to respond.

"Be safe." Ashely kept it moving.

Nosey bitch, Fantasy thought, as she hit the button for the fourth floor. *How the fuck am I gon' play this situation?* Running into Ashley really didn't help matters at all. Fantasy didn't need anyone to be able to link her to the Comfort Inn that Raymond was in.

****

Sean and Dee pulled into the parking lot and parked in the back. A silver Benz S 550 was two spaces down from them; the joint was sick—chrome rims and light gray tints. The tags read: Ray Ray. Looking at the tags, Dee thought, *them joints should read: Pay Day.*

Sean checked his pistol, made sure it was ready to go and said, "That's that nigga's ride right there, ain't it?"

"Yeah, that's it. He sittin' on that paper." Dee said as his phone went off. It was his cousin, Tony. Thinking out loud, Dee said, "This nigga Tony keep pressin' me for a move."

"Your cousin?"

"Yeah." Dee said, answering the phone. "What's good, homie?"

"I need to get wit' you. Got some serious shit to holla at you about." Tony said.

"Cool, I'm on a mission right now, I gotta get wit' you later though."

Tony sighed. "Okay, don't bullshit, I really need to holla at you."

"Okay, let me take care of this shit. I will hit you a little later." Dee said, checking his pistol.

"Bet." Tony ended the call.

Sean and Dee looked at each other and a weird awkwardness filled the air for a second. They both brushed it off.

Eyone Williams

Looking over his shoulder, Dee said, "Give it a few minutes and then we gon' go in and take care of this BI."

With a nod of agreement, Sean said, "Sounds good to me."

A few minutes later they were creeping up the stairwell to the fourth floor. They had walked in like it was nothing. No masks at all. They called it: Looking normal. They had made such moves work before.

When they got to the forth floor Dee turned to Sean and whispered, "We gon' move fast. Shorty should already be doin' her thing by now."

"I'm wit' it. Let's do the muthafucka', slim." Sean said, ready to get the ball rolling.

They headed down the empty hallway and stopped in front of room 406. Dee put his ear to the door to hear any sounds inside the hotel room while Sean watched their backs with his pistol out, ready for whatever.

Dee seemed to have his ear to the door for too long. Sean said, "Slim, what the fuck is up?"

"Shhhhh, I don't hear shit."

"Maybe they fuckin', fuck that shit, kick the door open." Sean said.

Dee stepped back and kicked the door open with extreme force. Both men rushed into the hotel room with their burners leveled to tear some shit up. They weren't ready for what they saw next.

"What the fuck?!" Dee said as he checked the bathroom. It was empty.

Sean ran to the window and looked out on New York Avenue to see if there was a sign of Fantasy or Raymond. No such luck.

"Man, I know that bitch ain't play us like that." Dee said in disbelief as he looked around the empty room.

Shaking his head, Sean said, "Let's get the fuck outta here." He headed for the door, not waiting for Dee.

"Shit!" Dee hissed, following behind Sean.

They hit the stairwell like they played special teams for the Washington Redskins. Two and three steps at a time, they dashed down to the first floor. The gig was up. They hit the first floor and bolted through the door like they were shot out of a cannon. They dashed out the front door just in time to see Raymond's Benz fly out of the parking lot and up New York Avenue. Fantasy was riding shotgun. It was clear, she had crossed Dee.

Sliding his pistol back in his waistband, Dee said, "That bitch gon' pay for this, slim, on everything."

Sean shook his head. He didn't feel good about the move from the start. "It is what it is, let's get the fuck out of here." He jogged toward the truck. Dee flowed behind, steaming mad.

****

Looking in his rear view mirror like the police was on his back, Raymond flew up New York Avenue weaving in and out of traffic. He was fucked up that thinking with his dick had almost gotten him caught up. His uncle Dexter always got on him about thinking with his dick; Dexter had told him a number of times that thinking with his dick was going to be the death of him.

Fantasy decided to play a safer card and try to win Raymond's trust by telling him what kind of plans Dee and Sean had for him. She swore that Dee forced her into every part of the plan. Raymond didn't believe a word that came out of a bitch's mouth, but Fantasy made too much sense. As soon as she told him what the deal was they got the fuck out of dodge and hit the back steps. Now Raymond wanted to know everything he could about Dee and Sean's whereabouts. As far as he was concerned, they were dead men. This wasn't the first time their names had come across his desk, so to speak.

Making a right on North Capitol Street, Raymond looked at Fantasy and said, "Where you goin'?"

Surprised, Fantasy said, "I thought I was goin' wit' you."

"Bitch, is you crazy? You ain't goin' wit' me. You must be outta' your muthafuckin' mind." Raymond pulled into the Exxon gas station on North Capitol Street and Florida Avenue. He pulled a few twenty- dollar-bills from his pocket and handed them to Fantasy. "Here, catch a cab."

Fantasy was fired up. "I save your life and this is how you do me?!" she snapped, snatching the money.

Raymond grabbed her by the throat with force in a flash. She gasped for air. "Bitch," he hissed, close enough to her face to kiss her. "I should slit your fuckin' throat for the stunt you tried to pull. You think I don't see through the shit you just did. If you thought you could get away wit' that shit you woulda' went through wit' it. You don't get no points from me for catching cold feet. Now get the fuck outta' me car before I change my fuckin' mind."

She managed to snatch away from him and jump out of the car. "Fuck you, nigga. I hope you die and burn in hell, bitch!" Fantasy took off running.

****

Sean and Dee pulled up in an apartment complex off of Silver Hill Road in Suitland, MD. Dee had a girl he was fucking with that lived in the building and he laid low at her spot from time to time. Dee and Sean were both fucked up that the move to snatch Raymond hadn't gone well. They decided to chill out for a while to regroup. Both agreed that Fantasy had to be dealt with. They would get to that in due time. However, the situation with Raymond was more pressing. They were sure that he would be yet another nigga that wanted them dead now that he knew that they had tried to bring him a move.

With a sigh, Dee looked at Sean and said, "My bad about that bullshit. I—"

"Don't even trip, slim, shit don't go as planned sometimes. We both know that. We'll get that bitch and deal wit' the nigga in due time. Right now we just need to chill for a second, think about another move or somethin'. My pockets hurtin' like shit."

"Bet." Dee gave Sean five.

"You gon' chill over here for a while?"

"Yeah, I ain't goin' nowhere right now. I gotta do some thinkin'." Dee said as he opened the door.

Eyone Williams

"Cool, I'll catch you a little later, I gotta take care of some shit over my baby mother's house."

CHAPTER 3

Dee got out and headed for the building as Sean pulled off. Shaking his head, Dee thought about how deadly the Raymond move could have been. *I'ma kill that bitch soon as I catch her*, he thought.

Dee walked in the building and knocked on the door to apartment 102. It was rented by a female friend of his by the name of Kameron, Kam as he called her. They'd been friends since their teenage years and had tried the relationship thing off and on as well. However, the friendship package worked much better for them.

Kam answered the door in nothing but her pink bra and panties. Her long, black hair was pulled back in a ponytail. She had a sexy glow on her brown skin that came from jogging in the summer sun. With a cute smile spreading across her face, she looked at Dee and said, "I was just thinkin' 'bout your wild ass." Kam headed toward the kitchen, switching like she was on a fashion runway somewhere.

Damn, she phat as shit, Dee thought, *must be the workin' out she doin'*. Dee shut the door behind him and locked the top lock. "You can't be walkin' 'round me like that, girl." He headed to the leather sofa in the living room.

Kam looked over her shoulder with a sly grin and said, "Oh yeah, what's that supposed to mean?"

"You know damn well what it means." Dee said, flopping down on the sofa. "You gon' make a nigga do somethin' big wit' your sexy ass."

With a sigh, Kam said, "You ain't gon' keep comin' over here gettin' in this pussy when you want to."

Dee laughed. "What makes you think that's what I'm over here for?" He grabbed the remote to the huge flat screen.

She stopped in her tracks, walked back in his direction and struck a sexy pose right in his face. "Who wouldn't want to get in this pussy?" she said as she licked her lips.

Even though Dee had a thousand things on his mind, he still looked her up and down with sexual hunger. She always turned him on. He felt himself begin to grow between the legs. "Yeah, I don't know who wouldn't want to get in that pussy either." he said as he reached out and rubbed her sexy thigh.

"You want to get in this pussy?" She licked her lips seductively.

"Yeah, give me a second to think real quick. I got some shit on my mind." Dee said.

"Okay, I'm 'bout to jump in the shower." She strutted to the shower throwing her ass, knowing Dee was looking.

Dee cut the TV on and switched the channel to On Demand videos. He selected Rick Ross' *Blowin' Money Fast* video. As the video came on, Dee's mind

Eyone Williams

was in another zone. Not only did he have to deal with the Raymond/Fantasy situation now, but he still had another mission at hand that he had to take care of and he wasn't sure how he was going to do that. The mission had him feeling uneasy, but he had agreed to it and it was no turning back, as far as he was concerned.

Dee's phone rang. He looked at the name on the screen and sighed. "What's up?"

"Where do you want the money sent?" a deep voice asked.

"How soon can you get it to me?" Dee sat up straight, giving his full attention to the conversation at hand.

"How soon can you take care of your end of the deal?"

"Tonight."

"You sure about that?"

Dee sighed. "Yeah, I'm sure, slim. You know I'm 'bout my work."

"All I know is what I've heard and –"

"And you ain't heard nothin' but the truth." Dee said in a slick tone.

The man with the deep voice laughed and said, "Where do you want the money dropped off? I can have it there in thirty minutes. Just give me a location."

"Popeyes on Silver Hill Road." Dee said, looking at his watch.

"Look for a dark blue Lexus, Virginia tags."

"Bet, I'll be there in thirty minutes." Dee ended the call.

He got up and headed to the bathroom. He opened the door and the hot steam from the shower hit him smack in the face. Through the shower glass he could see Kam's sexy-ass washing her body.

"You just gon' stand there and watch me?" Kam said.

Dee smiled. "Nah, I need to use your car for a second."

"The keys on the nightstand in the bedroom."

"Be right back." Dee shut the door and went to the bedroom to grab the keys to Kam's Lexus.

Moments later Dee was cruising down Silver Hill Road in the Lexus smoking an Al Capone. Scarface was pumping through the speakers. As he turned into the Popeyes parking lot his cell phone went off again. It was a text that Fantasy was sending to someone. *Ain't this a bitch!* He parked the car and looked at his phone again.

Fantasy: I'm over Tangie's house. I need you to come get me.

Donna: I'm out Largo, it's gon' be bout twenty minutes before I get there.

Fantasy: Just hurry up, I need to get out of the city. It's very important, I'll explain when you get here.

Dee had seen all he needed to see. He knew Fantasy's peoples, Tangie. Tangie lived on First Street, in Northwest, D.C. *I got your ass*, Dee thought. Everything inside him made him want to go smoke her ass on the spot, but he had to grab the money that was on the way to him for a job. As long as her text messages came straight to his phone Dee would put her ass in the dirt in no time.

Pistol on his lap, Dee kept his eyes open. Couldn't get caught slippin'. No one was to be trusted in his line of work. He'd seen twin brothers cross each other for the right price. Shit, he'd seen niggaz cross their own mothers for one reason or another. His phone vibrated again. This time it was Sean texting him.

Sean: I got another lick for us. Gotta put a bug in ur ear.

Dee: Cool. I'm wit it. Just holla at me slim.

Sean: Bet.

Dee slid his phone back in his pocket. Sean always had a move of some sort. Dee liked that about his partner in crime. The dirt that they did together kept them dealing with each other. Sean was down to get whoever, he didn't discriminate. Dee was the same way.

Minutes later, a dark blue Lexus with Virginia tags pulled up in the parking lot. A dark-skinned female was behind the wheel. She was looking around as if she was looking for someone. She pulled out a cell phone and made a call. Dee watched her carefully. He looked around to see if anyone was following her. It didn't seem like it.

Dee's phone vibrated. He answered, "Yeah."

A deep voice said, "My peoples are there. Dark blue Lexus."

"I see 'em."

"That's your move right there."

Dee ended the call and got out the car. Carefully, he walked up on the Lexus. He tapped on the passenger's side window. The door was unlocked. He got in slowly.

The female handed him a green backpack and said, "That's ten-thousand. You can count it."

"I'm good." Dee got out of the car without another word. He jumped back into Kam's Lexus and rolled out.

Back at Kam's house Dee counted the money sitting on her sofa. It was ten-thousand on the nose. After the job was done he would get another ten-thousand. *Money gotta be the root of all evil,* he thought, shaking his head.

"Deeeeeee," Kam called from the bedroom. "You gon' come fuck me or am I gon' have to do it myself?"

"I'm bout to give you what you want in one second." Dee stuffed the money back in the backpack and stashed it in the closest. Without another thought he headed to the bedroom. His dick was growing harder with every step he took. It was no doubt in his mind that some good, wet, tight pussy would ease his stress for a second.

Eyone Williams

When he walked in the bedroom Kam was laying in the bed with her legs wide open, playing with her pussy. Low moans escaped from her throat as she moved her mid-section up and down as if she was fucking. Seeing Dee walk in the room, she licked her lips and grabbed her plump breast with her free hand; she rubbed it and squeezed it before pulling it to her mouth and sucking on her nipple.

In her sexiest voice, she said, "Come on, Dee, fuck me, baby. Put that dick in me real good."

"You ain't gotta' ask me twice." Watching her finger herself and suck her own titties made Dee rock-hard as he undressed. When he was fully naked he walked around to the side of the bed and stared down at Kam's sexy-ass body. Tall, dark and lean with an erection at full attention, Dee was just what the doctor ordered for Kam. "Come here, girl." She eased to the edge of the bed. "Yeah, just like that." he said.

Looking up into his eyes as she slid a second finger in her pussy, Kam said, "Let me put it in my mouth." She left her breast alone and grabbed his dick with her soft hand and stroked it a few times, making Dee moan slightly. She licked the tip, still stroking it. He moaned louder. She licked from the balls to the tip of his manhood and back to his balls. The bottom, the sides, the top and back again. She got the whole thing nice and coated with the insides of her wet mouth. Watching his eyes roll back in his head made her pussy gush as she finger fucked herself faster. He put a hand behind her head and helped slide his dick in and out of her mouth. The tip of his dick hit the back of her throat with every thrust. "Ahhhh, shit, girl … ssssshhit."

Eyone Williams

She stopped pleasuring him for a second and looked up into his eyes. "I love this dick, Dee, you fuck the shit outta me? You gon' fuck me good."

"You know it." he pushed his dick back in her mouth. Nothing but wet slurping sounds came from her mouth as she made love with her head game.

Dee pushed her away. He was coming close to cumming. It wasn't time for that, not yet anyway. He climbed in the bed and got between her legs. Using his fingers he pulled her pussy lips apart and licked the inside. Sucked and pulled them. Licked her clit. Held it with his teeth and flicked his tongue up down, driving her crazy, making her squirm and moan.

"Ahh, that's right, eat this pussy, nigga. Uhhhhhhh … mmmmmmhhmmm, don't stop." She grabbed both of her titties and squeezed them. She pulled her hard nipples to her mouth and sucked them feverishly. "Make me cum, make me cum. Ahhhhhh, yeah, don't stop."

Dee stuck his finger inside her as he ate her pussy, sucking, licking, slurping and tasting her juices. She began to grind her pussy against his face and pull his head deeper into her pussy, wanting more of his mouth as he pleased her. Her moans got deeper. He could tell she was about to cum.

"Oh my God!" she screamed as she came all over his face. He kept eating her, sucking on her clit firmly, sliding his finger in and out of her faster and deeper. He loved the way she came for him. Her moans became begging yells. "Ahhhhh … sssssshhhhhit, don't stop, please don't stop!" Her body began to shake uncontrollably as she came with the force of a natural disaster. It was good, running throughout her whole body. She loved the way he made her cum with such ease by using his tongue. He was mean with it.

Raising his head with her cream all over his mouth and chin, he said, "Let me get in that pussy now."

"Fuck me from the back." she said, turning over with the quickness. She couldn't wait for him to enter her.

Dee pulled her ass up just a little and eased in the pussy. Her wetness made it easy, her tightness gripped him like a straightjacket as he stroked her raw. At first he was slow, in and out. As her moans grew louder he began to fuck her faster, getting deeper with every stroke.

"Ahhhhh, yeah, muthafucka, fuck me harder, give me that dick, fuck the shit outta me!" she moaned, throwing the pussy back at him. She could feel him deep in her stomach with every pounding stroke. He smacked her ass. "Sssssssssss, yeah, do that shit again." she moaned. He smacked her ass again. The stinging sensation turned her on, made her feel nasty. Made her feel like he was in control. Dee grunted and moaned as he put his all into it. Sweat began to pour as he went to work on the pussy. "Oh-my-God-you-are-fuckin-the-shit-out-of me!" she moaned her words in unison with his pounding strokes. Her eyes rolled back in her head as she felt another orgasm coming on, it was rushing her way like a speeding train.

Dee felt his nuts begin to tighten and knew that he was about to explode. His stroke got harder and faster as he tried to hold out just a little while longer. "Gggggrrrrhhhhh," he grunted, pulling out and cumming

Eyone Williams

all over her back and ass in thick gobs of semen. "Aaaahhhh, shit, girl." Dee was through, Kam always worked him good.

They both rolled onto their backs, sweaty and breathing hard.

Looking over at Dee, Kam said, "Can you go again?"

He laughed. "Yeah, give me a minute."

CHAPTER 4

Gucci Mane's *Trap House* was pumping throughout Sean's Temple Hills, MD, apartment. He was sitting on his bed counting stacks of money. Nine rows of cash in one-thousand-dollar stacks, wrapped in rubber-bands, sat on the floor in front of him. He was counting his stash. He had a fresh $10,000 to add to his stash now. Minutes earlier he'd met a dude at the Shell gas station down the street from his apartment to pick up the first half of the money he was supposed to be paid for a mission he'd agreed to. Now all he had to do was see the mission through. It was nothing to it but to do it, no matter how he would feel when it was done.

Sean had learned how to block things out of his mind a long time ago. When he was 17 he smoked his mother's boyfriend for smacking her. He had grown close to the boyfriend in a twenty-four month period but when it was time to knock his brains loose Sean didn't think twice about it. He laid in the darkness behind his mother's apartment and caught the boyfriend taking the trash out late at night. Sean shot him in the head five times at point blank range. He got away with the move and never let anyone know he did it. Even his mother had no idea why her boyfriend was murdered. She had forgiven the boyfriend for smacking her days before he was murdered. Needless to say, Sean could keep a secret and block some things out of his mind once he set his mind to something.

Eyone Williams

A short while later, Sean had all of his money in one-thousand-dollar stacks on his bed. Altogether, he was sitting on $67,000. It wasn't enough to live off, but it was something nice to have put up. He threw it all in a gym bag and put it in his closet. Pulling a shoe box off the top shelf, Sean walked back to his bed and took a seat. He pulled a black Glock .45 out of the shoe box. Admiring it, he turned it from side to side in his hand. Also in the shoe box was two 30-shot clips. He popped one clip in the Glock and slid the other in his pocket. There was no time for games, one wrong move and he would be the one in the box.

****

Fantasy was a nervous wreck. She didn't know what to do. She knew Dee would be out to kill her now. Getting out of town was her next move. She had no intentions on running into Dee any time soon. She had her cousin, Donna, pick her up and take her to her apartment in Gaithersburg, MD. She and Donna were close; she told her everything that had went down pertaining to the move with Dee and Sean. Donna thought Fantasy was crazy to get caught up in such a dangerous situation. Fantasy had always been that way.

Standing in the mirror doing her hair, Donna said, "Girl, you ain't gon' be satisfied until you get yourself killed fuckin' wit' them crazy-ass niggaz."

Fantasy sighed, sitting at the desk checking her Facebook account on the computer. "I know. I'm' bout to go down south for a little while, shit too hot up here right now anyway."

"Down south where?"

"Down Atlanta wit' Tammy." Fantasy said, changing her profile picture to a more sexier one where she had on a pink thong and bra.

"I don't know why you wanna' go down there wit' her, she stay in shit, too." Donna shook her head.

"Yeah, I know, but it's better than being up here right now." Fantasy said.

As Fantasy and Donna spoke, Fantasy's cell phone went off. It was her aunt Tamika.

"Hello." Fantasy answered.

"Nadia, have you heard from Tangie?" Tamika asked in a concerned voice.

"No, why, is something wrong?"

"Yeah, she went to the store a little while after you left and ain't came back yet. I been calling her back to back and she won't pick up."

"You know her, she probably runnin' her mouth somewhere." Fantasy said, thinking nothing of the situation.

"No, it's more to it than that, her car is still parked out back, she's not goin' nowhere in this heat without her car." Tamika said.

Eyone Williams

Fantasy thought about it for a second and became worried herself. Her cousin wouldn't walk anywhere in the heat when she had a perfectly good car with AC.

While Fantasy was on the phone, Donna heard someone at the door and went to see who it was. She looked out of the peephole and saw a police officer. Her heart skipped a beat. She had no idea why the police would be knocking at her door. Her first thought was to act like she wasn't home, but then she changed her mind.

She said, "How can I help you?"

"There's been an emergency in the neighborhood, I need to speak to you, miss." the officer said.

"Speak to me about—"

The door flew open with force, knocking Donna to the ground. She screamed in pain from the door slamming into her nose; it had to be broken. Dee stepped inside swiftly and slammed the door behind him. He pointed his 9mm Ruger with the silencer on it at her head and hissed, "Where that bitch, Fantasy, at?"

"I don't know!"

He shot Donna in the head twice at close range, wasting no time with her. Brains and blood stained the white carpet. Dee didn't even blink an eye. He was as cold-blooded as they get. The pistol made no more than a chirping sound when it went off. Quickly, he made his way to the bedroom.

In the bedroom, Fantasy had dropped the phone on the floor with her aunt still on the line. She began to panic when she heard Donna scream. Before she could make a move Dee was standing in the doorway, pistol in his hand smoking. The police uniform surprised Fantasy. Fear froze her in her tracks. Her life began to flash before her eyes. She wanted to scream but she couldn't get it out.

Dee rushed her and grabbed her by her hair. Jamming the pistol against her temple he said, "You thought you was gon' get away wit' crossin' me you little bitch?"

She screamed and went wild. "Please! Let me go! Let me go! Don't kill me, please!" She began swinging, and scratching, and kicking. Anything she could do to fight for her life. It did no good. Yanking her by her hair, Dee smacked her with the pistol and slammed her to the floor. Her screaming seemed to get louder. Dee didn't give a fuck, he came to do one thing and one thing only: Kill her ass.

"Shut the fuck up, bitch!" Dee stomped her in the mouth, kicking her front teeth in. She grabbed her mouth and rolled over. Blood was everywhere. "You's a dumb bitch! You gon' cross me knowin' what the fuck I was gon' do. How dumb could you be?" Dee kicked her in the back with no mercy. The kick sounded off like a bass drum. Standing over her, he fired three hollow tip slugs into her head. Brains went everywhere. Silence, death, and the smell of gunpowder filled the small apartment. Dee looked down at Fantasy and shook his head. He felt nothing, no emotion. He was a cold muthafucka' and he knew it. It was all her fault as far as he was concerned. If she hadn't crossed him she would still be alive, Donna would still be alive, and Tangie would be alive as well.

Dee caught Tangie coming out of her house a short while after Fantasy left. He snatched her and made her tell him where Fantasy was. When he was done with her he shot her in the head and dumped her body in the woods of Rock Creek Park.

Looking at Fantasy's body one last time, Dee frowned and, without a care in the world, left the apartment like everything was normal.

CHAPTER 5

Fantasy's murder was the top story on the nightly news. The Montgomery County Police Department was offering a $10,000 reward for any help in the arrest and conviction of the person who committed the double homicide in a Montgomery County Police uniform.

Sean was sitting in his cousin's living room smoking loud as he watched the news. He knew Fantasy's real name so he was on point as soon as he heard the names of the victims. Blowing smoke in the air, he shook his head. *Damn,* he thought, *that nigga Dee move fast as shit, slim about his business.*

Sitting on the sofa next to Sean was his cousin, Wood. Wood was the younger brother of Sean's older cousin, Day-Day. Day-Day was a street legend that was shot to death outside of a D.C. nightclub. Word on the streets was that Day-Day had $10,000 on his head for robbing a stash-house that belonged to Dexter Moore— the uncle of Raymond Moore. Although Dexter was locked up at the time of the robbery of the stash-house and at the time of Day-Day's murder it was understood that his hand reached far and wide, even from a federal prison.

"Damn, them bitches musta' done some foul shit to get punished like that." Wood said as Sean passed him the Dutch.

Eyone Williams

"No bullshit." Sean said. "Whoever did that shit ain't to be played wit', slim." Sean had seen Dee do far worse shit, he knew for a fact that Dee was a vicious motherfucker, to say the least.

"Fuck this news shit, you tryin' to see me in some Madden?"

Sean looked at his watch. It was 10:47 pm. He said, "Nah, I'll take your money on that Xbox at another time. I got a move to make. It's jive important, I'll get at you a little later, cuzzo."

"That's a bet."

The cousins stood and gave each other some love with some dap and a hug.

Sean hit the road. Focused on what he needed to take care of.

****

Life went on for Dee, sure the murders he'd committed earlier crossed his mind, but it was nothing to it. Less than an hour after the murders he was in Barry Farms smoking weed with his cousin like it was nothing. Barry Farms was in Southeast, D.C., and it was one of the most violent housing projects in the city. Nevertheless, Dee hung out in the Farms like it wasn't shit, even though he was from uptown. It was a plus that he had family in the Farms also.

Eyone Williams

People were outside at night time like it was still noon. Little kids and all, the Farms stayed live. Dee was leaning against a silver BMW 745i with black tints. He was surrounded by his cousin Tony, and few other niggaz from the Farms.

Tony got a phone call and stepped off for a hot second. Dee watched him carefully. Moments later Tony returned and pulled Dee to the side.

"So what's the deal?" Dee asked. He cousin had run across some information about some money being put up for somebody to kill Dee. Death threats were nothing new to Dee, however, if he could find out who the person was that had the money in the streets for his death he was damn sure going to take care of the situation.

"My man can't get me a name right now, but he know you my peoples so he brought the info to me. Slim be takin' money for hits so I know he know what he talkin' bout. It's gon' take a minute for me to get the name though." Tony said.

Dee nodded. "Cool, this is what I want you to do. If you can't get the info from your man for whatever reason I want you to take the hit. Do whatever you gotta do to get to the person."

"I can do that, it's all good."

"How soon can you do that, slim?" Dee asked.

"I can get right on it. Give me a little time, a day or so,"

Eyone Williams

"Cool." Dee looked at his watch. "I gotta' make a move real quick. Hit me when you hear somethin'."

Dee stepped off and jumped in a rented black Charger with tinted windows.

****

Sean was riding up Benning Road in the Northeast section of D.C. He had been trying to catch Dee for a while but Dee wasn't answering the phone. *What the fuck is up with slim?* Stopping at a red light on 17th and Benning Road, Sean put his phone down and pulled a pack of Newports out of his pocket. He lit one just as the light turned green. Making a right on 17th Street he headed to his girlfriend Asia's house which was two blocks away. Checking his mirrors to make sure no one was on his back he pulled up right in front of her apartment and parked. Carefully, he looked around. The street was dark and empty. He called Asia and told her to open the door before getting out. She was pleased to hear that he was right outside and told him to hurry up inside to get in the pussy. Sean smiled and hung up the phone. He grabbed his pistol, checked to make sure it was locked and loaded, and got out of the truck with the burner in hand.

Looking around, always watching his back, he crossed the street. Out of nowhere gun shots rang out, nonstop. He dropped the cigarette and his phone as he dashed behind his truck as bullets slammed into the side and through the windows. His heart raced as he fired

Eyone Williams

back in the direction of the gunfire. All he could see was the flames coming from the weapon. Whoever was shooting at him was coming his way, running. Crouched down, Sean eased back alongside the cars parked behind his truck and kept firing over his head. He couldn't get a good shot but he knew that his gunfire would keep the shooter at bay.

The shooting stopped for a second. Sean wasn't about to stick his head up, he knew what the deal was. He slid between two cars and eased out into the street to get a better look up the street. There was nothing. Police sirens hit the air. *Fuck, the police on the way!* He had to get back to his truck.

Across the street, creeping alongside the parked car, the masked gunman was trying to get a better shot. He decided to ease out into the street. As soon as he did Sean popped up firing, backpedaling with speed towards the alley. The gunman returned fire as he ducked. Shots flew back and forth with thunderous roars.

Two police cars bent the corner with screaming tires, blaring sirens and flashing lights. Officers jumped out and began firing. Sean fired at the closest officer to him as he hit the alley. Bullets flew by his head as he jumped a fence and disappeared into the shadows. The gunman fired shots at the police as well before running through the cut and disappearing into the darkness on the other side of the street, but not before picking up Sean's cell phone.

"Oh my God!" Asia screamed as she watched the gunplay from her window.

Eyone Williams

****

A short while later Sean was in a cab headed up Florida Avenue. He was out of breath, paranoid as shit. He was smoking a cigarette like it was the last one in the world as he tried to calm his nerves. He'd seen death face-to-face once again and walked away alive. Yet and still he was fucked up that he hadn't seen the move coming. He checked his pocket for his cell phone and couldn't find it. *Shit!*

"Where to?" the cab driver asked, for the third time.

"Sixty-four New York Avenue." Sean said, looking over his shoulder to make sure nobody was following him in the cab.

"Okay, sir." The cab driver said.

When they arrived at Sean sister's apartment on New York Avenue he paid the cab driver and jumped out of the cab. Wasting no time, Sean jogged up to the front door and let himself into the building with his own set of keys and quickly made it to his sister's door. He let himself into the apartment and found that she wasn't home. The first thing he did was look out of the window. *That nigga Raymond must've put a nigga on me and Dee that fast. I gotta find that nigga as soon as possible.*

Asia, Sean's girl, crossed his mind. He jumped on the phone and called her.

"Hello." Asia answered the phone sounding worried.

"Is everything okay?" Sean asked.

"Yes, I'm okay. What the hell is goin' on? I saw what happened, are you okay?" Asia was still shaking from the fear of what she'd witnessed.

"Don't worry, I'm good. I need you to calm down, okay, baby?"

"Okay, okay. Where are you?"

"I'm over my sister's house."

"The police are all over the place."

"What they doin'?" Sean asked.

"They searchin' the street."

"Okay, just chill out. I'll holla at you in a minute."

"Are you okay."

"I'm good, I told you that. Let me hit you back. I gotta take care of some shit." Sean ended the call. He sat down and lit another cigarette. Raymond was the only thing on his mind.

He wasted no time calling Dee. The phone rang a few times and then Dee picked up.

"Yeah," Dee said.

"What's good, slim? I been trying to catch you all night."

"I been on a move. Where you at?" Dee asked.

Sean hesitated for a second. For some reason he felt a funny feeling in his gut when Dee asked him where he was. "I'm uptown over this little bitch house. I need to holla at you, homes."

Dee picked up on the hesitation. "Over a bitch house?"

"Yeah. Ay, look though, a nigga just tried to bring me a move. I think the nigga Raymond already put a nigga on us."

"Maybe, fuck it. It is what it is. You know how shit go." Dee said.

"We need to get at slim as soon as possible, we can't be playing wit' his ass."

"I'm hip. I'm already on it. You know that."

"Meet me at the Exxon on Florida Avenue as soon as you can." Sean said.

"Cool. I'll be there in bout fifteen minutes."

"See you then." Sean hung up the phone. He sat in deep thought for a second. Shit was hitting too close to home. For the first time in a long time Sean felt as though he needed a break. Ducking death was becoming a full-time job. However, business had to be taken care of first.

CHAPTER 6

Dee sat on the sofa in Kam's living room with a thousand things on his mind. His pistol sat on the coffee table along with a ski mask. In his hand was a cell phone that he was going through. One number caught his attention: 703-723-3399. He wondered why the number was in the cell phone. It was time to stop playing games and get down to business.

Dee's cell phone went off. The call was from: 703-723-3399.

"Yeah," Dee answered.

"What's the latest on your end?" a deep voice asked.

"Shit is under control. Just make sure you have my money right. Feel me?"

"Do the job and money is not a thing. Don't get cold feet."

"Cold feet ain't my forte. I'll call you when it's done." Dee ended the call.

Seconds later, the other cell phone Dee was holding went off. It was the same 703 number. Dee let it ring. Thoughts of all kinds of snake shit went through his mind. No one could be trusted in the streets as far as Dee was concerned. Not even him.

Out of the blue, Dee had been contacted for a murder for hire job. At first he turned the job down, he couldn't see himself doing it. Someone wanted Sean dead and that someone was willing to pay $20,000 for the murder. However, Dee changed his mind about taking the job when he was able to listen to a recorded conversation between Sean and an unknown individual where Sean was placing the blame for two murders on Dee. The two murders were murders Sean had committed alone. Sean had crossed him, it was no getting around it.

Shit was in full swing at this point. Dee had tried to hit Sean in front of his girl's house and had missed, he hadn't expected Sean to be ready

At the moment, Dee wondered why the same number that was calling him was calling Sean's phone as well. He also had to wonder if Sean was hip to the fact that he was trying to kill Sean. As he thought about it he pushed it out of his mind. He knew Sean, so he thought, and if Sean knew he was trying to kill him Sean wouldn't play a bunch of secret games about it.

Nevertheless, it was the moment of truth. Dee popped another clip into his pistol and headed out the door.

****

Sean was through playing. It was about to go down. He planned to kill Dee, get it over with, collect the rest of the money he was owed, and then find and kill Raymond. In that order.

Eyone Williams

For Sean, the decision to kill Dee wasn't hard at all. When presented with reliable information that Dee was the actual shooter in the murder of his cousin Day-Day, Sean agreed to kill Dee. All that was left to do was pull the trigger.

Sean walked the short distance from New York Avenue to Florida Avenue to meet Dee at the Exxon gas station. He scoped out the gas station carefully. A few people were inside; three cars were outside—a black Charger with tinted windows, a blue Nissan Maxima, and a Silver Ford F-150. He stopped at a pay phone across the street to call him. For some reason Sean was nervous, something just didn't feel right. In his mind, Dee had no idea what was coming, yet and still Sean was nervous and he couldn't understand why. He got butterflies in his stomach. That was a feeling he hadn't felt in years. Normally he was cold as ice when it was time to put in work. Nevertheless, he shook the feeling off and called Dee.

"What's up, slim? Where you at?" Dee answered.

"I'm at the Exxon. Where you at?"

"I'm at the Exxon, I'm in the black Charger."

"Oh, I see you. Here I come." Sean said. He hung up the phone and headed across a busy North Capitol Street. His heart beat faster with every step he took. As he approached the Charger he couldn't see inside due to the dark tints. He walked up on the driver's side of the car slowly. Easing his pistol out, he wasted no time. He opened fire and let five shot go into the driver's side window. The gunshots sounded off like cannon blasts. Brains and blood flew all over the windshield. Sean couldn't believe his eyes. It was a woman inside. He was in shock. He couldn't believe he'd hit the wrong person. Bystanders panicked and scattered. Cars pulled off with screaming tires.

Out of nowhere, Dee appeared in a ski mask and ran toward Sean firing shots. The first few shots hit Sean in the back, dropping him. He never saw it coming. Dee ran over top of him and fired two more shots into the back of his head. For a split second, Dee looked down at Sean's lifeless body and felt something close to remorse. *Fuck it.*

Dee had gotten out of the car and hid behind the Dumpster when he pulled up at the gas station to see how Sean would approach the car. He never thought the situation would go down in such a way. He had cost Kam her life.

An off-duty police was inside the gas station. He came out with his pistol drawn and yelled for Dee to freeze. In a flash, Dee turned and aimed his pistol at the officer. Shots went off again. Bullets tore through Dee's chest, knocking him backward as he continued to pull the trigger. Slugs from Dee's pistol hit the officer in the vest that he was wearing. More shots flew. The gunfight had turned the gas station into a war zone. Dee hit the ground lifelessly, pistol in hand. He took one last breath as his eyes rolled back in his head.

****

A week later, Dexter Moore was sitting in the visiting hall of the United States Penitentiary, Lee County. He was talking business with his nephew, Raymond.

Dexter said, "I told you not to worry about Dee and Sean. I had a cake baked for them all along. I never thought it would go down like that, but fuck it. I couldn't have planned it that well if I tried to."

Raymond smiled.

Dexter had hatched the plan for Dee and Sean to kill each other weeks prior. They both had crossed him one too many times by robbing members of his drug organization. He figured if they were trying to kill each other that one would succeed and then he would just have someone else kill the other. That would be the end of them. However, fate took things into its own hands and ridded Dexter of both of his problems at once.

With an admiring nod, Raymond looked at his uncle and said, "It's chess, not checkers."

Dexter nodded. "That's right, it's chess, not checkers. All you gotta do is out think these niggaz and fate will do the rest. That's how this shit goes. Don't play wit' them niggaz. You see how I carry shit. A nigga got one time to cross me and that's his ass."

Hazel Eyes

Pinky Dior

Chapter 1
Half job

Danita just put her two girls to sleep, as if they were still babies. Every night before she went out to do a mission or went to sleep, she would always kiss them goodnight and turn off their bedroom light. Before walking out of their room she quickly turned around in her tracks and smiled as her eyes wandered from both of her daughters, Hazel and Hazee. She stared at Hazel who's hair was a bright blonde and flowed down both sides of her caramel complexion face as she layed on her back. She looked over at Hazee whose hair was jet black just like hers, but pulled back into a ponytail. Hazel was her oldest daughter, she was eighteen. Her youngest daughter Hazee was sixteen years old. She sighed in relief as she entered the hall way, closing the door behind her. She ran her fingers through her thick jet black hair which was straightened; she headed back to her bedroom to grab her black addidas duffle bag. She was already dressed to go out to do a mission for her boss, Dinero. She tossed the bag over her shoulders and then removed her long hair that was caught underneath the black straps.

As Danita headed down the hall there was a loud, obnoxious knock on her apartment door. She was startled as she jumped back; slowly she walked over to the door. She looked through the peephole and noticed it was Dinero. He didn't look too happy. Danita unlocked the bottom lock, then the top lock. She didn't even get a chance to open the front door before Dinero had pushed the door wide open. Danita quickly backed up so the door wouldn't hit her, she was struggling to maintain her balance. Dinero quickly grabbed her by the neck with a tight grip, pulling her close to him. His grip was taking her breath away, making her feel faint. He lifted up her entire body with his hand. Her pink heels kicked back and forth as her feet left the ground. The heavy duffle bag she wore on her shoulder dropped to the ground. She grabbed and scratched at his hands as she tried to get him to release the tight grip which he had around her neck, almost cutting off all of her breathing.

"You fucking stupid bitch!" he retorted. "You didn't even fucking kill him!"

Danita's eyes got so big you could see her vessels popping out. Tears formed in her eyes. She couldn't breathe. He quickly released the tight grip from around her neck as her petite body fell to the floor. She coughed loudly as she grabbed at her neck and rubbed it, trying to sooth the damage he'd just caused. Danita breathed heavily in and out as she tried to catch her breath. She slowly lifted her eyes up and looked at Dinero. He now had his gun pointed directly at her head.

"Why are you doing this?" Danita uttered, still trying to catch her breath.

"You know why bitch?" He smacked her in the face causing blood to trickle down the side of her mouth.

"Because you didn't kill him!" he barked.

Danita held the side of her face as she stared at her white carpet which now was stained with blood. She slowly looked up from the stained carpet into Dinero's eyes. He was steaming mad, if looks could kill Danita would have been dead two times over.

"I ... I killed him." Danita assured him. "I ... I saw him on the floor with multiple gun shots to the chest ... he's dead."

"He's not fucking dead Danita!" he yelled, shaking his head. He looked at her with a murderous look. She tried to pull her duffle bag close to her body. He cocked the gun and pointed it at her head. "Don't you fucking move." Slowly, he kneeled down beside her and unzipped the duffle bag. He reached inside and removed her loaded gun. He removed a thick rope as well. Getting up, he grabbed her hands and tied them behind her back. Danita screwed up her face and a soft moan escaped through her parted lips as he tightening the knot around her wrist. He slowly walked around her and stared her into eyes.

"Dinero ... I sware I killed him ... he wasn't breathing." Danita sniffled as snot started to creep from her small nostrils.

"He's still fucking alive!" he barked. "What the fuck else am I going to tell you? I gave you a mission to kill this motherfucker and you half kill him, you did a half fucking job and I don't accept half fucking jobs! That motherfucker is after my head now, because I sent one of my best fucking hit women to kill this stupid bastard! And you fucked up this one ... real bad and now you have to pay Danita ... I'm sorry." He held his finger on the trigger and Danita started crying out, praying to God in Spanish. She knew she was about to die. He was about to pull the trigger until he heard something in the hallway and looked up
****

Pinky Dior

Hazel layed on her back with her hands folded across her flat stomach. Her eyes were wide open when she heard her mother's tiny voice from the hallway. It was mixed with tears and loud outbursts. Hazel pulled the covers back from her body as she looked over to make sure her little sister was asleep. She slowly walked to the door and opened it. She stepped out into the hallway and tip-toed down the hall. She stopped in her tracks as she stood in the middle of the corridors of her mother's apartment. As she stood from a distance and watched her mother sitting on her knees with her hands tied behind her back with a thick rope around her petite wrist. Hazel looked up from her mother and brought her eyes to Dinero, Dinero's eyes were no longer focused on Danita, they were locked on Hazel. Her mother noticed he wasn't looking at her, she slowly looked back over her shoulder and wished her daughter would have never came out of her room. Dinero motioned with his four fingers for Hazel to come in the living room. Hazel hesitantly walked down the hall entering the living room. She noticed her mother had blood trickling from the inside of her mouth down to the bottom of her jaw. Her silky smooth hair was no longer straight and neat, it was now dishelved and out of its normal place.

"Come here Hazel." he said in a demanding, but calm tone. Hazel nervously walked over to Dinero, who was supposedly her stepfather. That's what her mother told her but it was all a lie, Dinero was her mother's boss. Hazel stood in front of Dinero as he slowly turned her body towards her mother. She held back the tears as she removed strands of blonde hair from her face and placed it behind her ear. She knew her mother was in some type of trouble, she was baffled about why her mother was on her knees and tied up with blood on the side of her face. She had never seen Dinero being violent toward her mother or anything of that sort. He always showered her and Hazee with expensive gifts, such as diamond earrings with the matching necklace and bracelet.

Dinero gently grabbed her right hand. Hazel looked down and noticed he was placing a gun in her hand. He squeezed her hands on the gun as she gripped it into her hand. Dinero had his hands on both of her hands which contained the gun and he brought up her hands and pointed it at her mother. Hazel gulped down hard as sweat formed on her forehead and started to drip down her face within seconds.

"Shoot her!" Dinero said calmly, as he let go of her hands. Hazel stood there with the gun in her hand. Her hands were shaking and trembling with fear. She stood there with a blank expression on her face as she stared at her mother. She didn't know what her mother had done, but whatever it was she didn't deserve to die for it, as far as Hazel was concerned.

"Please, Dinero, don't do this." Danita begged him.

"I said shoot her!" he raised his tone. "If you don't I will kill Hazee."

Hazel couldn't believe he was giving her such an ultimatum. *Danita or Hazel?* She loved both of them and didn't want them to die, but she didn't have a choice.

"Just shoot me." Danita sniffled, as the tears crept down her cheeks.

"Mama why—" Hazel was cut off by her mother's loud tone.

"I said shoot me!" she stared her daughter in the eyes. "I'd rather you and your sister live than me live with the burden of this sick bastard killing my daughter." She eyed Dinero, he had a devilish smirk on his face. "I love you Hazel."

"I love you too, ma." Hazel hesitantly placed her finger on the trigger, slowly pulling back on it. "I'm sorry, ma."

"Don't be." her mother cracked a smile and closed her eyes. She didn't want to see her daughter pull the trigger and kill her. A tear crept down her cheek as she hesitantly pulled back the trigger, sending a single bullet through her mother's forehead. Her fingers started trembling as she dropped the gun to the floor and fell to her knees as she took her mother into her arms.

"What did I do?" Hazel cried out as she looked down and saw blood rushing from the bullet wound in her mother's head. She had killed her mother. God would never forgive her for what she'd done, as far as she was concerned. She looked up and saw her younger sister, Hazee, standing a couple of feet away from them as she stood there in shock. Hazel didn't want to be the one to tell her that she'd killed her mother. Hazel wished she could go back in time, she also wished she could have turned around when he placed the gun in her hand and killed Dinero when she had the chance. Hazel knew she wouldn't be proud of killing someone, but it would have been better if she had killed him instead of her beautiful mother. She knew she didn't have a choice to kill her mother. Dinero would have killed Hazee. He

Pinky Dior

probably would have killed all three of them just because they didn't follow his orders.

Hazel looked down at her mother, her mother's eyes were wide open in a blank stare. Her black hair that was drenched in her own blood stuck to her head as if she had dyed her hair a different color. There was blood all over the carpet and all over Hazel's white t shirt. She rocked her mother back and fourth in her arms and looked up at Dinero with a hateful look in her tear-filled hazel eyes. She wanted to go hard and attack Dinero. He looked as if he didn't have a care in the world that Danita was dead. He had a look in his eyes that said he loved watching someone die. If he could taste her mother's blood he would probably enjoy its savor. Hazel knew that her life from that day on would never be the same, she felt like she was a cold-hearted monster.

Chapter 2
Laid to rest

Hazel couldn't believe her mother was gone. She blamed herself and told herself it was all her fault. She couldn't blame anybody else. She could have turned the gun on Dinero, but she couldn't think straight. It had been a couple of days since she killed her mother. She stood in front of the vanity mirror as she sucked in her full lips, tears streamed down the side of her face that was so red from all the crying and wiping she'd been doing. Hazel turned away from the mirror, she hated seeing her reflection. She wished she could get a pair of scissors and just end her life, but she had to live for her little sister. There was a slight knock on her door, she didn't even respond. Hazee walked in and walked over to Hazel.

"Are you going to mama's funeral?" Hazee questioned.

"No I can't sis ... I can't show my face." Hazel said as she shook her head side to side. Hazee didn't know what that meant, she wondered why her sister didn't want to go, but she didn't bother asking. She just consoled her sister who was hurting badly.

"Sis, everything is going to be alright." Hazee tried to assure her sister.

"Nooo ... she's gone." Hazel broke down into tears, "It's my entire fault." Hazel admitted, but she had lied and told Hazee last night that her mother was murdered by an intruder. She felt bad lying to her little sister, but she had no choice because she knew Hazee

Pinky Dior

wouldn't understand and would hate her for life. Dinero walked in and gave Hazee a quick glance, he had an intimidating look in his eyes. Hazee hugged Hazel and kissed her on her cheek. "I love you sis." Hazee said before exiting the room. She avoided eye contact with Dinero as she exited the room and went back into her room. Dinero closed the door behind him and walked over to Hazel.

"Are you okay?" He lifted up her chin. Hazel looked up at him with her nose flared up, she had hatred in her eyes.

"Does it look like I'm okay?" Hazel shot back as she stared him in the eyes.

"No, that's why I'm asking you." He smirked. "What's wrong?"

"My mother is dead … because of you." Hazel held back the tears as she jerked her head back, she felt her words getting choked up.

"No your mother's dead because of you." he said smartly. "You pulled the trigger," he pointed his finger at her, "Not me." he said before walking away, closing the door behind him.

"FUCK YOU!" Hazel screamed as she threw the chair at the door. She scrunched up her face, with her nostrils wide and flared. She stared at the door as she breathed in and out heavily. With tears streaming down her face. She was disappointed in herself and really wanted to go to her mother's funeral but she couldn't even go because she felt guilty and felt it would be best if she didn't. So she stayed home, blaming herself.

Sitting in her chair, Hazel stared out the window as the rain poured down and splattered all over her bedroom window. Tears streamed down her face, all she could think of was her mother, Danita. She was upset with the fact that she didn't go to her mother's funeral, but she knew God wouldn't forgive her so why go? She stayed in the house for a week straight without talking to Dinero or her little sister. She just didn't understand how Dinero could shower her and her little sister Hazee with expensive gifts and show them so much love, but still force her to kill her own mother. She was baffled as to why he wanted to kill her mother. She wanted to ask him why he made her do it, but she felt as if he wouldn't tell her the truth. Hazel dazed off as she stared out the window and didn't hear Dinero walk in. He stood behind her and caressed her neck. Hazel breathed in as she closed her eyes and opened them back up. He then moved down her chest grabbing her full sized breasts and caressed them. Hazel calmly removed his hands and got up from the chair, she stood in front of the wall and looked him in the eye. He inched in closer to her as he touched the side of her face and caressed it. Her nose flared up as she jerked her head back from his touch that sent chills down her spine.

"I want you Hazel." he whispered seductively. "I've wanted you since you was a little girl ... I need you." he cooed as he stepped in closer, she tried to back up but she couldn't go anywhere, her back was pressed up against the wall. He kissed her on her neck as he grabbed her vagina through her spandex jeans.

"Please don't do this." Hazel begged, as she tried to fight back. But then again she loved the way he found the way inside of her pants and started rubbing her clit through her pink fabric. She bit on the bottom of her lip as her body trembled with fear.

"You know you like this." He kissed her neck, using a little bit of his tongue, kissing it slowly, making Hazel get wet. Hazel always had a thing for Dinero, but she knew that her mother wouldn't approve. He was supposedly their step father, but the relationship that her mother had shared with Dinero was nowhere near a relationship. He never stayed the night, they never slept together or anything of that nature. He was forty years old, but he looked as if he was somewhere in his late twenties. He had a pretty caramel complexion with curly hair and full lips along with a muscular body. Hazel and Hazee used to joke about how he looked and they both had crushes on him when they were younger. Dinero lifted up her chin as Hazel hesitantly stared in his eyes, he inched in closer and pressed his full thick lips up against hers parting her lips with his tongue. Now wet and horny, Hazel threw her arms around his neck as she wrapped her legs around his waist and passionately kissed him. She didn't know what she was doing, but his touches and kisses were irresistible. He gently laid her on the bed as he ripped off her clothes within a matter of seconds. He then took off all his clothes just as fast.
Hazel looked up at the ceiling as she felt his big dick slip into her tight pussy, filling her to the limit. She moaned as she felt him going in deeper and deeper. She loved it but at the same time she was resisting it as well. She had to, she wanted to hate this man.

"Take your shirt off." he demanded. Hazel was going to reply no but the look in his eyes told her she better do it. She slowly pulled her shirt over her head and tossed it on the bed. She felt her body shaking.

Goose bumps covered her body as she squeezed the sheets on her mother's bed. He grabbed her breasts and pushed them close together and ran his tongue across her nipples, teasing her. Hazel let out a soft moan as she bit on the bottom of her lip; Dinero continued to sex her but rougher than before. Hazel wished she could go back in time, because she knew for a fact she wouldn't be in her mother's bed, especially having sex with the man who made her kill her own mother. A tear slid down her cheek as he sped up his pace. Feeling himself about to explode, Dinero pulled out his manhood and let his semen shoot out the tip of his dick all over her stomach. Hazel rolled over and sat up on the bed grabbing a towel off the floor. She wiped Dinero's cum from between her legs; everything about the situation made her feel worthless and ashamed of being in her body.

How could I have sex with this man? The man who brought me and my sister presents? The man who was supposed to be my step father? The man who made me kill my own mother? Why am I doing this? Hazel thought to herself as tears formed in her eyes.

"What are you doing?" Hazel blurted out as tears blurred her vision. "What do you want from me? What is it that you want?" she said repeatedly, never thinking that she was asking the same questions.

"I need a favor." he said. "Well it's not really a favor. It's a demand." He chuckled at his comment. "See your mother worked for me." he said as he got up and pulled on his pants. Hazel didn't understand what he was getting at. She stared at him with a confused look on her face.

"What do you mean my mother worked for you?" she asked.

"She worked for me, your mother was a hit woman." he informed her. "I give her a mission and she would go kill a person and get paid. She was good at it, too, one of the best I've seen in many years."

"So what do I have to do with this?"

"Everything," he smiled. "Now that your mother is dead it's your responsibility to take her job and finish it."

"Yeah, just like it was my responsibility to kill my own mother?" she asked sarcastically.

"You pulled the trigger." he said shrugging his shoulders. "Anyway this man is to be dead before twelve o clock and I want it done. No matter what it takes!" he said as he tossed a piece of paper on the bed. Hazel picked up the piece of paper and saw that she was to kill a dude by the name of Vice. Also on the paper was the location of where she was to find Vice.

"It's fifty thousand if you finish the job...If you don't...then you're dead." He grinned as he tossed the gun on the bed, it landed next to Hazel's lap.

"If I was you I wouldn't leave town, your mother owes me and it's up to you to finish the job." he said. "Plus it's not like it's your first body." He winked at her as he left her alone in the room with the gun in her hand and the piece of paper that determined if she lived or died.

Pinky Dior

Hazel sat in the car as Dinero's driver pulled up in front of the Boston Park Plaza Hotel. The driver gave her instructions and she told him that the man was expecting company already but he had worked plans out to have a stripper for his birthday. He told her he would give her ten thousand while he got Hazel to finish the job. She agreed and took the ten thousand dollars and stayed as far away from Vice as she could. Hazel was nervous as she stepped out the car with her six inch heels clicking across the concrete. When she approached the hotel the double doors slid open as she walked in clutching a bag close to her side. She smiled at people who looked at her and the man who admired the way she was wearing a long trench coat, showing off her sexy legs. She pressed the elevator button as she stared up and watched the numbers as they dropped, getting closer to the lobby. Once the elevator doors open, she quickly got in and pressed the button for the door to close.

Arriving on the sixteenth floor, she headed for the presidential suite. Hazel pulled the coat closer to her body as she looked around and was amazed at the beautiful hotel surroundings. She had never been in such a hotel before. She walked down the hall and looked for number 564. Hazel gulped down hard as she knocked on the door. She waited for Vice to open the door. When he opened the door he noticed that it was a different stripper. Vice was a short, chubby Italian guy with a little bit of hair on his head. He was wearing a robe, holding a glass of champagne in his hand.

"They didn't tell me they were sending a different stripper." he said. "What the hell with it?" He shrugged his shoulders as he motioned for her to come in.

Pinky Dior

Hazel stepped in the room and looked around. She placed her bag on the chair as she unbuttoned her coat and dropped it to the floor. Vice bit down on the bottom of his lips and looked Hazel up and down admiring everything about her. She was dressed in a pretty purple baby doll gown from Victoria's Secrets that was transparent.

"Damn girl you look good." he said as he sipped on his glass of champagne.
"You look better than the last bitch they sent."

Hazel rolled her eyes as she turned around and smiled.

"So you ready to get down to business?" she questioned.

"Hell yeah I'm ready to get down and dirty." he chuckled. Hazel's eyes widened as she cracked a smile, shaking her head.
"Let me use the bathroom real quick." he said as he put his glass on the table and gave her one last seductive look before heading into the bathroom.

Once the door was closed and locked, Hazel quickly removed the gun from her bag as she walked over to the bed and slipped it under the pillow. She patted down the pillows, making sure they looked untouched. She quickly turned around when she heard the bathroom door open and he emerged from the bathroom wearing nothing. Hazel wanted to laugh so badly, but this wasn't a laughing matter. Vice was a chubby man with a huge gut and nasty-looking chest hair. Hazel gulped down hard as he walked over to her and stared her in the eyes.

Pinky Dior

"You ready for this?" he asked, grabbing his dick that was so little and disgusting looking. Hazel scrunched up her face as she looked away and put on a pretend smile.

"I was born ready." she said.

Vice crawled into the bed as he got under the covers and waited for Hazel to join him. Hazel knew she had to kill him before she even got a chance to spread her legs. There was no way that she was having sex with him. Hazel climbed into the bed and sat on top of him, placing her legs on the outside of his. She bent down as she kissed him on his neck, she then reached under the pillow and grabbed the gun, but she let go of the gun because he kept grabbing her hand. He let out a soft moan as she licked his neck, making him hard. Hazel rolled her eyes as she easily slipped her hands from his hands and grabbed the gun. She pointed it at him as he dropped his mouth wide open in shock, his eyes were bulged out. Hazel cocked back the gun and shot him once in the forehead just to make sure the job was done, she shot him in the chest several more times. She couldn't afford to fuck the mission up, if so she knew she would be the next to die.

Hazel didn't even stay to watch for his last breath, she grabbed her bag and quickly got out of there as fast as she could. She rushed down the hall and pressed the button to wait for the elevator. She hopped in the elevator and pressed for the lobby. She impatiently tapped her foot on the floor. She couldn't wait to get as far away from the hotel as possible. She avoided making eye contact with people who entered the lobby, but she kept a pleasant smile on her face. She didn't want to seem nervous or look out of the ordinary. Hazel quickly walked through the double doors as they slid open and there was Dinero waiting for her. She opened the car door and hopped in.

"That was quick." he stated, not believing it was done that quick. "Ten minutes?" He looked at his Rolex that was shining on his right arm.

"It's finished." Hazel said bluntly, as she turned her head and extended out her hand, "Where's my money?"

"You'll have it tomorrow evening." he assured her. "I will pick you up tomorrow so we can go out to eat and talk." he said. Hazel didn't know what kind of games he was playing, but if he didn't have her fifty G's by tomorrow he would end up being the target.

Chapter 3
My first love

Soft merengue music filled the exquisite 5 star restaurant located in downtown Boston as Hazel made her way through the restaurant. She stopped in her tracks as she stood up on her tippy toes increasing a line in her Prada heels, scanning the restaurant for Dinero. She noticed him in the back of the restaurant sitting at a table. The lighting was low, smoke surrounded him. You could only see the black hat he was wearing and a face behind it. But she knew it was him because he put up his index finger and slowly put it down once he saw her walking towards him.

She clutched onto her Prada bag as her heels clicked down the brown shiny marble floors. Hazel slid into the booth as she looked up at Dinero who was smoking a cigar. Dinero admired her and he wanted her so bad. Her beautiful long blonde hair fell down the side of her face and had bouncy curls on the bottom of her hair. Hazel was reluctant to meet with Dinero because she'd already finished her mission and didn't want anything else to do with him after that, but of course she needed her money.

"Hello Dinero," Hazel said nonchalantly.

"Misses Cruz," A wicked smile appeared across her face.

"It's Hazel." she corrected him. She hated being called by her last name. He just stared at her, admiring her beautiful caramel complexion that was flawless, then he looked down to her thick lips wondering how it would feel if she performed oral sex on him with her sexy lips. Hazel rolled her eyes, she was getting agitated with the silence and him staring at her.

"You got my money?" she questioned, staring him directly in his eyes.

"Oh of course I do." he smirked. "I was just admiring how beautiful you are, you look just like your mother." he said as she rolled her eyes again at him. He stuck his hand into his jacket, pulled out a huge white envelope, and slid it across the table. Hazel grabbed the envelope and opened it.

"It's all there." he winked with a smirk on his face.

Hazel looked inside and saw it was all stacks filled with hundred-dollar-bills.
"Yeah it better be." she said rhetorical, "or I might have to put a hit out on you." she winked back at him in return, as she halfway smiled.

"Oh I like that!" He bit on the bottom of his lip. "I love a woman who takes charge, that your mother did, but the last mission she couldn't do, and since you came along you handled your business...well your mother's business as she should've."

Hazel grilled him with her nose flared, biting her tongue, holding back her words.

"Anyway, I got another job for you to do." he said without asking her.

Hazel chuckled.

"I'm all set here, I'm through, I got my fifty thousand, now you leave me and my sister the hell alone." Hazel snatched her purse up from the table. As she got up to leave Dinero grabbed her arm. She looked back at him with a deadly look, staring him in the eyes.

"Sit your ass back down!" he demanded through gritted teeth. He noticed he was a tad bit loud. He looked around and noticed people staring at him with weird looks on their faces.

"Come on honey sit down, I'm not ready to go yet." He toned his voice down and smiled as he turned his attention back to Hazel.

She looked back at him as she snatched her arm away from his grip and noticed he had flashed a gun that was inside his coat. Hazel plopped back down into the booth as she waved her hand and pursed her lips together.

"What do you want?" her heavy Spanish accent kicked in as she leaned back against the cushion of the seat.

"I have a mission for you." he said.
"Here ..., let me pour you a glass of wine to get you a little loosened up." Dinero insisted as he grabbed the bottle of red wine and poured it into her glass.

Hazel rolled her eyes, she couldn't believe what he was trying to pull.

Pinky Dior

"And what's that?" she grabbed the glass of wine and brought it up to her full glossed lips and savored the taste or red wine.

"My mission is done."

"Well I'm offering you double this time." Hazel chuckled. However, Dinero was serious.

"A hundred thousand?" her eyebrows shot up and her lips pursed together.

"Yes a hundred thousand dollars, you can move you and your little sister up out the hood…for good." he snarled.

"So who is this guy you want me to kill?" she asked calmly.

"I want this guy dead! He owes me a lot of money and I want him dead." he barked.

Hazel gulped down hard as she saw the hatred in his eyes. If looks could kill she would have rolled over and been dead by now. She could tell that he wanted whoever it was dead, just by the look on his face. He slid her a piece of paper across the table. Hazel picked up the piece of paper and slowly opened it. As soon as she read the name on the note her heart began to pound in her chest. She couldn't believe it. It was her first boyfriend, Antonio. She held back the tears as she excused herself from the chair and walked into the bathroom. She placed both hands on the side of her face as she stared into the mirror, tears started to fall. She couldn't believe it was her first love, Antonio, that Dinero wanted dead. She didn't know if he knew who he was and how much he meant to her, he probably wouldn't even care, and if he found out they knew each other he would probably kill her. But on the other hand she hated Antonio for leaving her for another woman and having a baby.

Hazel wiped away her tears as she pulled herself together and headed back to the table wearing a smile on her face. Dinero smiled and watched her as she sat down, trying to get a look at her ass before she sat.

"I'm in." she said nonchalantly.

"Good, I'm giving you a day to handle this."

"One day?" she questioned.

"What do you need? Longer?" he asked with a questionable brow.

"No, no." she smiled.
"All I have to do is make one simple phone call." she smirked. She knew all she had to do was call him and ask for him to meet her somewhere, but she knew she wouldn't be able to just kill Antonio. She needed time to plan it out, especially with him. And she wanted him to die slowly.

"Alright one day it is." he said before getting up and walking away.

Hazel sat there, looking straight ahead in a daze. She brought the glass of wine up to her face as a tear slid down on her face. Hazel didn't want to continue to kill people and do missions for Dinero. But a hundred-thousand dollars kept popping up in her head, and it was an offer she couldn't turn down.

After dinner, Hazel arrived home and headed straight to her mother's bedroom. She sat on the edge of the bed as she flipped open her cell phone and went straight to the contacts. She looked for her ex-boyfriend Antonio's phone number and when she came across his name her heart dropped and old memories began to resurface. She tried to hold back the tears that were forming in her eyes. She hated him for the fact that he left her for some other chick, and when she was sixteen he made her get an abortion. Antonio was her first love, her first boyfriend, they even shared their first kiss together. Hazel hadn't been able to talk to another guy since her and Antonio broke up. He tried calling her a couple of times after she found out he was cheating, but she was tired of his ways and didn't want to be a part of that anymore.

She pressed the green button, to dial his number as she slowly pressed the phone against her ear and waited for him to pick up. She nervously tapped her foot on the floor. She hadn't talked to him since she was seventeen years old, and that was a year ago. Her heart pounded faster when he picked up the phone.

"Hello?" Antonio answered, sounding sexy.

"Umm...hey Antonio," Hazel smiled, "It's me Hazel."

"Of course, aint nothing changed I still got your number locked in my phone, waiting for the day you would call me...I missed you too."

"Well that's why I was calling, because I miss you." She lied, but deep down inside she still had love for him.

"Aww how sweet, do you still have love for your boy?" He chuckled.

"Please boy," Hazel blushed, "Don't push it."

"Well what's up then? Are you trying to see me or what?"

"Are you changed?" She asked bluntly, "Or are you the same Antonio?"

"Come on ma, I'm changed. I'm fucking twenty years old; I don't got time for the games, now whassup?" He smirked.

Hazel playfully rolled her eyes, hoping and praying that he was different. "Alright, meet me tonight at the hotel. The one you took me to the first time we did it." she informed him.

"I'll be there, you don't have to ask me twice." "See you there." she said seductively, as she hung up the phone.

Chapter 5
I love you

The hotel room was dimly lit with vanilla scented candles that flickered in the darkened room. Hazel emerged from the bathroom wearing a pink towel wrapped around her body. She dropped the damp towel to the carpet, and walked over to the table where all her lotion and body gels were. She lathered up her body with warm vanilla lotion from Bath and Body works and then sprayed on the vanilla spray on her neck and palms rubbing them both together, spreading the aroma. She slipped into a pretty cheetah satin slip which hugged her thick body perfectly, it plumed up her firm breasts, bringing out her hips and phat ass which poked out of the side and back of the slip. It complimented her pretty caramel complexion, with her bright blonde hair that was wild and curly giving her that exotic kinky look.

Hazel walked around the room, making sure everything was intact. She lit one of the candles that went out and walked over to the bed and grabbed her 38.revolver off the night stand and placed one knee on the high bed as she slipped the revolver under the fluffy pillows that were perfectly set on the bed along with smaller pillows in front of the bigger ones. Hazel looked over at the clock and noticed it was 11:45 and Antonio was supposed to meet her here at 11:30 and he wasn't here. She got impatient as she ran her fingers through her thick curly hair. Right before she was about to sit down, she heard a knock at the door. She smiled at the fact that it was Antonio. She let him. She bit on the bottom of her lip as he walked inside.

"Damn, you look good." She smiled as she walked over and adjusted the knob on the wall just a tad bit for him to see her face. She walked over to him and wrapped her arms around his neck and began kissing him passionately, parting his lips with her tongue. He was in shock the way she threw herself at him, he'd never seen her like this, but it turned him on even more. He loved the fact that she was dressed in a sexy cheetah slip that brought out all the features in her from her face to her ass. He wrapped his arms around her waist as he inched down and grabbed her ass.

"You like that?" Hazel pulled her lips from his and stared him in the eyes.

"Hell yeah I like that ass." He smiled. "That's my ass."

Hazel playfully rolled her eyes as she started unbuttoning his pants and pulled them to his feet. Antonio stepped out of his pants as he pulled his shirt over his head and tossed it to the ground. He was now naked, showing off his muscular toned body. Hazel bit on the bottom of her lip as she eyed him up and down. She missed everything about him, especially that thing between his legs. She quickly pushed him down on the bed and climbed onto the bed on all fours and purred like a cat. Antonio pulled his body against the pillows as his manhood got hard instantly. She pulled her lip over her wild hair exposing her pretty set of d cup breasts that were firm and didn't sag. She climbed on top of Antonio. Grabbing his manhood, she guided him into her tight vagina and sat on his dick. Hazel grabbed a handful of her hair as a moan escaped her parted lips. She started riding him slowly, back and forth on his hard rock dick. Antonio held onto her hips as he switched up the motion.

Hazel was bouncing up and down on his dick as her breasts bounced up and down. Antonio lifted his head up as he cupped her breasts and ran his tongue across her aroused nipples, going side to side. That turned Hazel on even more, she moaned and sped up the pace the faster he licked.

She pushed him back down as she smiled, leaning over as she plopped her ass up and down, making smacking noises as her ass hit his thighs. He held onto her hips, with his head reclined against the fluffy pillows. Hazel felt as if it was the right time to make a move. She was still riding him, as she reached for the gun that was under the pillow. She gripped the 38. Revolver tightly as she slowly removed it from under the pillow, bringing it up to her side.

"I'm about to burst ma!" He exclaimed.

"Good." Hazel said nonchalantly, thinking it would be fireworks. After he busted inside of her she had the gun on the side, and was slowly rising it up.

"I love you ma." He uttered as he released the rest of his semen in her.

Tears formed in her eyes as it automatically brought back memories from when he first said he loved her.

"I-I love you too." Hazel uttered the words as a tear slid down the side of her cheek. She slid the gun back under the pillow as she collapsed onto his chest. There was no way she could kill Antonio, she knew for a fact that she was still in love with him, he was her first love.

Pinky Dior

The next morning, Hazel laid up with Antonio, making love again. The thought of them making love, and the fact that he kept saying he loved her, touched her deeply. She knew she loved him, but when he said it he was lying. Hazel pulled herself off of him as he sat up with a perplex look on his face, wondering why she stopped and he was about to nut.

"I can't do this." Hazel said as she held back the tears as he removed the sheet from her body.

"What are you talking about?" He was baffled.

Hazel got up, grabbed her bag off the floor, and went to the bathroom. She ran her fingers through her hair. *What the fuck am I doing? Why can't I kill him? A hundred thousand dollars is on the line right now, but I can't kill him.* Those questions and thoughts ran through her mind as she got dressed and emerged from the bathroom. Antonio was getting dressed when he Hazel emerge from the bathroom carrying a duffle bag on her shoulder. She walked over to the bed and grabbed her gun as she eyed it and lowered it to her side.

"Hazel, is there something that's bothering you?" he said as he walked over to her and held his hands in the air. Hazel had the gun aimed directly at him.

"What are you doing?" he questioned with a baffled tone.

"Don't you fucking come near me!" Hazel barked, "You're supposed to be dead right now, but I still love you." A tear slid down her eye, as her hands

Pinky Dior

were shaking, "I can't kill you so you need to stay low, watch your back … get out of town if you can … Dinero is going to kill you if I don't." She assured him as she backed up with the gun still pointed to him.

"I'm confused Hazel …"

His words trailed off as Hazel rushed out of the hotel room and rushed out of there. She couldn't do it, she loved Antonio and no matter how much he put her through when they were younger, she just couldn't. She hopped into her Honda civic and headed for Dinero's house. Tears blurred her vision, causing her to almost hit a car. They laid on their horn as it caught Hazel's attention. She wiped away her tears and put two hands on the steering wheel, trying to stay focused on getting to Dinero's house safely. She pulled up in front of the house, not thinking of the repercussions that she would have for giving up on a mission. She grabbed the duffle bag which had a lot of tools and gadgets inside and hoped out of the car. She threw the bag over her shoulder as she walked up to Dinero's house and rang the doorbell. A security guard opened the door and he tilted his head to the side, motioning for her to step inside.

He escorted her to his office, and closed the doors behind her. Dinero swirled around in his chair with a thick cigar hanging out the side of his mouth. He blew smoke through his mouth and nose and then removed the cigar from his mouth and plucked the ashes in the tray.

"Is it done?" He questioned.

"I'm out." She said calmly, as if it wasn't a serious matter, "I can't do this, so I suggest you find somebody else to do your dirty work and leave me and my sister the fuck alone. I'm done with you Dinero, I did my part, I did what you told me to do and I killed that bastard that my mother didn't, isn't that enough?" she questioned.

"No it isn't, we had an agreement." he said calmly.

"Well you know what Dinero? Fuck you and fuck this mission. I don't care how you get it done, but I can't kill him." Hazel said as she walked up and dropped the duffle bag on the table, "If you want me dead, here I am. Kill me?" She cooed as she held her hands up as if she was surrendering.

He looked at her with a devilish look on her face as she slowly turned around and made it to the door. She sighed in relief when she didn't hear gunshots, she was sure he would shoot her in the back. Reclined in his chair, Dinero stared at Hazel as she walked out like everything was okay. He thought she would have learned from her mother's mistakes but it was clear that she hadn't. Dinero picked up his phone and made a phone call.

Chapter 6
Running scared

Hazel lay in her mother's bed with her 38. revolver, gripping it tightly in her hand as she slept. She decided to sleep with her gun just in case Dinero tried to put a hit out on her. She squeezed her eyes together as she tossed in turned in the queen sized bed having a bad dream. The clashing sound of shattered glass hit the floor and woke her up. Hazel jumped up and grabbed her purse as she peeked down the hall. She saw that there was a man walking down the hall with a gun. She immediately started shooting at him. She ran backwards as she tried to reload her gun. Pain shot through her body when a bullet hit her in the arm.

"Argh!" Hazel roared in pain as she turned around and dashed through the back door. She ran around to the front of the house. Bullets flew by her head as she looked over her shoulder and saw the gunman running after her firing his pistol. Firing back at him, she made it to the car and jumped inside. She stuck the key into the ignition and pulled off with the tires screaming. She looked back in the rear view mirror and saw the gunman standing in the middle of the street firing rounds. A bullet shattered the back window as she ducked and almost lost control of the car. She quickly turned down the next street, getting away from the gunman. She knew it was Dinero's work, he had put a hit out on her. All of a sudden her cellphone started ringing, she grabbed it from the cup holder and saw it was Dinero calling.

She flipped open her cell phone and didn't get a chance to say anything.

Pinky Dior

"So you think you can just drop a mission like that and call it quits?"

"Fuck you Dinero! Why don't you come kill me yourself!" she challenged him.

"You stupid bitch!" he barked. "How about I send your sister to kill you?" He laughed hysterically.

"Don't you hurt her!"

The thought of him saying anything about her sister, sent chills down her spine. She heard her sister's voice in the background and knew that Dinero had her. He must have kidnapped Hazee. Hazel could hear him smacking her sister around. That enraged Hazel.

"You better not touch my sister or I will kill your ass."

"You couldn't even fucking kill the man I wanted you to, but you had the nerve to jump when I told you to kill your mother!" he said smartly as he chuckled.

"Fuck you Dinero I swear I'm going to kill you." Hazel said with hatred in her voice.

"You can run...but you can't hide Hazel." he assured her, "Boston is small and I know everyone." He smiled devilishly.

She didn't have any words for Dinero. She quickly hung up the phone as she closed it and tossed it back into the cup holder.

Pinky Dior

She looked over as she took a quick look at her arm, and noticed it was leaking with blood, as it stained her white t shirt. She pressed down on the gas, as she made her way over to the project buildings to one of her mother's friends. She met her through her mother and was told that she was a doctor. Hazel knew that if she went over to her house that she would help her. She didn't want to go to the hospital because they would ask too many questions. Hazel quickly parked the car in front of the apartment buildings as she got out the car. She held onto her arm, applying pressure onto her wound. Rushing towards the apartment building, she forgot what number she lived in, but she knew she lived on the first floor. Her eyes scanned on the apartment list and tried to remember what her mother said her name was. A light bulb went off in her head and remembered her name was Debra, Debra Olsen. Hazel squinted her eyes as she scanned the list and seen her name, Debra O, apartment 101. She noticed the front door was open, and proceeded into the building. The hallway had a strong aroma of piss and cigarettes. She made her way down the hall and stopped in front of apartment 101. She banged on the door, as if she didn't have any sense.

"WHO IS IT?" the lady yelled.

"Debra, it's me...Danita's daughter." Hazel moaned in pain, as she held her arm.

She hoped that she remembered her. All you could hear was the door unlocking, three times. Debra opened the door as she had a gun in her hand as she lowered it when she noticed who it was.

"What are you doing here?" she questioned.

Pinky Dior

"I've been shot." Hazel said.

"Come on in."

Hazel walked in and Debra closed the door behind her as she turned the lamp that gave off a little light. "Sit down, I'll be right back." she pulled out the chair from the kitchen table and put it next to the lamp. Hazel sat down as she hid her gun in her lamp, reclining her back against the wooden chair. Debra returned back into the living room with a first aid kit, bandages and a bottle of alcohol. She sat on the edge of the couch as she extended her arms over and pulled back Hazel's shirt. Hazel winced in pain.

"It may hurt, but just sit still." Debra stated, Hazel tried to sneak a look, as she looked out of the corner of her eye, to see what she was doing,
"I advise you not to look." Debra cracked a smile, as Hazel turned around and squeezed her eyes shut.
Hazel bit down on her lips, as she moaned in pain as she felt her removing the bullet from her arm. She tried not to scream, it was so painful, she'd never been shot and didn't know what to expect. She just wanted it over as fast as possible. Debra finished up as she applied alcohol around her wound; Hazel winced in pain, as she tried to remain calm as possible. Debra put a white bandage around the wound and taped it up along the sides.
The house phone started ringing.

"I'll be right back." Debra told her as she got up from the couch and went to answer the phone.

Pinky Dior

"Hello?" Debra answered.
"Hello Debra."
"Hi Dinero."

Hazel eavesdropped on the conversation and listened closely, and she was shocked when she heard Dinero's name.

"Listen to me carefully...I know Hazel is going to come to you because I sent someone to kill her and I know for a fact my man hit her. So if she comes to you ... kill her." he demanded.

"Don't worry about it, she's here now." Debra smirked.

Before Hazel could dash for the door all the lights went out. Debra came out with an AK-47 and started shooting like a mad woman, Hazel quickly jumped on the floor as she looked around but she couldn't see shit. But she remained calm and quiet.

"Where are you?" Debra sang, "Come out and play." she said hysterically laughing.

Hazel felt as if Debra was close to her, and that's when she had stepped on her hand. Hazel quickly pulled her hand from under her foot and pulled her by both of her feet as her body fell to the ground. She started shooting as the bullets pierced through the ceiling. Hazel got up and searched for a switch. She saw Debra on the floor as she had the gun pointed at her. Hazel wasted no time as she cocked back her gun and shot her four times in the chest. Hazel got up out of their as quickly as she could. She rushed towards her gun as she looked over her shoulder to make sure no one was behind her or had spotted her. Hazel didn't know where to go so she decided that the safest place for her to lay was in the hotel. She drove all the way downtown and got a room at The Boston Park Plaza Hotel. Once she got settled into her room all she could think about was her sister Hazee, hoping that Dinero wouldn't kill her. Then her mind drifted off to Antonio, she decided to check up on him in the morning to see if he wanted to leave Boston.

The apartment buildings were filled with cops, sirens flashing everywhere and nosey neighbors outside. You even had some neighbors talking to 7 news and they were already airing the story about the murder of Debra Olsen. One of her daughters came to visit her mother this morning, coming from Connecticut when she found her mouth dead lying in her own pool of blood. Dinero had called back Debra the night he told her to kill Hazel, but he knew something hadn't gone right. He sat outside in a black car that had twenty percent tints all around the car, and you couldn't even see inside. He stared at everybody who was standing in front of the apartment buildings. He noticed the female officer heading towards his car, as she looked both ways before crossing the street. It was a short Puerto Rican female officer. Dinero rolled down the window.

"Who is it?" he questioned, referring to the person who was found inside.

"An African American woman, she's in her early thirties, tall and brown." the officer said describing her the best way she could and then she looked down and held her ID in her hand,

"Debra Olsen." Dinero picked at his chin hairs as he stared straight ahead. He couldn't believe Hazel killed her.

"What do you want me to do?" she asked.

"You know Antonio Sanchez?" he looked over at the officer as she nodded her head.

"Yeah I remember him." she said remembering Antonio, from when he used to get pulled in to the station for violating his probation.

"I want him dead." he demanded, "And his little girlfriend Hazel...she might be at his house this morning, I don't know where that bitch is hiding but I have a strong feeling that she's over at his house. She's trying to protect that son of a bitch!"

"How much are we talking?" She questioned,

"Fifty thousand dollars,"

"I can lose my job, you know that Dinero." she informed him, "But I've been working for you, for many years and the money is good." She winked at him as a wide smirk appeared on his face.

"Get it done." he said as he rolled up the window and watched as she walked away. He loved the way her phat ass fit snuggle in her uniform pants. He always dreamed of banging her, but she was married and he had to respect that. Although he knew all he had to do was make a hit out on him and make her all his, but he knew it wasn't worth it. All he wanted was Antonio and Hazel dead.

Chapter 7
Shots fired

Pulling up in front of Antonio's house, Hazel put the car in park as she grabbed her gun and got out the car. She held the side of her arm that was still aching with pain from where she was shot. She walked up the stairs and was tempted to ring the doorbell, but she had saw the door was slightly open. She arched her eyes brows as she pushed the door knob in. she pointed the gun around the living room, hoping Antonio wasn't in any type of trouble. Thoughts crossed her mind that Dinero had already sent someone to finish the mission she couldn't complete. But those thoughts were soon cut short, when she heard moaning and bed rocking coming from upstairs. Hazel pointed her gun as she walked up the stairs and inched over to the door where the noise was coming from. She kicked in the door with her gun pointed at the bed. Tears formed her eyes as she caught Antonio in bed with another woman.

They didn't even hear her bust open the door. She fired her gun in the air making the female scream. Antonio pulled back the sheets. Hazel saved his life and he was sleeping with another bitch. Tears whelmed up in her eyes but she didn't let them escape. She fired her gun and hit Antonio in the chest four times. The naked woman screamed as she tried to get out of the bed and get low to the floor, as if that was going to save her. Hazel slowly walked over to the side of the bed where the woman was curled up in the corner with tears streaming down her face begging for her life. Hazel tilted her head to the side as she cocked the gun back and let off three more rounds in her chest. She headed

Pinky Dior

downstairs and stopped in her tracks. She glanced out of the window and saw a cop car pulling up out front.

"Shit." she yelled as a female officer made her way to the front door.

She started ringing the door bell. Hazel had to think fast. It was all or nothing. She answered the door and acted as if she was in danger.

"There are two dead bodies up stairs and another man has the gun." she fake cried as she closed the door behind the officer. The officer didn't know if she was Hazel or another woman since she did say there was another woman upstairs. She thought she was getting off easy and getting easy money if Antonio and Hazel were already dead.

"Stay here." the officer demanded as she pulled out her gun and ran upstairs. Hazel stood behind the officer with a smirk on her face as she pointed the gun towards her back and fired without a blink of an eye. The officer was riddled with bullets, she fell face first on the steps. Hazel snatched the officer's gun and her radio. On the police radio Hazel could hear a dispatch going out about her and her location. She made a run for the door. When she opened up the front door two black male officers were walking up the steps.

"Put your hands up!" one of the officers yelled. Hazel played no games with him; she shot him right in the face. The other officer opened fire. Hazel side-stepped the first shots and fired blindly striking the officer in the chest. He fell to the ground and Hazel rushed him, firing shots, hitting him in the head and neck.

Hazel ran down the stairs and jumped into the patrol car. She put the car in drive and headed straight for Dinero's house. Pulling up in the patrol car right in front of his house, she grabbed the police shotgun from the middle of the car and got out. Enraged, she headed straight up the stairs and rang his door bell.

Dinero came to the door wearing a red robe. "Who is it?"

Hazel fired the shotgun at the lock on the door, blowing it open. Dinero fell to the floor.

"What the fuck!" he shouted, covering his head. "Turn...the...fuck...around." she said between gritted teeth as she cocked the pump. "Get the fuck up!" she demanded as he slowly got up. "Move nigga! Don't make me tell you again!" They reached at the top of the stairs and Hazel pushed him inside the room.

Hazel noticed there was a woman who was sitting on the bed holding her legs as they were scrunched up to her chest. She was frightened just by the look on her face. Hazel pointed the shotgun at her chest and fired two times, blowing her small frame against the wall. Blood and guts were everywhere.

"What the fuck?!" Dinero yelled as he turned around and saw the bloody woman laying slumped across his bed.

"Shut the fuck up and turn the fuck around." Hazel hissed with murder in her eyes.

"What the fuck do you want, bitch?!" he shouted.

"Open the fuckin' safe." she jabbed him in the back with the front of the shotgun.

"What safe? I don't have a..." he turned around to get a look at her. Hazel cut him off as she hit him in the mouth with the butt of the shotgun, knocking his front teeth out.
"Aarrgghh!" He fell to his knees, holding his mouth.

"Motherfucker, don't play no games with me!" she barked "Get up and open the fucking safe."

He held his mouth as he slowly got up and removed the panting off the wall. It revealed a safe embedded into the wall. A wide smirk appeared across Hazel's face as he slowly turned the knob on the safe. She knew he had money, but how much? She didn't know. She knew for a fact Dinero was making good money. Once she heard the click she held the pump closer to his head just in case he tried to do something stupid.

"How much do you want?" he questioned.

"I want all that! So put that shit all in a bag and don't try anything stupid." Hazel slowly walked over to the side of the room still pointing the pump at him. She slowly kneeled down and picked up a Louis Vuitton bag that was sitting on the floor. She unzipped it and noticed it belonged to the dead woman. She emptied all the contents onto the floor and shoved the bag against Dinero's chest.

"Put all the money in there, all of it." she demanded as she pressed the pump to the back of his head. As he started to put the money in the bag she got impatient, feeling like he was trying to stall.

"Hurry the fuck up I don't got all day!" she spat. He quickly tossed all the stacks of money into the duffle bag. She snatched it from him as she zipped it up and tossed it over her shoulder.

"Who's the bitch now, motherfucker?" she spat.

"How could you do this?" he questioned.

"How could I?" she snapped. "You was trying to kill me...the doctor...the officers...yeah well they are all dead now, including Antonio." Dinero clapped his hands as if he was proud of her and her accomplishments. Hazel arched her eyebrows with a perplexed look on her face.

"Shut the fuck up!" she said with an attitude. "You made me kill my own mother and if I didn't you would have killed my little sister. Now it's my turn to kill you." Hazel said with her finger on the trigger, ready to blow him away.

"Good job! But you won't get away with this I promise." He assured her as he winked.

Hazel laughed at him.

"Get on your knees." she demanded. "Just like my mother was, I will make you die the way she died, so get the fuck on your knees." she raised her tone.

"I rather die like a man than on my fucking knees like a bitch!" He barked.

"Alright, I guess we got to do this the hard way." Hazel sighed as she shrugged her shoulders. She lowered the shotgun and shot him in both knees. His legs snapped like toothpicks.

"Argh!" he screamed as he dropped to the floor. It was a bloody mess.
"You fucking bitch!"
"Save it you fucking wuss!" Hazel snarled.
"This is for my mother!" Hazel raised the pump and shot him in the head, blowing his brains all over the room. His body fell over sideways as he layed on his arms. Hazel walked closer towards him as she kicked his body over, so he was facing her. She shot him three more times in the chest and watched his body jerk up and down on the floor. He died with his eyes open. Hazel then ran down the hall calling out her sisters name.
"Hazee!" Hazel yelled, "Hazee." she continued running down the hall and she could hear muffled sounds coming through a door. Hazel listened closely as she walked down the hall and heard the noises again. She tried to open the door, but it wouldn't open up. She noticed that it was locked, and you needed a key to unlock the door. She stood back and pointed the pump directly at the door knob and shot it twice. She then kicked the door in. Her sister younger sister Hazee was on the floor with duct tape on her mouth and her hands behind her back. With tears streaming down her bruised face, all you could hear is her screaming through the duct tape.

"Hazee are you okay?" Hazel rushed over to her sister and snatched the duct tape from off her mouth, "Did he hurt you?" Hazel questioned as she cut off the duct tape with a razor.

"Not really, he just smacked me around a couple of times." Hazee sniffled as she stood up and looked in the mirror. Her hair was unruly from Dinero smacking her around and pulling her hair.

"Thank God you're alive." Hazel hugged her sister tightly, "I thought he was going to kill you, let's get out of here, the cops are probably looking for me." Hazel automatically assumed.
"The cops? What did you do?" Hazee questioned.
"Don't worry about it, I will tell you later, let's go." She rushed out of the room and ran down the hall. She didn't notice that Hazee had picked up a gun that Dinero had left on top of the dresser, in the room he had her in. Hazel stopped in her tracks when she didn't see her sister behind her. Hazee walked into the hall and wondered where Dinero was at. She peeked in his room. Her mouth fell to the ground. She was in shocked as she saw the woman lying in the bed, murdered and Dinero laying on his back with his brains blown out. She looked over her shoulders and noticed Hazee staring into the room where the woman and Dinero were murdered.
"Hazee! Let's get the fuck out of here!" she yelled, getting aggravated. Hazee turned towards her sister and followed her downstairs. They hopped in the patrol car and Hazel threw the bag of money in the back seat as she started up the car and peeled off. She knew that it was only a matter of time before the cops were onto her so she had to get out of the area ASAP. She pressed down on the gas as she accelerated down the

street, switching in and out of lanes. She sped down Blue Hill and didn't even notice that there were undercover cops following her.

"Pull the fuck over." Hazee said as she pulled out the gun and pointed it towards her sister's head.

"Hazee, what the fuck are you doing?" Hazel said shocked, almost loosing grip of the steering wheel when she saw the gun pointed at her head.

"You killed mama." Hazee said with tears forming in her eyes. "And don't lie to me." she said between gritted teeth, "I know...I know...you killed mama, he told me how you stood there with the gun pointed at mama and you just shot her. For what Hazel? Why?" She cried as her hands started to tremble.

"I didn't want to kill her, I didn't Hazee." Hazel said softly, "He made me kill mama, I had no choice."

"What the fuck you mean you had no choice?" Hazee snapped.

"That was our mother." The tears streamed down her face nonstop, "Your fucking cold hearted, mama would of never did nothing like that to you or me."

Hazel took a deep breath as she pulled over in an empty parking lot and parked in the middle of the lot, not in an actual parking space. She turned and looked at Hazee.

"Look Hazee, you don't understand...I didn't want to kill our mother, Dinero made me kill mama and I didn't want to do it but mama told me to kill her because if I didn't he said he would've killed you. So mama told me to do it Hazee, I didn't want to, I had no choice but to kill her and I've been taking it pretty hard on myself lately." The tears poured from her eyes as she stared at Hazee who still had the gun aimed at her head.

"Yeah, yeah bitch, you fucking should!" Hazee didn't believe one word she said.

"I'm sorry Hazee, if you want to just kill me." She said nonchalantly. "What type of person deserves to live after they killed their mother?" her words cracked. Hazee bit the bottom of her lip as she refrained herself from crying but she couldn't. She believed her sister just because she knew what type of conniving person Dinero was and he would do something like this. She reached her arms around and hugged her sister as they cried in each other's arms.

"I'm really sorry sis, I didn't know." Hazee cried in her sister's arms, as she felt bad that she was really going to shoot her sister.

"No, I should be sorry." She pulled back from the embrace, "I should of told you the same day what happened, but I knew you would hate me and I love you little sis, and either way someone had to die that day and if I could go back in time I would've killed him instead." She wiped away her tears.

"Yeah but you can't go back in time." Hazee informed her sister, "What's done is done, you just have to accept what you've done and keep it moving." She said nonchalantly as she shrugged her shoulders. "But I still love you and I know mama loves you the same."

Pinky Dior

Hazel cracked a smile, her sister's words made her feel better.

"Thanks sis, I love you too." Hazel said, "Let's get out of here." Before she could put the car in park there was a cop car that had pulled up in the parking lot with their flashing lights. Both of the Boston Police hopped out of the car with their guns drawn.

"Come out with your hands in the air!" one of them yelled into an intercom.

"Shit!" Hazel said as she banged on the steering wheel.
"What the fuck did you do Hazel?"

"I walked in on Antonio and found him sleeping with another woman and I killed both of them, I know Dinero sent a paid cop to kill me and I killed her."

"Get out the car now." they yelled.

"You killed a cop?" Hazee asked surprisingly.

"She was going to kill me anyway."

"So what are we going to do?" Hazee asked in a worried tone as she looked out the window. The officers still had their guns drawn. They noticed that Hazel wasn't getting out the car, she placed the car in drive and tried to press on the gas but one of the officers let off a couple of rounds and shattered the glass, hitting Hazel right in the head. Hazee screamed as she witnessed her sister getting killed by cops. The blood splattered on her face, she touched her face as she examined her hands which were covered with her sister's blood. Hazee

Pinky Dior

thought the cops would stop after they killed her sister but they didn't, they kept firing into the car, hitting Hazee in her shoulder. She roared in pain as she looked down and pulled up her short sleeve shirt, she noticed that she was only grazed by the bullet. Hazee still had the gun in her hand as she positioned it on her lap. She reclined back in the chair as she noticed two cops walking over to the car. She closed her eyes pretending to be hurt.

"We got two down." one of the officers said into his radio.

Hazee peeked through the corner of her eye as she noticed the officer opening up her door. She quickly picked up her gun and shot the officer in the chest and turned quickly and shot the other officer before he got a chance to shoot her. She looked over at her sister, as tears welled up in her eyes. Her head was leaking with blood, as her whole head was deformed. She couldn't believe her sister was gone, and her mother, meaning she had no one. The rest of her family was in Dominican Republic. Hazee moaned as she looked behind the seat and grabbed the bag that her sister had put back their earlier, she wondered what was inside. She unzipped it revealing stacks of money. Hazee got out the car, as she tossed the bag on her shoulder. She looked on the ground and the officer was still trying to move. She lifted up the gun in and shot him once in the chest, then she walked over to the side of the car and she seen the other officer leaning up against the car, gasping for air as he tried to call for back up on his radio. A devilish smirk across her face, she bent down and shoved the gun all the way into the cop's mouth.

"You killed my sister! And you almost killed me, now it's your turn to die."

All you could hear was the officer's muffles. She smiled, as she pulled the trigger and blew his brains all over the car. She got up and heard sirens in the distance. She quickly rushed over to the cop's car, got in, and pulled off. Hazee didn't think things would go down this way, her mother's dead and now her sister. Hazee had nothing else to loose. She looked over at the bag of money that was in the seat and the gun that was in her hand. Hazee sped down the street as she turned on the police sirens and dipped in and out of lanes. Although her family was gone, everything that her and her sister been through in the last two weeks, Hazee knew that this had made her a stronger person. They created a monster.

Order Form

DC Bookdiva Publications

#245 4401-A Connecticut Avenue, NW

Washington, DC 20008

dcbookdiva.com

Name: _____

Inmate ID _____

Address: _____

City/State: _____ **Zip:** _____

QUANTITY	TITLES	PRICE	TOTAL
	Smokin Mirrors	$15.00	
	A Beautiful Satan 2, RJ champ	$15.00	
	A Killer'z Ambition 2, N. Welch	$15.00	
	Dynasty 3, Dutch	$15.00	
	Que, Dutch	$15.00	
	Tina, Darrell Debrew	$15.00	
	Trina, Darrell Debrew	$15.00	
	Secrets Never Die, E. Williams	$15.00	
	Lorton Legends, Eyone Williams	$15.00	
	The Hustle, Frazier Boy	$15.00	
	A Killer'z Ambition, Nathan Welch	$15.00	
	A Beautiful Satan, RJ Champ	$15.00	

Sub-Total $_____

Shipping/Handling (Via US Media Mail) $3.95 1-2 Books, $7.95 1-3 Books, 4 or more titles-Free Shipping

Shipping $ _____

Total Enclosed $ _____

Certified or government issued checks and money orders, all mail in orders take 5-7 Business days
to be delivered. Books can also be purchased on our website at dcbookdiva.com and by credit card at
1866-928-9990. Incarcerated readers receive 25% discount. Please pay $11.25 per book and apply the same shipping terms as stated above.